PHOTOS OF YOU

When Ava Green turns twenty-eight, she discovers this will be her last birthday. The cancer she thought she'd beaten three years ago is back, only this time it's terminal — and she's not going to waste any of the time she has left. She's been dreaming of her wedding since she was a little girl, but there's only one problem: there's no groom. Her friends and family decide they will help her throw the wedding of her dreams, without the vows; and as word spreads, the whole country seizes the story of a woman whose dying dream is simple, uniting to give her a wedding to remember. But when photographer James Gable volunteers to help document the whole event, it becomes painfully clear that it's never too late to discover the love of your life . . .

TAMMY ROBINSON

PHOTOS OF YOU

Complete and Unabridged

AURORA
Leicester

First published in Great Britain in 2019 by
Little, Brown Book Group London
First published in Australia & New Zealand in 2018
by Hachette New Zealand

First Aurora Edition
published 2019
by arrangement with
Little, Brown Book Group
and Hachette New Zealand

A catalogue record for this book is available
from the British Library.

ISBN 978–1–78782–139–2

Published by
F. A. Thorpe (Publishing)
Anstey, Leicestershire

Set by Words & Graphics Ltd.
Anstey, Leicestershire
Printed and bound in Great Britain by
T. J. International Ltd., Padstow, Cornwall

This book is printed on acid-free paper

For Holly, Willow and Leo,
who bring the joy into every day.

And for love, and the courage
to follow your heart.

Prologue

The End, it begins

In my dreams I go everywhere.

I am limited only by my imagination, but as my Year 7 English teacher once remarked, I was blessed with a rather robust one of those. Original and dramatic, she said; proudly, as if it were all down to her guidance and tutoring rather than the genetic card I was dealt. I wonder what she would say if she could see me now.

Such a shame, such a waste.

She wouldn't be wrong.

In my dreams, I travel to places I have never been but always wanted to go. On the one hand, it is preferable. There are no customs queues, pickpockets to keep a wary eye out for or tetanus shots to be had. Yet on the other hand, none of it is real. I will never see these places for myself.

Days have begun to merge. The passage of time is marked by the administration of pain medication. I don't remember the last time I left this bed, or this room. I am near the window, I am grateful for that. I watch clouds roll on by, and then . . .

Blink.

. . . they are replaced by stars.

I hear them. The voices. Muffled, tearful, weary. I hate what I have put them through. Continue to do. Is it my fault? That I am still

1

here? Am I hanging on when I should be letting go? Have I failed at the very thing that comes to us all?

Blink.

I dream of him. With the water on his skin and the sunset in his eyes. The timing was all wrong. And yet, the timing was perfect. I wonder where he is, and what he is doing.

Blink.

I tiptoe amongst the stars, along the Milky Way. Hitch a ride on a comet, dance with the man in the moon.

I am star dust; blow on me too hard and I will disintegrate.

1

I stopped listening a few minutes ago, right around the time he uttered the three words I had been most longing not to hear.

I'm so sorry.

I watch as his mouth moves and a few other words filter through, even though I feel like I am underwater or listening to him from inside a vacuum.

Secondary

Bone

Incurable

Limited options

On their own, none of those words are particularly malevolent, but together they paint a grim picture. The cancer is back. And this time it's not going away. Numbness steals over me like an anaesthetic and I feel my whole body settle in cold stillness. This can't be happening.

I should be listening. As far as speeches go, the one he's currently giving is right up there in terms of importance. I know I'll be fielding a million questions later, none of which I will have the answer for if I don't listen. Except one, if anyone is brave enough to ask it.

Are you dying?

Yes.

'Ava?'

I realise he's been saying my name and blink. 'Sorry?'

'Do you have any questions?'

'No.'

Yes. Why me?

'I know it's a lot to take in and you'll need time to process it all.'

He gets to his feet and comes around the desk, perching on one corner to look down at me sympathetically.

When did doctors stop wearing white coats? They barely even look like doctors any more. Half the time they look fresh out of high school. Like this guy, Dr Harrison. Under any other circumstances I would have been flirting with him. He was seriously good-looking in a cultivated, obvious way. I was willing to bet money that he had nurses falling all over him.

'Is there someone I can call? To come and pick you up?' he asks.

I blink again, realising I am staring at his lips. Wondering what it would be like to kiss them. Inappropriate, but if there's one thing I've learned it's that what one anticipates is an appropriate reaction in a situation like this and what actually happens can be two very different things.

'No, thank you,' I tell him. 'I'll be fine.'

Except I won't.

'OK. Take a few days to think about what I've said and then we'll discuss options going forward.'

I snort bitterly. Options. Discussing options when the end result is unavoidable feels futile, but I don't say that. Ironically, I don't want to hurt him.

4

GETTING MARRIED.'
  The rain stops.
  My mother looks from me to Amanda.
  'To her?' she says.

4

'There must be *something* they can do? A drug trial? Did you ask him about any new drug trials?'

Only my parents, Kate and Amanda and I are left. My mother all but hurried the guests out the door, plates of food pressed into their hands, shortly after my marriage announcement. She knew something was up, and it was confirmed when I started crying and seemed unable to stop. I sat at the dining table with the tears streaming into my nose, my mouth and my hair, until I was a sodden, damp mess that gaped like a goldfish every time one of them asked me what was wrong, incapable of words.

In the end my mother poured neat whiskey down my throat and that stopped the tears, at least long enough for me to tell them.

My father hasn't said anything since, not a word. He is staring at the wall as if he can see through it, to some other place, another dimension, one where his only daughter hasn't just told him he'll be burying her before the year is out.

Kate and Amanda are crying. Quietly, unobtrusively, low sniffles and pained breathing. My mother gave them glasses of whiskey for the shock too, Amanda is already on her third measure, her coping mechanism any time she has bad news is to get completely shitfaced. I feel like joining her. Anything that will help numb the sense of impending doom I feel, and the guilt that threatens to choke me for putting my parents through this.

My mother isn't taking the news lying down. Even though I have told her everything the doctor told me, she is insistent I must be wrong. That I've misheard something, that in my shock I missed out on a vital piece of the conversation. She is angry that I went without her, as if her presence today would have changed the very outcome of the meeting.

I shake my head. 'No. I didn't ask.'

'Right. We'll go see him again tomorrow, together. You're in too much shock to ask the questions that need to be asked.'

I take another gulp of whiskey. 'Fine.'

'We're not giving in to this,' my mother warns me. 'You have to fight, just like last time.'

The thought of going through all that again is unbearable. But what choice do I have? I nod.

My dad stirs for the first time and looks at me. 'Should you be drinking? In your condition?'

'She's not bloody pregnant,' Mum snaps, and he bows his head.

I put a hand on his arm. 'It's OK, Dad, it can't get any worse than it already is.'

He nods and pats my hand. His face has gone that pale yellow colour of the first spring daffodils, only on skin it isn't anywhere near as pretty.

5

'How long does she have?'

Dr Harrison gives my mother a look I'm sure he's cultivated especially for mothers like her.

She'd bustled into his office today determined to change his mind, like my terminal diagnosis was just some half-cocked idea he'd come up with on his own.

'You must have made a mistake,' she said.

He hadn't.

'Surely there's a way to cure this?'

There wasn't.

'You're telling me, that all you doctors with your collective wisdom, you can't find a way to save my daughter?'

That's exactly what he was telling her.

Finally, after exhausting all her prepared questions and failing to get a different answer, she had blusteringly accepted it, in as much as a mother can accept being told her only child is not long for this earth, and had just asked him the question I'd been longing to but had been too afraid.

'That's hard to say,' he says carefully.

'Come on, you must have a ballpark figure.'

'We don't like to give people false hope.'

'How about if we promise not to hold you to it?' she says exasperatedly. 'Give us some idea, please.'

'I really couldn't hazard — '

'Do you have children of your own, Dr Harrison?' my mother interrupts.

'No.'

'Well could you just right now, just for a minute, pretend that you do. And then put yourself in our shoes. How. Long.' My mother's teeth are gritted, her expression steely.

'A year maybe, eighteen months. Could be less, could be longer.'

'With all due respect, Doctor.' I lean forward to speak up for the first time. 'There's a big difference between twelve months and eighteen. A whole extra six months in fact. There's a lot I could do with that time. I could take a world cruise in six months.'

My mother's head swivels to look at me. 'Is that on the cards?'

I shrug. 'I dunno. Probably not. But I'd like to know my options. I'm not going to go ahead and book something if it's unlikely I'll be around to enjoy it.'

Dr Harrison rotates his pen between his left thumb and forefinger, a nervous habit he's probably not even aware he has. He looks to his computer screen for help but the inconsiderate thing has gone into sleep mode.

'I wish I could be more specific,' he says finally. 'I really do. And I understand the desire to have a time frame. I'd be the same in your shoes. But these things can change depending on circumstance. General health, the treatment options you choose. It's just not something we can predict with any great accuracy.'

33

I sit back in my chair and exhale. 'It's OK, I understand.'

My mother looks at me with a stunned, helpless expression. 'This can't be it, the final say on the matter. We'll get a second opinion.'

'Absolutely. You're welcome to do that, of course,' Dr Harrison says, twirling his pen. 'I can recommend someone, if you like?'

'No.'

'Ava — '

'No, Mum. Dr Harrison knows what he's doing. I trust him.'

'It's not *about* trust. This is your life we're talking about.'

Normally I'd react to a statement like that. But I know she doesn't mean it the way it sounds. She's hurting too.

'I'm aware of that,' I say levelly.

Her shoulders collapse inwards like someone just punctured her lungs. My normally youthful mother suddenly looks every year of her age. 'Of course you are. Sorry.'

'It's OK.'

'No, it's not. None of this is OK.'

'That's got to be the understatement of the year.' I smile, trying to break through her seriousness. Not that the situation doesn't deserve her gravity, because of course it does. But if I only have a few months left I'll be damned if I'm going to spend them being miserable all the time. The odd pity party is allowed, expected even, but I'm not going to wallow there. She gives me a hopeless little smile. This isn't fair on her either.

'When would you like to start treatment, Ava?'
Dr Harrison clicks his mouse to bring up a calendar, relieved to be back on familiar territory.

'As soon as possible,' Mum answers him. She looks at me. 'Right?'

I look out the window at the sky. It is fiercely blue today, and almost empty bar a few scraps of cloud clinging to the hills. I feel like my senses have been heightened by my diagnosis, and I'm painfully aware that out there *life* is happening, all around. I hear traffic, voices, birds, and the distant hum of an aeroplane thirty thousand feet above my head. Out there, new life is being created, people are taking their first breath, just as others are taking their last.

'Just so we're clear.' I look Dr Harrison straight in the eyes. 'You can't cure me, is that right?'

He shakes his head. 'No.'

'And these treatments, chemo and the like, they would merely be prolonging the inevitable?'

'Not necessarily prolong, no. It's difficult to say. Best-case scenario we would buy you some time, yes.'

'But nothing is definite.'

'No.'

'So what's the point?'

Mum stiffens. She has sensed where I'm heading.

Dr Harrison scratches his head. 'With treatment we can prevent some of the complications that may arise. We also hope to improve your quality of life, and of course manage your pain.'

'Basically you want to be able to look in the mirror before bed and say you did everything you could.'

He gives me a look that says I'm not being fair. 'We do everything we can for all of our patients, Ava.'

'I believe you. But, Dr Harrison — ' I shuffle forward so I'm sitting on the front of my seat, my elbows on his desk — 'I need you to cut the bullshit.'

Mum snorts and covers her eyes with her hands. She's used to my bluntness, and while normally she'd make an effort to stop me, she correctly senses this is one of those moments in life when she needs to let me be an adult on my own terms.

Dr Harrison looks both amused and wary. 'I'm not bullshitting you, Ava.'

'Good. So the kind of chemo you're suggesting is aggressive, yes?'

He nods.

'The kind like I had last time? That will leave me feeling so wretched and broken I'll *almost* beg for death?'

He swallows but says nothing.

'I appreciate that you're offering me options,' I say. 'But I don't want to waste a minute being falsely optimistic, and I don't want to spend what little time I have left up here, having X-rays, and scans, and endless blood draws. Vomiting my guts out and losing control over my body and any dignity I still have. And I *definitely* don't want that port back in my chest for you to pump drugs into me that will do just as much damage as they *may*, on the off chance, do some good.'

'It's your choice,' he says finally. 'Of course it is. And believe it or not, I do understand where you're coming from.'

'I doubt that.'

'Just so we're clear,' he says, leaning forward himself. 'You're making the decision, as is your right, to forgo treatment.'

'I'm making the decision to plan for the worst and hope for the best. I'm making the decision to not spend my last days here in a futile effort to buy myself more time when that time would be spent barely living anyway. But also, I'm making the decision to keep my options open, because I might change my mind in a week and be back here begging for you to help me.'

He gives a small smile. 'I'll be here.'

6

I spend a few days after the appointment at home, wallowing and feeling sorry for myself, watching crappy daytime TV and eating anything at all that takes my fancy. I figure there's no point any more in either trying to watch my figure or heal my body through healthy choices.

But it's not in me just to quit outright. And even if it was, my mother wouldn't let me. She comes around to browbeat me into accepting treatment through an efficient mix of nagging and parental guilt.

I am camped out on the couch wearing the same clothes I have been wearing for the last three days straight. Track pants and a slouchy top that, conveniently, works as either day wear or sleep wear, allowing me to slip effortlessly from one to the other.

'I just want to be alone,' I tell her mournfully when I open the door wearing my most pitiful expression.

'Tough,' she says, pushing past me.

I watch as she picks her way through the detritus of my life, gingerly collecting up dirty plates and containers off the floor, her disapproval obvious.

'You just have to try, Ava. Just try. Miracles happen every day, who's to say one won't happen for you?'

'No, they don't.'

'Yes, they do.'

'Name one miracle. Nothing religious,' I say, making no effort to help her.

'What about that boy who was born completely blind but miraculously gained his sight after bathing in — '

'Sounds religious.'

'OK. What about that woman who had triplets after the doctors had said she could never carry a baby because her uterus was shaped like an upside-down seahorse — '

'Nothing religious *or* out of one of your trashy magazines.'

She squints as she thinks. Eventually she sighs. 'I can't, not specifically off the top of my head. But that doesn't mean they don't happen. You just have to believe.'

'Gee, if only all the cancer sufferers around the world had you to coach them,' I say sarcastically.

She pauses to arch her eyebrows at me. 'I'll allow you to speak to me that way just this once, because of everything that's happening. But try it again and see what happens.'

'Sorry.'

She picks up a particularly hairy plate and peers at it. 'What on earth was this?'

'Chinese, I think. Or pizza.'

She shudders. 'Right, get in that shower and get dressed. I've made an appointment with your oncologist and I don't want us to be late.'

'Jesus, Mum, I'm not five. I don't need you to make my doctor's appointments for me.'

'Well someone had too.' She sits down beside

me and takes my hands in hers. 'I know you're scared. But you have to let them try and fight this, Ava. You have to give it everything they've got.'

'I'm not scared. I'm terrified.'

'Oh my baby girl,' she whimpers and pulls me in for a hug. 'I know. And if I could swap places with you I would, in a heartbeat. But we just have to do what we always do, OK? We have to put one foot in front of the other and we have to carry on, not give up. We just have to try whatever we can to prove them wrong, to buy you some time. Because who knows when a cure will be found. New drugs are invented every day.'

'I just don't know if I can go through it all again, Mum. It was hard enough the first time.'

'I know. I know it was. But you're not alone. We're *all* here for you, all of us. Your friends and family. And if you won't do it for yourself, then do it for us. We need you here. Your father's barely eaten a thing since your birthday party. All those leftovers just going to waste.' She looks around the room again and frowns unhappily.

'I've been thinking that it might be a good idea for you to move back in with your father and me, so we can look after you.'

'And give up this place?'

She snorts. 'Newsflash, it's hardly the Taj Mahal.'

'I like my little flat,' I protest.

'Oh darling. It's grotty, admit it. Even the cockroaches take one look and leave. I hate the thought of you being here all alone. Come home and I promise I won't fuss.'

I tilt my head to one side and give her 'a look'.

'OK,' she admits. 'I'll probably fuss, I can't help it. It's what mothers do. But I'll try not to go over the top.'

'I'll think about it,' I say to mollify her.

'OK. I won't pressure you. Well, not much. And you'll come see the doctor?'

'Yes. I'll go and see what he has to say.'

'Thank you,' she says. 'Now get in that shower, seriously. You stink.'

I'm in the shower when a thought occurs.

'Mum,' I holler.

She opens the door and sticks her head around. 'What?'

'Aren't seahorses the same shape upside down?'

She looks surprised and draws an S shape in the air with her finger. 'I think you're right.'

'Told you those magazines are full of shit.'

She gasps. 'Blasphemy.'

'It's really not.'

We go back to Dr Harrison, my tail between my legs, and I ask him to help me. He comes up with a treatment plan that works for us both. I refuse the same chemotherapy I had last time — fat lot of good it did as it turns out — but agree to try an oral chemotherapy drug.

To my mother's delight, I also take her advice and give notice on my flat. To her dismay, I move into Kate's instead of back home under her motherly bosom. I love my parents more than anything on this earth, but I can't go backwards. Not now. I have to look forward. So when Kate suggested I move in with her, I jumped at the

41

offer. Who wouldn't want to live next to the beach? I made sure first, though, that she knew what she was in for. That it wasn't going to be like one big house party and that there would probably be just as many bad days as good. I made her promise that if it got too much she would tell me.

I try hard not to dwell on the fact that this is most likely my final stop before hospice. It just doesn't feel real.

7

The majestic colours of autumn bleed away into the barren starkness of winter. All but the most hardy of plant life withers and dies. I go into hibernation and watch it happen from my window, leaving the house only for hospital appointments and when my mother drags me to the supermarket to buy fresh fruit and vegetables. They, too, wither and die inside my refrigerator. I have no appetite for food and no energy to eat, let alone cook. I am bitter, and I can't seem to shake it.

Why me?

Why again?

It's too cruel to understand, though I spend hours trying. I am tortured by the things I haven't done with my life. Things that weren't even really possibilities until the possibility was taken away from me.

Sail the Atlantic Ocean
Climb Kilimanjaro
Cross the Sahara Desert on camel back
Raft the River Nile
Fly across the Tasman in a hot air balloon
Kayak solo down the Grand Canyon
Hike the Appalachian Trail

I could have been an explorer. An inventor. In a parallel universe there is a Nobel Prize for literature with my name on it.

In another, I cured cancer.

I spend hours obsessively searching the internet and compiling an exhaustive bucket list, which I then tear into a thousand tiny shreds and sprinkle out the kitchen window, watching as the wind carries them away like snowflakes.

I would have been happy just to be loved.

The oral chemotherapy does what it says on the box and drains me to new levels of exhaustion and lethargy. I don't care if it drains me to the brink of death, as long as it takes the cancer cells as well. My skin dries out like a lizard, scaly and brittle. I slather it with moisturiser to no avail. I feel old and withered myself.

I end up admitted to hospital twice. First, when the vomiting and diarrhoea leave me dangerously dehydrated, and the second when routine tests show my blood count is low and I need a blood transfusion. The IV line blows a vein and I end up with a swollen and bruised hand. I tell the nurse she is a sadist. She looks at me sadly and says nothing, which makes me feel bad. Not bad enough to apologise though.

I am sick of needles. My skin is marked with the faint scars of all the needles that came before. I worry I look like a junkie. A cashier in the supermarket once looked at me with disgust, and it wasn't until I got home and looked in the mirror that I realised my pale skin, shadowed eyes and bruised arms could be taken either way.

I watch my favourite movie, *Love Actually*, six times in one day even though it is not Christmas, because I worry that I won't still be around at Christmas to see it when it comes on TV. There are one hundred and forty-two days, nine hours, fifty-six minutes and twenty-three seconds until Christmas. I find a website that gives me a countdown and make it my new screensaver. Morbid, for sure. But it gives me something to aim for.

Reluctantly, I put any more thoughts about the wedding on hold. My mother is convinced the treatment will buy me more time, and I allow some of her optimism to rub off on me.

8

Spring insinuates itself upon the land quietly and unassumingly. New growth splits the soil. Animals prepare to birth. The circle of life continues.

I go to my appointment filled with hope, while telling myself I am a fool for doing so.

The scan reveals the last-ditch treatment has had no effect on the cancer. In fact, like a tenacious weed, it has spread, sending offshoots to find new strangleholds. Better prepared this time, the doctor refuses to be drawn by my mother into giving out any time-frames.

'I'm sorry, Ava,' he says. 'Please don't think we're leaving you to deal with this alone. There are still treatments we can offer.'

I don't say anything. I just get up and walk out. Although shuffle is more appropriate, given I am wearing the plastic slip-on shoes I reserve solely for scan days because of the ease in which they can be taken on and off. I shuffle past signs that I have read a hundred times: *Birthing Unit, Radiology, Surgical Day Unit, Cafeteria.*

'Ava?' My mother catches up and falls into pace beside me. 'Darling?'

I shuffle past men, women and children. Of all ages and in varying states of disarray.

'You don't want to talk, I get it,' my mother says, her breath catching in her throat. 'Let's go and get a coffee somewhere, eh?'

When I see the big glass automatic doors that lead outside I shuffle faster, as if I have sniffed out freedom on the other side.

Outside, I blink. The sun is brighter than I remember it being when we arrived, and I have no idea how much time has passed while I was inside. How many minutes I have just wasted.

'Ava?'

But one thing I *do* know; now that I am out, I don't intend on ever going back in.

9

The French door leading out to the deck sticks, like it always does, until I throw all my body weight into it and then it opens with a reluctant 'pop'. I nearly drop my green tea but manage to hang on to it. The morning sky is the colour of apricot and lemon, like a pretty Italian sorbet. There's a perfect stillness in this moment, right before the world wakes and the pace becomes frantic and harassed and people forget to stop and just breathe. I know because I was like that once.

'Morning,' Kate says, joining me outside with her freshly plunged Brazilian-imported coffee. I love the smell of it, but not so much the taste. She scans the coastline with a satisfied smile, as well she might. If this view was mine to wake up to for the rest of my life I'd be the same.

'Any plans for the day?' she asks, blowing on the surface of her coffee gingerly to cool it down.

'Wedding planning.'

Her eyebrows arch. 'So you're really serious about this whole wedding idea?'

The night before we'd had a few drinks and I'd brought up the subject again. The treatment had been unsuccessful in halting the spread of the cancer, and I was more determined than ever not to waste whatever time I had left. As far as I was concerned it was full steam ahead with the wedding.

'Yes. Now more than ever. I know it's hard for you guys to understand, but it's what I want.'

'Hey, I have no issue with it, but I think your mother's worried the cancer has spread to your brain.'

I wince. That's the thing with Kate being a GP. She's become desensitised and says things without thinking how they might sound.

'Harsh, Kate.' Amanda emerges from inside and blinks in the daylight as if she's been locked in a cellar for nine years.

'What, the sunlight?'

'No, you and your brain cancer comment.'

'Oh right.' Kate looks at me guiltily. 'Sorry, Ava.'

'Fuck, this view is something else,' Amanda says, collapsing down on to a deckchair and looking around. She lifts her feet on to the small glass outside table in front of her and leans back contemplatively. 'Seriously I'd never leave home if I had this to look at every day.'

'I *have* to leave home to earn the money to *pay* for this view,' Kate points out.

Kate earns a decent salary due to a nationwide GP shortage, and one of the first things she did upon graduating and accepting a position back in our hometown was make an offer on this place. It sits almost on the tip of the small peninsula that shelters our small town from the open sea. The houses along this couple-of-hundred-metre-long stretch of land vary in style and price, due to the fact some have been here for decades and some are newbuilds. More and more of the old beach houses are being

49

bulldozed to make way for city folks' holiday homes, each trying to outdo each other with sleek angles and new materials and ground-breaking architectural designs.

We're just half an hour and one large, windy hill away from the country's third largest city. Half an hour from a heaving metropolis of glass and concrete, where people walk so fast my mother says it's a wonder their ankles don't catch fire. Here the pace is much slower, ankles pause in the street to catch up with neighbours and friends. Deadlines are loose and appoint-ment times vague.

Kate's pride and joy is a neat 1950s-style bach. A square box shape, it's fashioned from weatherboard that she had repainted a nonde-script grey, with cream on the wooden window frames. The section it's perched on is steeply sloped, with a path that leads from the house down across the lawn and through a short section of native bush to the relatively private beach.

'What are you doing out of bed so early?' Kate asks Amanda as she drains the last of her coffee cup. 'Not used to seeing you before noon.'

'Couldn't sleep. Damn tui outside my bedroom window kept chirping.'

'Budgies chirp,' I tell her. 'Tuis sing. And beautifully. You should be grateful.'

'Yeah so grateful that I'll throw a shoe at it if it wakes me again tomorrow. I need coffee,' she groans.

'You have legs.'

'They're on strike.'

50

'I'll get it,' Kate laughs, poking Amanda's thigh with her foot as she goes inside. 'You are my guest after all.'

Amanda has been living in the city for years. She moved there to kick-start her music career and never looked back, only returning for special occasions. Normally when she's back for visits she'd stay with her parents, but when she knew I was going to be staying here she insisted on staying too.

'The three amigos, back together again,' she insisted, ignoring the fact that everything had changed.

I lean against the balcony railing and enjoy the feel of the sea breeze on my neck. My hair is up in a loose messy bun and I am still in my pyjamas. Days like this I struggle to believe I am sick. I don't feel sick. I certainly don't *look* sick.

'*Will my hair fall out again?*'

That was one of the first questions I asked the day Mum dragged me back to see my oncologist and we decided on a course of action.

Not, *Will it make me sick?* or, *Will it work?*

Call me vain, but I'd hated the way I looked the first time around. No empowering head shave parties for me, I clung to my locks for as long as possible, until chunks started to come out in my hand and there was no longer enough to do a comb-over and hope that no one would notice. I'd been expecting it, and it was hard to come to terms with. My hair, along with my breasts, represented my femininity. With one gone and one faulty and pockmarked by illness, I felt sexless. Unattractive. It rocked me to my

51

core. What I *hadn't* been expecting was the rest of the hair on my body to fall out too. My eyebrows, gone. Eyelashes followed, except for one stubborn one in the middle of my right eyelid. I waited and waited for it to declare defeat and fall out, like the rest of them, but it never did. In the end I couldn't stand looking at it, this one stubborn lash that mocked me every time I looked in the mirror, so I plucked it out myself.

I went wig shopping with Kate and Mum. We tried to make light of the situation by joking around and trying on different styles and colours that were so far removed from my pre-cancer look. I could be anyone, Kate said. Like an exotic spy. Yeah right. Some spy. I couldn't even stand for too long before I became exhausted and had to sit, like the invalid I was, in front of the mirror while they fetched wigs and tried hard to keep the pitying looks to a minimum. In the end I got one similar to how my hair was before in colour, although much shorter. Less maintenance, Mum said.

I never wore it. When I tried, I felt like Julia Roberts in *Pretty Woman*, when she was dressed as a prostitute and everyone stared at her like she was a freak. I *felt* like a freak. So I stuck to bandanas if I went out. At least then it was obvious I had no hair for a reason, rather than someone choosing to wear a bad wig.

After the chemo finished and my own hair grew back, it was thicker, curlier.

'About this wedding.' Kate comes outside again and passes Amanda a coffee.

I brace myself against the railing, prepared for her to try to talk me out of it. 'What about it?'

'I want to help.'

'Me too,' Amanda says.

I look from one to the other. 'Seriously?'

'Of course. If this is what you want then we want to help give it to you.'

'Oh wow. You guys are the best.' I well up with emotion.

'Only thing is,' Amanda says tactfully, 'you're kind of missing something important.'

'You mean a groom?'

'Yeah.'

This is where I got stuck trying to explain it to my mother too. I don't blame them. When you think of a wedding you automatically think of a happy couple. The man in the penguin suit and the woman in the meringue dress. The plastic couple on the top of the cake. The exchange of rings and the 'will they or won't they' moment as they cut the cake and threaten to wipe each other's face with it. It's kind of a team sport, this wedding business. A team of two.

'Obviously that would have been the ideal situation,' I say. 'Although maybe not, given that any man I'd be marrying would be signing up for imminent widowhood.'

'Good point.'

'But it's not about that for me. Not any more. I'm not looking for any of the stuff that comes after the wedding. I just want the day itself. I want the chance to wear the dress, and feel like a movie star getting my make-up done by a professional because, let's face it, I'm kind of shit

53

at the whole make-up thing.'

They murmur their agreement.

'But we can do all that without calling it a wedding,' Kate says. 'We can go dress shopping, and do the salon thing. Get some proper photos done. Have a party and invite everyone. But to call it a wedding? I mean, you're not talking about walking down an actual aisle, are you? What for?'

I take a deep breath. 'My funeral. Kind of. But while I'm still here.'

'Explain,' Amanda says. 'It's too early and I haven't had enough coffee.'

'I don't want a traditional funeral. I don't want everyone in black, standing around discussing my life while they eat mini pies and drink watery tea at the local funeral parlour while I lie in a box nearby unable to participate in any of it. What's the point of that?'

'To say goodbye? And celebrate your life with a proper send-off?'

'*Exactly*. Celebrate *my* life. So why wait to do that until I'm gone? Why not do it while I'm still around to enjoy it, and make a bit of a party out of it at the same time.'

'OK,' Kate says. 'So what you're saying is that you want a wedding *instead* of a funeral?'

'Yes.' I click my fingers at her, excited that she's got it. 'I want to have *my* big day, celebrate *my* life, and say my goodbyes myself.'

'You know,' Amanda says thoughtfully. 'That kind of makes sense, in a weird, twisted way.'

'I knew if anyone would understand it'd be you two.' I smile gratefully. 'And the first job I'm

54

going to need you both to do, is to help me convince my mother.'

10

'Absolutely not.'

'Please?'

'No. Uh uh. No way. Not happening.'

'Why not?'

'Because — ' my mother shakes her head firmly — 'no daughter of mine is getting married in the local surf club rooms.'

'Ah.' I hold up a finger. 'But I'm not actually getting married, am I?'

'Whatever you want to call it — and you're the one insisting on calling it a wedding, by the way — we can do better than a few streamers and balloons and trestle tables.' She shudders at the thought.

'It was good enough for Bill and Barbara's golden wedding anniversary last year,' Dad comments. 'Remember, we had a lovely time.'

'Yes it was a perfectly adequate venue for that. But not for *this*.'

'Since when did you become a snob?'

'It's not snobbery to want the best for your daughter's . . . ' she pauses to swallow . . . 'big day.'

Even though she smiles brightly I can see how much of an effort she is making not to cry. How much she is struggling with this. Planning a funeral for your only child is a big ask of any parent. But this is not an ordinary funeral. My mother is having difficulty pretending it is easy

56

for her to celebrate when I am dying, but she's doing a decent job of trying to hide it.

'Where then? It's not exactly as if we have metropolitan venues on every corner,' Dad says. 'It's the surf club or the Chinese restaurant. They're the only places in town that might be big enough.'

'I don't know yet,' Mum admits. 'But we'll find somewhere more appropriate.'

'I really don't mind the surf club,' I venture cautiously.

'I said no. And that's my final word on the matter.'

Dad and I exchange a knowing look. When my mother has made her mind up about something there's no way of swaying her.

'I forgot how scary you can be, Mrs G.,' Amanda says.

'Pfft,' Dad laughs. 'She's not scary.'

Mum swivels to give him 'a look'.

'I'll just put the jug on, shall I?' He backs out of the room.

We are camped out around my parents' round dining-room table, with magazines and brochures spread out in front of us. In the end, my mother took little persuading to get on-board with the wedding idea. She could see how much I wanted it, and there was no way she'd deny me anything, not any more.

'What's our budget like?' Kate asks, her reading glasses perched on the end of her nose. She has a pen poised over a brand new spiral-bound notebook and is clearly in her element.

'I have some money saved,' I say. 'Not a lot though.'

'How much?'

'Five grand, closer to five and a half.'

Amanda sucks in air between her teeth. 'Is that enough for a big farewell party?'

'Probably not,' I say.

She frowns thoughtfully. 'What if we . . . '

'What? What if we what?' Kate asks when Amanda trails off mid-sentence.

Amanda shakes her head. 'Nothing.'

'I called this morning about refunding the airline ticket,' Mum adds. 'The lady was nice and agreed these are extenuating circumstances. That will add another couple of thousand. Plus your father and I can rustle up a bit more.'

I put a hand on her arm gratefully. 'No, Mum, the ticket money is enough.'

'We'll see.'

'So seven grand, give or take?' Kate asks.

I nod, feeling inadequate.

She scribbles it down in her notepad. 'OK.' She nods. 'It's a good start. I nominate myself to be in charge of expenses, so any and all, and I mean *all*, expenditures related to the wedding must come through me. No matter how trivial you might think, it all adds up and I'm not having the budget blown out on my watch. I want receipts for everything. *Everything*. Understood?'

My mother, Amanda and I look at each other and then burst into laughter.

'Too much?' Kate asks wryly.

'You might want to dial the crazy down a

notch, yeah,' Amanda says.

'Well anyway.' Kate consults the pad in front of her. 'I think the best way to do this, unless someone has a better idea, is to make lists for everything and then delegate. I've taken the liberty of preparing these ahead of time,' she continues, pulling a Filofax folder to her lap and undoing the clasp with barely concealed glee. She lifts out different coloured manila folders and lays them out on the table. On the front of each is a sticker with a task written on. I read a few.

Dress
Venue
Food/Drink
Photographer
Music
Flowers/Props

There are others too, but I can't read them all from where I'm sitting. Seeing them, I realise the magnitude of planning that needs to be done, and I lean back in my seat, exhaling softly, suddenly feeling very tired.

'What's wrong, what is it? Are you in pain?' My mother is on me in an instant, her face creased with worry. She places the palm of her hand on my forehead to check for fever, the way she did when I was little and coming down with something.

'A mother's hand is a better judge than any thermometer,' she'd say back then, pulling me in against her and kissing my head soothingly. I can still recall how comforting that felt, listening to her heartbeat through her chest against my ear.

'You're a little hot,' she says now. 'Maybe we should take you to the hospital.'

'I'm fine.'

'You *are* a little flushed,' Kate adds.

'Want me to start the car?' Amanda asks, pushing her chair out.

'Guys, I'm fine,' I reassure them. 'Really. Stop fussing. Can we please get back to the job at hand?'

'I call dibs on food/drink and music,' Amanda says, picking up the folders.

'Naturally.'

'I'll scout out some venues,' Mum says.

I open my mouth to speak.

'And no, *not* the surf club rooms, either,' she adds. She picks up another folder. 'Also I'll have a chat to Christine about who did the flowers for her daughter Maxine's wedding. They were nice. Do you remember them?'

'No.'

'Really? They were lovely. Roses, I think. And those little blue things. I don't know all the names. Remember she had those funny stick things in the middle of the tables with the lights on?'

'I wasn't there, Mum.'

'Weren't you? Are you sure?'

'Positive.'

'Right, well, anyway,' Mum carries on. 'I'll do some research on the internet. Find out what's in season and what's not. Leave it with me.'

'Dress is obviously your department,' Amanda

says to me. 'Although of course we'll all come shopping with you if you'll let us.'

I nod, because I don't trust myself to speak. It just keeps hitting home, and I wish it wouldn't. I'd love nothing more than to pretend that this is a normal wedding we are planning. To get caught up in the details and carried away by the frivolity of it.

'Great,' Kate says, picking up her papers and shuffling them. 'We'll reconvene here on Saturday, that should give everyone enough time to rustle up some initial quotes etc.'

'Are you absolutely *sure* this is what you want?' Mum asks me.

I nod again.

'OK.' She smiles. 'Then let's organise you a wedding.'

11

'Wake up. Look.'

The voice is muffled but insistent.

'Ava, wake up,' it says again. Then something starts bouncing on the bed beside me, whacking lightly at my foot. I ignore it, burrowing my head deeper into the pillow. It took me hours to get to sleep the night before, and most of the nights before that. Cancer has a way of making you question everything, never letting your mind shut off.

Will I live long enough to finish this book I just started?

To see the final episode in this series?

To use all of this bottle of hand moisturiser I just purchased?

If we are all Here For A Reason, what was my reason? To live a life only remarkable by its complete lack of anything spectacular, then fizzle out at the grand old age of twenty-eight leaving only a handful of people to mourn the world's loss of me? I didn't leave a legacy like Shakespeare, or whoever it was that invented the wheel.

I didn't even have love. Not the real stuff, the good one. The one you read about.

'What's going on in here? Is she OK?' Kate's voice joins in, sleep still weighing down the syllables. I hear fear in her voice and that prompts me to roll over and blink open my eyelids.

'She is fine,' I say. 'Although she is wondering what the hell's going on.'

'Just shut up and look,' Amanda says, thrusting her phone in front of my face. It takes my eyes a moment to focus.

'What am I looking at?'

'Duh, my phone. Check it out.'

I groan. 'Seriously? It's too early in the morning to expect me to admire photos of whoever you hooked up with last night, Manda. Actually, if you've only just crawled out of his bed then it's too early for you to be Facebook stalking him. Go away.'

'I didn't hook up with anyone last night,' she retorts. 'I was too busy kicking your arse at poker remember? Now look.'

I finally sit up and rub the sleep out of my eyes, letting my sight adjust to the light in the room. Then I take the phone from her hand and peer at the screen.

'HELP MAKE AVA'S WEDDING A KICK ARSE AFFAIR TO REMEMBER!!'

There is a photo of me blazoned across the top as a cover photo. It is not one I would have picked, given the choice, but I'm guessing Amanda only had the option of what was on her phone. She's gone with a photo of the three of us taken at my recent birthday party, only she's cropped her and Kate out so it's a zoomed-in picture of my face wearing a slightly manic smile. I can see a small bit of food stuck between my teeth.

'Shit, Amanda, what the hell is this?'

'Yeah OK, so it's not the best photo, but we

can change that.' She takes the phone back off me and scrolls down to click on the about button. 'Here, read this.'

Ava Green is my best friend, and she's recently been diagnosed with terminal cancer. She's a top chick, actually she's the best, and it's bullshit that she's going through this, because it's not fair. Her dying wish is to throw a big wedding party as a farewell celebration of her life, but she's broke, as am I, so I'm putting this out there to you, the good kind folks in the Facebook universe and saying, HELP please! If you can donate in any way, shape or form we'd be grateful! Comment or message me if you'd prefer to stay private, and please share this page with your friends and family so we can spread this wide and far! Thank you and peace out!

I groan and pass the phone to Kate. 'Did you know about this?'

'Know about what?'

She sits on the end of the bed and reads what I just read. When she's finished she tuts. 'Geez, Manda, you could have mentioned you were doing this. At the very least I could have proofread it and come up with something a little less crude and a little more elegant.'

'Well I'm sorry I'm not as poetic as you.' Amanda rolls her eyes, taking the phone from Kate.

'Says the songwriter.'

'Exactly. If you've listened to any of my songs you'll know I say exactly how I feel. I don't sugar-coat anything.'

'I've known you since you were four. I don't need to listen to your songs to know you think blunt honesty is the same as tactful — '

'*Anyway,*' I interrupt. 'Back to the whole point. What were you thinking? This is embarrassing. Delete it, quick, before anyone sees it.'

Amanda adopts a smug expression. 'Too late.'

'What?'

She giggles. It sounds incongruous coming from her. 'This page has barely been up a week and it's already going viral. It's been shared in four countries that I can see, by — ' she peers at her phone — 'three thousand, four hundred and twenty-nine people and counting. Over five hundred comments and quite a few messages. I haven't even read them all yet.'

I stare at her. 'What?'

'Which part did you not understand?'

'Any of it?'

'OK. Remember when we were at your house with your mum, talking about the budget?'

'Yes.'

'Well I had an idea to help us raise some funds so we can throw you a proper party. I mean, anything that's anything is on Facebook now. It's the way to connect with the world.'

'Well *disconnect* it, please. I don't want anyone feeling sorry for me.'

'Oh please. If you can't accept charity when you're dying, when can you?'

'But I don't need charity.'

'Wrong choice of word,' she says, conciliatory.

'It's not charity, Ava, if people want to help you.'

'It is if they don't know me and only want to help me because I'm sick.'

'You're so stubborn.'

'I'm not. How did all these people even see it? If you only just created it?'

She smiles modestly. 'I shared it on my band's page. We may be on the wrong side of famous still, but we have *a lot* of dedicated fans. They all started sharing it and well, it's all gone a bit nuts.'

'I can't believe you did this without asking me.'

'Look.' She holds the phone out to me again. 'I'll delete it if that's what you really want. But before I do, read some of these comments first, OK? You have a lot of people thinking of you and sending positive, healing thoughts.'

'That reminds me,' says Kate drily, clicking her fingers. 'I meant to put an order in for healing thoughts at the surgery yesterday. We're fresh out of stock.'

'Oh, ha ha,' Amanda says. 'You're so funny. There's nothing wrong with the power of positive thinking.'

'Except it can't cure cancer.'

'No, it can't cure cancer. Obviously. Just shut up, OK? This is for Ava.' She gets to her feet. 'I'll make you a cup of that green crap you drink while you have a look.'

After they've left the room I prop myself up in bed with an extra pillow, and with some trepidation I start scrolling down the Facebook page. She's right; there are loads of messages. I even recognise the odd name from my past, an old school friend, an ex-colleague. But the vast majority are strangers.

Sorry to hear you're sick! Kia Kaha, thinking of you xx

I lost my mom to cancer. Of course she was much older than you. It's a horrible disease and I'm really sorry you have it. I'd like to donate to your wedding party, do you have a fundraising page? Or an account we can deposit into?

So sorry to read about your illness. I think what you're doing is a great idea. Go out with a bang! I don't have any money to spare sorry, but I do have my old wedding dress just hanging in the wardrobe going to waste. It's a size 14 and I'll attach a photo. If you'd like to wear it get in touch!

I'm so busy sifting through the messages I don't notice Amanda slip in to leave a cup of green tea on my bedside drawers, and I only realise it's there once it's stone cold. The whole time I'm reading, more comments are arriving on the page. Most are thoughts of goodwill. But more and more are offers of money, or goods and services for the wedding. Four DJs have offered their services and an assortment of beauticians. There are even offers of venues.

Hey there from the marvellous Marlborough Sounds! Cancer sucks, I lost my sister to it last year. She was only 36 and a mum to two young boys. Seeing what she went through was hell and I wouldn't wish it on anyone. My husband and I own a winery, it's a small family business in a stunningly picturesque area. Google Anchor Bay Winery and you'll see. If you'd like to hold your wedding here give me a call, we'll come to an arrangement.

'You see?'

Amanda is peering around the door frame. When I don't immediately yell at her or chuck her phone in her face she comes into the room and perches again on the side of the bed.

'I'm still not thrilled that you did it,' I tell her. 'But I know your intentions were good.'

'Exactly. And look how many offers of help we've had.'

I shake my head. 'I still can't accept any of this. It's too generous. There are so many other people out there more deserving than me.'

She sighs and picks up my hand. 'Ava, sweetheart, I love you, but sometimes you can be a total pain in the arse.'

'Hey,' I protest.

'Sorry, but it's true. These people *want* to do something for you.'

'Only because I'm sick.'

'Yes, only because you are sick. But what's wrong with that?'

I shrug. 'It just feels weird.'

'Look at it this way. You'd really be doing *them* a favour.'

'Oh really, and how do you figure that?'

'It's simple. People like to help other people. It makes them feel good about themselves. People *like* knowing that they've made a difference in someone's life. It's called being kind and it's actually a worldwide movement right now.'

I look at her doubtfully.

'Seriously. Look it up if you don't believe me. With so much awfulness in the world people like to show kindness to strangers. Why shouldn't *you* reap some of that? Huh?'

She can sense I am weakening.

'And,' she carries on, 'think of how amazing we could make this wedding for you if we let all these people help.' She picks up her phone off the bed and flicks her finger down the screen.

'Offers of dresses, free hair styling on the big day. Look, this old guy has even offered his beach house for your wedding night. Wait.' She frowns as she reads and then jabs at the screen. 'OK, delete that one. Think he's got the wrong idea. But, Ava, please. Let *me* let these people do this for you. Please? You're my best friend — '

'Ahem.'

Kate shuffles into the room and I realise she's been listening at the door. She sounds all choked up as if she has been crying.

'OK, *one* of my best friends,' Amanda corrects herself, reaching out to take one of Kate's hands as well.

'I want this day to be everything you've dreamt of and more,' she says. 'I want it to be amazing. Just like you.'

I look at Kate. She smiles through her tears. 'I don't see any harm in it. Like she said, people like to help other people.'

'OK.' I nod. 'As long as I get to decide what we accept. No monetary donations. Just stuff that might help with the wedding.'

'Deal.' Amanda squeals, bouncing up and down on the bed.

There's the ping of a new message and she picks up the phone and reads it. I see her eyebrows arch and she looks at me.

'What?'

'One of the largest magazines in the country has just messaged. They saw the page and want to do a story.'

'No.' I shake my head. 'No way. Not happening.'

12

Before my initial diagnosis, back when I was blissfully wading through life confident in the belief I could do anything I wanted and had all the time in the world left to do it in, I fought my morning wake-ups with all the determined grit of a bare-knuckled streetfighter.

The blaring alarm made me get up and face the day long before I was ever ready. I hated that thing with a passion, but it was a necessary evil. Without it I had no internal alarm to rely on. My love for sleep and the comfort of my bed were too strong, my pillow a siren call. The alarm's raucous blaring made for a bad start to the day, and it often took a couple of hours, a few coffees and a guiltily bought, instantly regretted, cream doughnut to awaken me to an acceptable level to deal with people and the world.

Now I regret those lost hours. I sleep now because my body tells me I have to, but my thoughts and fears often wake me while the rest of the world slumbers peacefully on. At least, those on the same side of the curve as me.

I had no idea how enchanting the pre-dawn world can be. How deliciously mischievous it feels to be up before anyone else. I don't stay in bed any more, it's too easy to notice in the stillness every ache in my body, every twinge, and think, Is that more — ? And then I picture it, the cancer a little malicious army of soldiers, identical in dress and appearance, marching in perfect unison through my bones and my blood, advancing to claim new territories.

No, I get up when I wake, now. Softly, so as not to disturb the other two. I make myself a green tea and if it's cold I open the curtains, curl up on the couch and watch the world awaken from within my sanctuary. But if it is warm, or I am feeling particularly scared of what is coming and need reassurance that *I am still alive*, I go out, on to the deck, and let the morning chill steal my breath and tiptoe across my skin, springing goosebumps up in its wake.

I watch the stars fade out as the sky lightens, from black to inky denim to baby blue, the horizon hazy with the colours of a new dawn. And I smile, and I breathe, and I give thanks that I have made it through another night and been gifted with one more day. Because it *is* a gift. I know that now.

Some of the people I have met through the cancer network, which stretches its tentacles far and wide, have referred to cancer itself as A Gift. For differing reasons; it truly made them appreciate their loved ones, their job, the very fact they have life. Being ill gave them the kick up the arse they needed to finish that book they started writing ten years ago/buy that motorcycle/jump out of that plane/end that dead-end relationship/mend those bridges. It has given them perspective.

I don't agree.

My cancer has not been a gift. Yes, it has changed the way I view or interpret certain situations and circumstances, and it has caused me to physically slow down and focus on what is the most important thing to me, day to day, even sometimes hour by hour. But if I had a choice between being terminally ill and living the way I used to live, with blinkers on, I'd take living any day. Hands down.

Perspective is good. But a fat lot of good it will do you when you're lying in a hole in the ground.

'Morning.' Kate emerges from the house, coffee in hand, blinking in the unadulterated pureness of the morning light.

'Another stunning day in paradise,' Amanda says, joining us. She is wearing sunglasses, as if she is not ready to face the light of day. Last night her band played a gig as a favour to the publican of our local. A short, rotund guy named Gary, he has known us since we were fourteen and hiding in the bushes outside his pub balcony, ready to pilfer unconsumed alcohol from glasses, and cigarette butts from ashtrays.

'Ugh,' she groans, collapsing into one of the deckchairs. 'You know the day after recovery gets harder the older we get? I'd hate to see what we'll be like when we're forty.'

There's an uneasy silence while we digest her words.

'Shit. Sorry, Ava. Shit.'

She is stricken with her thoughtlessness but she needn't be. I don't expect everyone to filter every word before it comes out of their mouth on the off chance it might upset me.

'Recovery wouldn't be so bad if you didn't get

shitfaced every time you sing,' I tell her.

She shrugs. 'You know it helps.'

Only a select few people in the world know how much Amanda struggles with stage fright.

'I suppose I'd better shower,' I say reluctantly.

'What time are they coming?'

'Nine-thirty.'

'Isn't that rather early for journos to be out and about,' Kate comments.

'Early bird catches the story, or something like that.'

'I thought it was worm.'

'Far too early for me anyway,' Amanda grumbles.

Standing in the shower and letting the hot water massage my body, I take a few deep breaths, trying to quell the nerves I feel at being interviewed for a major women's magazine, one with a readership of roughly half a million women each week. Five hundred and ninety-four thousand, to be precise. I know this because I stupidly googled it last night when I couldn't sleep. Now I'm terrified about saying something stupid for all those women to read.

The only reason I agreed to this interview in the end was to raise awareness. Specifically, that it can also be a young women's disease. Free mammograms are only offered to women over the age of forty-five in this country, and while I've read the stats and agree that yes, more women in that age group are affected, there is also a troubling trend of young women such as myself being diagnosed. Worse, we are often misdiagnosed, or diagnosed too late, once the cancer has metastasised and become harder or, as in my case, unable to be cured.

Some doctors, such as the one I saw, don't place enough seriousness on lumps or bumps or dimples or any other such symptoms of the disease when it presents in someone under the age of thirty-five.

And that has to change.

'You have the opportunity to make a difference here,' Amanda had said, when she and Kate were trying to sell the idea to me. Cunningly, they'd roped my mother in on the cause. Her love of glossy printed pages is tremendous, and the thought of her only daughter being on the pages of one was enough to make her actually, *physically*, quiver.

'Just think, darling,' Mum said. 'They'd make you all glamourous for the photo shoot. They bring their own wardrobe and make-up people you know. And hairstylists. You'd look amazing.'

'*And* you could make a difference to someone's life. By increasing awareness,' Amanda said again with a pointed look at Mum.

'Oh yes. And that,' Mum said.

She had a point. If I could save just one person from going through what I've been through and am now facing, by catching their own cancer in the early, highly treatable stages, it'd be worth any misgivings on my part.

I don't know what exactly I'd been expecting but the reporter, when she arrives, isn't it. She blows into the house like a southern wind, all purple hair and sweeping kaftan, the bracelets on her wrists jangling like wind chimes. She stops in the centre of the lounge and does a three hundred and sixty degree turn, and then nods to herself. 'Yes. This will do.'

'You must be Ava,' she says to me, tilting her head to the left and adopting the same sympathetic expression most people who know my plight wear.

'What gave it away? The deathly pallor?' I joke, but she thinks I'm serious and freezes like a possum caught in a spotlight.

'Er, well . . . '

'Relax, I'm joking.'

She throws back her head and laughs too loud and for too long.

'I'm Nadia,' she says when she recovers, a hand pressed against her chest. 'And these are Sophie and Kelly. They're here to do your make-up and hair and wardrobe for the photos. Don't worry, they're very good at what they do. When they've finished working their magic no one would even guess that you're . . . '

'Dying?' I supply helpfully. 'I think that's kind of the point of the story, isn't it?'

'Coffee, anyone?' Kate interrupts to break the awkward silence that follows. 'Or tea? I have herbal.'

'Are they . . . here . . . yet? Am I too . . . late?' Mum's voice arrives first, then her body follows. She bustles inside and collapses against the back of the couch, out of breath. When she sees Nadia she flushes. 'I know you,' she says, straightening up and pointing. 'I've seen your picture in the magazine.'

Nadia smiles regally.

'You're my favourite journalist,' Mum gushes. 'I read all your human interest stories, every week. First page I flick to. Well, after the gossip pages, of course. That Dominique Taylor sure can sniff out a good story. Is he still with that guy off the telly? That dancing show?'

'Mum.'

'What?'

Nadia steps forward and holds out a hand so covered in heavy rings I'm surprised she can manage to lift it. 'Nadia Hepburn. It's a pleasure to meet you, Mrs Green. I can't even begin to imagine what you're going through.'

'Oh, I'm not going through it. Ava is.'

'Well, I know that, I just meant . . . ' Nadia looks at me helplessly. I smile back. She's on her own.

I almost say no to Sophie and Kelly and their magical, talented fingers, but when they finish their work and I look in the mirror I am so glad I didn't. I don't look like me. Well, I do, but a better, much nicer version.

My blonde hair, curly and untameable since it grew back after the chemo, has been gently coaxed and styled, pinned back on one side with a pretty diamante clip. It flows sweetly over the top of my head and down the other side in sleek finger waves, a nod to the hairstyles of eras gone by. My make-up is subtle but effective, and Nadia was right; if you didn't know I was sick you would probably never guess. With smoky eyes and plump, outlined lips, they have elected not to camouflage the tiny freckles that scatter across the tops of my cheeks. Fairy footsteps, my mother called them when I was growing up. Back when they were the biggest thing I had to complain about.

Although she has produced a small rack from her van with an assortment of outfits, Sophie cups her chin in her hand and looks me up and down shrewdly for a good two minutes before declaring she has 'just the thing'.

That thing is a dress I would never have bought in a million years, or even tried on for that matter. Long, flowy and coral pink in colour, it is in a style that Sophie refers to as 'Bohemian Chic'.

When I look in the mirror after their efforts are exhausted, I actually gasp a little, and my mouth forms a wondrous 'O'. My reflection is beautiful. *I* am beautiful. I see someone who looks in the throes of their youth.

I see life.

Mum takes one look and promptly bursts into theatrical tears.

'Oh, love,' she wails through sobs. I get the impression that if she had a handkerchief she'd be sobbing into it. Once a person has a taste for amateur dramatics it's hard to let that go. 'You're absolutely stunning.'

'Thanks, Mum.'

'Seriously,' Amanda says. 'You look like a model or something. I don't think I've ever seen you look this good. Did you guys use paint or something?' She peers at my heavily contoured right cheek.

Sophie snorts.

Kate rolls her eyes. 'Don't listen to her.'

'She gets her looks from me, you know,' Mum says, nudging Nadia with an elbow. 'And her smarts. *And* her even temperament. In fact, I'm not sure what her father contributed, really. Well, I know *what* he contributed, if you know what I mean.' She nudges Nadia again. 'Shouldn't you be writing all this down?'

'Oh, I record most of my interviews these days,' Nadia says. 'Much easier and less likely to miss something. Then I can type it up later at my own leisure.' She looks at her watch. 'Where on earth is that photographer?'

I notice a look pass between Kelly and Sophie but think nothing of it because my stomach has gone all queasy at the thought of posing for photos.

'I don't think I can do this.'

'You can't back out now,' Nadia says, a little too sharply. 'This is our lead story for next week's issue.'

'I'm not backing out.' Amanda bristles protectively beside me. 'I just need some air.'

'Oh, of course.' Nadia nods sympathetically. 'Off you go. I need to speak to your mother and friends anyway. Get their side of the story.'

Mum follows me out to the balcony. 'Are you sure you're OK? Are you in pain?'

'I'm fine,' I reassure her. 'The pain is OK, nothing I can't handle. I really do just need some air. Too many people in one small room. I'll be back in a minute.'

'Do you want me to come with you?'

I give her an arched eyebrows look. 'Are you kidding? And miss out on being interviewed by your second favourite journalist?'

She winces. 'I said that, didn't I. I was star-struck. Didn't think before I opened my mouth.'

Nadia's voice calls out. 'Mrs Green? If you don't mind I have some questions?'

Mum looks at me questioningly.

'Go,' I reassure her. 'I'll be back soon.'

She kisses me on the forehead and ducks back into the house. I wait until she's gone, slip off my flat shoes and head quietly for the stairs that lead down to the lawn.

13

The grass is still damp from this morning's dew under my bare feet. A month ago it was crunchy with frost, and in another month or two it will be dry and brown from the heat of high summer. That thought is immediately followed by another: Will I still be alive to see it?

I hate that it is becoming my norm. To question how many seasons I still have. How many days, how many hours and minutes. Sometimes, when I am alone, I can hear seconds tick by in my head. Loud and relentless, a reminder that time stops for no one.

Under the trees the air is damp and humid, but it's a short walk of twenty metres and then I am clear, perched on the top of a small dune, only a metre high. Spread out before me, in all its breathtaking beauty, is the beach.

I close my eyes and breathe in a deep breath of salty air and when I exhale it back out a giddy little laugh escapes with it. The scent is delicious. It smells of my childhood and hot days punctuated with sweaty adventure, of teenage kisses with spotty boys in the tussock grasses of the sand dunes. Of flip-flops carelessly stolen by the tide, driftwood statues, sandcastles and jellyfish stings. Floating idly on my back in the clear water like a starfish, before gleefully riding the breakers to shore on a body board gifted by Santa. Picking through rock pools with a plastic bucket clenched in hand. My mother's voice, warm ham sandwiches and lime cordial, sand in my hair and zinc on my nose.

Memories, thick and fast, like a slideshow. Both painful and joyful. I have lived a life. I have lost a life. It was never mine to begin with. On loan, temporary, subject to recall.

I jump down on to the sand and walk down towards the water. The ocean is calm today, a kind of moody turquoise colour like one of those three dollar rings from gypsy fairs that change colour depending on whether you're happy or sad. Supposedly. Kate, a believer in science rather than the occult, said it was more to do with the temperature of your skin. I remember feeling secretly proud when mine would turn black, like I was a rebel of sorts. A misunderstood soul.

The water is cool but not cold. It laps around my feet and I lift the dress, quickly tucking it into my knickers at the sides of my thighs so it comes up to just above my knees. I see tiny fish dart away as I walk along the shore a little. I can't go far, I know they'll be looking for me soon. But I needed this.

Growing up in a small town right on the ocean, I took it for granted. It was just always there after all, so it wasn't a novelty like it was for the truckloads of out-of-towners who'd arrive every summer and lay claim to the beach, departing after the Christmas holidays leaving nothing in their wake but litter and the odd broken heart. When something is readily available it often loses its allure, and as my friends and I got older that's what happened. So it's been a while since I've been down here, especially on my own, and it's only now I realise how much I have missed it.

I pick up a few shells and try to skim them across the surface like we did when we were kids, but I am rusty and out of practice and they fail dismally at the first hurdle. Bending down to forage for more, I hear a noise that is out of place, a clicking sound. Puzzled, I turn to the path and at first I see nothing obvious, but then the light shifts and I make out the outline of a man, standing in the shadows of the trees at the bottom of Kate's property. He has a camera, and it is trained on me.

As soon as he realises I have seen him he lowers it and smiles ruefully.

'Sorry,' he calls out, emerging from the trees and jumping easily down the bank to stride down the beach towards me. The length of his legs means he is in front of me in an instant, a hand thrust out in greeting. His fingers are long and look well lived.

'James,' he says. 'I'm your photographer for the magazine shoot, not some random stalker.'

His smile is broad and honest, and I find myself tracing the outline of his lips with my eyes. They are a plum colour, emphasised even more by the light blond stubble on his jaw. I'm not normally a fan of facial hair, but his is trimmed and discreet and suits him. He is the very epitome of the saying, 'larger than life', and fills my vision, the beach, my world. Tall and athletic, he is wearing a snug black T-shirt and jeans that are possibly a size too big, given that they slouch around his hips and reveal a sliver of tanned skin. He is also barefoot, and has rolled his jeans up to his calves. Up close I realise he is older than he first appeared, evidenced by the fine lines around his eyes and mouth. His skin is beginning to show signs of weathering, and has the kind of colour cultivated by a great deal of time in the outdoors and exposure to the elements. The brilliance of his green eyes against this is penetrating, and his hair is a palette of blond tones, similar to that which Kate spends a fortune every month trying to replicate. It is shorter on the sides than the top, which is brushed roughly to one side.

I've had boyfriends, although not recently. My longest relationship lasted for three years, spanning the ages of nineteen through twenty-two. We had tentatively started discussing the possibility of engagement, but then something, and also nothing, happened. We simply drifted apart like wispy clouds on a summer's day. The sum of the parts that made up Us disentangled so stealthily and so slowly that it wasn't even painful. We just looked at each other sadly over the breakfast table one morning and realised that We had Come to An End. No fuss, no tears. Well, maybe the odd one when I watched a particularly soppy rom-com or drank myself maudlin. We're still on good terms and I bump into him in the supermarket occasionally. He is married with three children, and despite looking beleaguered as they run circles around the trolley and attempt to throw food in without him

84

noticing, he looks happy.

After that I dated a few guys, enough still to count on one hand. The length of time each relationship lasted varied between one (awkward) date and six months. I had just begun to see someone when I got my cancer diagnosis, the first one. To his credit he tried to do the right thing and play the part of caring boyfriend. He drove me to some of my appointments and bought me flowers when I started treatment. But then shit got real, and I got *really* sick, and neither of us had the strength to pretend that we cared enough to take things any further. Considering we were still in the first flushes of our relationship and he had yet to see me in my less than best knickers or with more than a day's growth of hair on my legs, I couldn't blame him. Nothing takes the shine off a new relationship more than your girlfriend breaking out with festering mouth sores from chemotherapy.

So it's been a while since I've *been* with a man, and although I am dying, I am not yet dead. I have the same desires and urges as the next woman, and the man in front of me is awakening all of them.

I realise he is also scrutinising me, waiting for me to speak. I am not typically brave when it comes to situations like this, so I try to think of something Amanda would say.

'Well.' I tuck my hair behind one ear and try hard to look nonchalant. 'If I had to choose someone to be stalked by, and you were in the line-up, I'd pick you.' Then I blush, hoping he won't notice with all the make-up I am wearing.

'Are you serious?'

'Sorry,' I say, cringing. 'Sorry. I don't know why I said that. That's not the kind of thing I would normally say.'

'Really?'

'Really.'

'I find that hard to believe. You said it so eloquently.' The upward pull of the corner of his lips suggest he is teasing.

'Yeah right.'

'If it's not the kind of thing you normally say, then why did you say it.'

I screw up my face because when I look up at him the sun blinds my eyes. 'I'm not sure. I just thought I'd try being someone else for a minute. Someone fearless and uncontrolled by normal societal decorum.'

'And how's that working out for you?'

'Terribly. How about we try again.' I hold out my hand and adopt a serious expression. 'Hi there, I'm Ava. And you must be James. I've heard so much about you.'

His cheeks dimple with amusement. 'You have?'

'No. Not a thing. Again, I don't know why I said that. For some reason you're making me nervous. But I'm guessing you have that effect on a lot of women.'

'Not that I'm aware of, no.'

'Seriously? But look at you. You're like . . . you know.' I gesture towards him and wave my hand up and down.

'Tall?'

86

'Yes. Tall. That's exactly what I was getting at.'

'So not insanely good-looking then?'

I snort laughter unintentionally before resuming a straight face. 'Sorry? Good-looking? Oh, well I guess. I mean, I personally hadn't noticed. But I suppose *some* might say — '

He laughs. The sound is loud and uproarious in the quietness of our surroundings, but it is a wonderful sound. The sound of life.

'As far as first impressions go I'm not doing so well, am I?' I smile up at him ruefully.

'On the contrary, you've complimented me twice. What more could a guy ask for?'

We hear my name called, muffled by the trees and distance, but clear nevertheless. I am being summoned. I give James a rueful smile.

'I guess I'm wanted.'

'I guess you are.'

'Shall we . . . ?' I gesture towards the house.

'After you.'

I start walking back up to the beach and he falls into an easy stride beside me.

'Am I in trouble with Nadia for disappearing?'

He shrugs. 'Who cares.'

'She's kind of intimidating,' I admit.

'Most journalists are. The trick is to remember it's *you* doing them the favour. Without you, they have no story.'

'I suppose that's true.'

'Besides, Nadia's like that with everyone. I don't work for her magazine often but every time I do she seems to have a new assistant.'

'So you're freelance? That must be exciting.'

He nods. 'Overseas publications mostly. I'm

doing this as a one-off favour for the editor, an old friend.'

'I'm sure he's grateful.'

He gives me a funny look. 'She. Marilyn Southgate. You haven't heard of her?'

'I don't really read a lot of magazines. Not my thing.'

His eyebrows shoot up. 'Maybe you shouldn't mention that in your interview.'

We have reached the trees and he steps back and gestures with one hand for me to go first. A gentleman. I find myself breathing shallowly, and I'm not sure whether it's because of the physical exertion or his presence. Either way, I don't want to go first, conscious of his eyes on me as I walk slower than someone my age should. But I don't want to make a fuss so I smile meekly and start up the track. I hear his breath quicken as he walks behind me and it makes my senses hyper-aware. I can hear the breeze rustling through the canopy of leaves above us, and the sound of birdsong as a tui goes head to head in a singing competition with a bellbird. Behind us the ocean provides the backing track. The air leaves particles of moisture on my skin as I move through it and I hope fervently the dress doesn't react badly to a little dampness; I have no desire to be in Sophie's bad books. I have barely gone twelve steps before the heat and the thick air combine to make me feel light-headed.

'Are you OK?'

I don't realise I have slowed right down to almost a stop until James is at my side, his voice and face betraying his concern. He reaches out to place a steadying hand on my arm and I suck in my breath sharply at his touch, as fleeting as it is before he removes it again. What is it about him that has this effect on me? I've never had this kind of reaction to a man before. Lacking the breath to speak, I simply lean back against a sturdy tree trunk and nod.

'Do you want me to get someone for help? Your mother?'

I shake my head fervently. That's the last thing I need, her overreacting.

'I'm OK,' I manage to say softly. 'I just need to rest a minute.'

'OK.'

'You can go on without me, I'll be there soon.'

He tilts his head. 'I'll wait, if it's all the same with you.'

I nod.

I concentrate on my breathing, counting each breath in and holding it before releasing. It works and I start to feel my pulse settle and my head clear.

'Better?' he asks, when I straighten up. He fills my presence with his vitality and health, and I don't want to be sick in front of him, or weak. I want, just for one day, to pretend otherwise. I allow myself to imagine that I am a model and on location for an exotic photo shoot. I am his muse, his Yoko Ono. He is infatuated with me.

'Yes, thank you. Must be the heat.'

'Look, Ava.' He shuffles one foot in the dirt and decaying leaves. A twig snaps. The tui takes flight, its wings powerfully thumping through the air. I feel a sense of dread at what's coming, and my dream evaporates and swiftly follows the tui into the ether.

'I don't really know what to say, you know, about what you're going through,' he continues awkwardly. 'But I also don't want to *not* say something, either. If that makes any sense.'

Cancer firmly inserts a foot between us, refusing as always to remain in the background.

'It's OK,' I say. 'I understand. I probably wouldn't know what to say either if the situation was reversed.'

'For what it's worth, you seem like a really nice person.'

'Oh I am,' I say, without a trace of modesty but with more than a touch of bitterness. 'I help old ladies across the road, pay my taxes on time, step over worms after a rainstorm. I'm as nice as they come. And that's why it doesn't make any sense.'

'No. It doesn't.'

'It's bullshit.'

'It is.'

'And not fair.'

'No.' His expression is hard to read as he looks at me. 'You're not like I thought you'd be.'

'Oh really? And what exactly were you expecting?'

'I'm not sure.'

He holds my gaze, and I like the way he doesn't flinch from the harsh truth. The ugliness of the disease is in the way it tries to alienate you from the healthy, those not afflicted. Whether they mean well or not, when you are dying, some people tend to act like you are already dead. And

I get it, I do. Everything changes. It's inconvenient. I remember at one family event, a wedding I think it was, not long after I was first diagnosed, I complained to my mother that I may as well have sat at home for all the attention anyone paid me.

'I feel like I'm a zombie in a horror film,' I complained. 'No one will look me in the eye or engage in conversation. When I went to the toilet they parted in front of me like the bloody Red Sea. What are they scared of? That I'm contagious?'

'Be gentle, Ava,' she'd said. 'They don't know what to say.'

And I'd looked at her, anguished, and said, 'Can't they just say hello?'

14

'What do you mean viral? Like herpes?'

Amanda snorts.

'Jesus, Mum,' I sigh. 'No, not herpes.'

'Oh. Well that's good then. I was worried for a minute.'

'It's a social media thing, Mrs G.,' Kate explains. 'Sometimes, for whatever reason, certain photos or stories appeal more than others. Then they get shared over and over until they're, like, all over the world and thousands of people are reading.'

My mother frowns as she tries to understand. 'So when you say Ava has gone viral, you mean . . . ?'

'People everywhere are following her story. And I mean everywhere. The magazine article got shared over two hundred thousand times alone.'

'Two hundred thou — ? Are you serious?'

'Deadly.'

Mum flinches and looks at me.

'Sorry, Ava,' Kate says. 'Poor word choice.'

'Don't worry about it.'

'Here, look.' Kate hands Mum her tablet and shows her where to read the comments underneath the online article. Mum fishes in her purse for the glasses she refuses to use in public, and starts reading.

It is two weeks since the magazine published

the article. Since it came out, the Facebook page Amanda set up has been inundated with offers. Everything from dresses to flowers to venues to money. A limousine company even offered to drive me to wherever I chose to have my 'ceremony', as long as I let them use my face on their advertising brochures afterwards. I politely declined.

And now, to top it all off, Kate has just fielded a call on my phone from Marilyn Southgate, the magazine editor. The readers love me, apparently. The plucky young cancer patient whose only dream is to have a big wedding party before she off and snuffs it.

Not her exact words, obviously. But that's the gist of it.

'No,' I say pre-emptively.

'You haven't even heard what I was going to say yet,' Kate points out.

'I don't need to. I know where this is going. I have a sixth sense for some things.'

'No you don't.'

'Yes, I do.'

'OK, what did Marilyn want then?'

'She wants to do another story. An exclusive of the wedding.'

'Kind of,' Kate concedes.

'Ha. Told you.'

'But that's not all she wants.'

'I don't care what she wants, the answer is no.'

Mum sits down on the bed, narrowly missing my knee. Everything aches today, but I don't tell her that. She doesn't need to know.

'Sweetheart,' she says. 'Have you read any of these comments?'

'No.'

'You should. They're very lovely.'

I'm feeling sulky and sorry for myself, so I don't answer.

'Marilyn wants to do a serial article,' Kate says cautiously. 'Yes, she wants to cover your big day, but also the lead-up and the organisation for it. An article a week, with photographs. They don't want just to leave people hanging.'

What people?

'No.'

'That's not all.' She takes a deep breath. 'They wondered if you might be interested in doing a weekly little column, an advice kind of thing.'

'Advice on what? I'm not an expert on anything. She's mad.'

'Sort of like, musings . . . about things you've realised while you've been sick. What's important in life and what's not. You now don't focus so much on the materialistic stuff. That kind of thing.'

'No.'

'Just think about it.'

'I don't need to. It sounds like an extraordinary waste of the little time I have left. In fact, the whole thing does. Cancel the wedding. I don't know what I was thinking.'

With some effort, I roll over in bed and bury my head in my pillow so they can't see the tears that trickle across the bridge of my nose to leave damp patches on my pillowcase.

Amanda clears her throat. 'I think maybe we

94

should give Ava some space.'

A hand gently strokes my hair, I don't know who it belongs to but I'm assuming it's Mum. Sure enough. 'Is that what you want, love?' she asks. 'Or do you want me to stay.'

I know I'm being a brat, and that these three women would do anything humanely possible for me and therefore do not deserve to be treated the way I am treating them. But I also know that *because* they love me they won't take offence, no matter what I throw at them.

'I'm sorry,' I mumble into my pillow. 'I didn't sleep well. Maybe a nap might help.'

'OK.' Mum kisses me on the head and I feel her weight lift off the bed. Before she leaves the room though she pauses. 'Do we need to see Dr Harrison about increasing your pain medication? Is that what kept you awake?'

'No,' I lie. 'The pain is fine, Mum.'

She sighs deeply. 'You're lying, Ava Green. I know you, remember? But we'll discuss it later. Sweet dreams, baby girl.'

The door closes.

When I wake up the room is dark, and I realise I have slept the afternoon away. Regret floods in quickly. More time wasted. It is hard not to jealously protect the days when days may be all I have left. Not years, I know that much. But weeks, months? How long is a piece of string? A wrinkle in time? A ripple in the ocean?

The house is quiet. Too quiet. I think they have all gone out and left me and I am confused. But then I hear soft murmurings of noise drifting in through the French doors, and smell something that gets my stomach rumbling.

The back lawn is lit up with the light of a thousand fairy lights. They are strung from tree to tree, along the deck and even around the clothesline. The barbecue is fired up and the smell of sausages is heavy in the air. The picnic table has been set and has candles in jars along the centre. I can see that Kate has picked some of her prized roses from the front garden and they are arranged prettily in a jar in the middle. It is a magical sight that takes my breath away and I emit a soft 'Oh!' that makes the assembled people turn. There are more bodies in the shadows than there should be, and I wonder who else is here.

'Ava,' Mum says, looking up. 'There you are. Are you feeling any better?'

I nod, walking down the steps to join them on the lawn. 'What's all this in aid of?'

She turns to see what I mean. 'Oh the lights? They're for you. We wanted to do something to cheer you up a little. Difficult, I know, in the circumstances. But we must try nevertheless.' She gives me a watery smile, her face slipping with the grief lying just beneath the surface.

My dad, Kate and Amanda's parents are here, as well as Kate's older brother Craig, his wife Stephanie and their four kids. Growing up, Craig was like an older brother to Amanda and me too, in that he both looked out for us and tormented us at the same time.

It's a small gathering of people that I consider family, and it's just what I needed.

'You guys are the best.' I smile.

'We know,' Amanda says, through a mouthful of sausage. 'What?' she says when we all look at her. 'It's quality control, I have to try them first.'

We sit around the table together and we eat — sausages and home-made salads and bread rolls — and it's a pleasant night. I sit quietly mostly, content to observe and listen to the many stories and conversations going on around me. The kids run around the lawn shrieking and playing tag and I remember similar occasions when I was growing up when I did the same. Barefoot on the grass, bellies full, the stars overhead. Soft music plays from the stereo inside, and the scent of the sea is particularly strong tonight. I feel at one with nature, connected to both the earth and the heavens, but then I guess I do have a foot currently in both camps. My dad sits beside me and I nestle in against his chest, his arm around me. My mother fetches a blanket for my knees; it's more of a gesture because it's not overly cold. She is looking after her daughter as best as she can.

'Do you remember when you got that scar?'

My dad's gentle voice brings me out of my reverie.

He is looking at my hand, which is cupping a wine glass and resting on the table. I look at the scar he is talking about and realise I haven't noticed or thought about it for a long time. Even though of course I do remember how I got it, I stay silent, hoping he'll tell the story. He doesn't disappoint.

'You were so tiny,' he says. 'Only five or six. But you insisted on coming fishing with me, wouldn't be persuaded against it. Your mother said if I let any harm come to you she'd kill me herself, with her bare hands. Luckily for me she wasn't serious eh?'

'I wanted to bait the hook myself,' I prompt him.

'Yes, you did. You certainly weren't squeamish like some other little girls. You stuck your hand in the bucket of fish guts and chose the biggest piece you could find, then you stuck that hook in so hard — '

'It went out the other side and into my thumb,' I finish, smiling.

'I've never heard someone scream so loud,' he chuckles. 'Jesus, you gave me a fright. I thought for sure you'd lost a body part from the amount of blood. I started planning on a new life somewhere your mother wouldn't be able to find me.'

He reaches over to rub the long white scar gently.

'Two stitches,' he says. 'And you didn't flinch. Not once. You were so brave.'

'I had you to hold my hand.' I smile up at him.

'You always will.' His voice chokes up with emotion. He doesn't say much about what's happening, my dad. But you can see it in his eyes, that he's hurting.

'You're still so brave,' he carries on. 'Ava, your mother showed me the things people have been saying after your magazine article. Very nice things. There's a lot of people keeping you in their thoughts you know. Maybe, if enough people do . . . ' He trails off.

I lean back to frown at him. 'Don't tell me Mum's got you believing in miracles too.'

'Of course not,' he says. 'Although for her it's not so much about believing as it is *hoping*.'

'It's false hope. She'll only get more hurt in the long run.'

'You can't blame her for wanting things to be different.'

'No.' He's right. Of course I can't.

'Anyway, I was thinking. This wedding idea of yours. I know I thought it was a bit odd to start with. But the more I think about it the more I've come around to the idea. And I think you should let the magazine document the journey. It'll be like a legacy of sorts.'

'Yeah, I just don't know, Dad. Won't it be a bit morbid? All those people reading, watching, waiting for me to die?'

'I think it's the opposite. They'll be watching you live out your life, on your terms. Ultimately it's your decision of course. But people have taken a shine to you. Which is only natural, because you're just wonderful.'

I stifle a smile. 'You might be a touch biased, Dad.'

'So what if I am? Anyway, you get your looks and your zappy — ' he clicks his fingers — 'personality from me, although don't tell your mother I said that. She likes to take all the credit.'

We exchange an inside smile at the joke.

'Just think about it,' he says, echoing Kate's earlier words.

'OK.' I nod. 'I'll think about it. For you.'

'Good girl. Now come here.' He pulls me in close and kisses the top of my head, just like he did when the doctor sewed up my finger. If only this was as easy a fix.

15

All credit to Nadia, because writing is much harder than I thought. I sit down one day to write my first 'advice' column, although the word makes me cringe because really, who I am to give advice to anyone. I'm not an expert on anything, unless you consider the TV show *Friends* a specialist subject. I have a bit of an addiction to reruns of that particular show, and even though I've seen every episode at least three times, I'm still not sick of it. I could easily rattle off the story arc of every character through seasons one to ten, but, unfortunately for me, that's not the kind of thing they're after. I sit and stare at the laptop screen for a while, then I stare out the window instead for a change of scenery, hoping for inspiration. None comes. In the end, after I call my mother and complain that I can't do it and they'll just have to accept that, she advises me to just write the kinds of things I'd like to have known about, before I was diagnosed. Or observations of life since. What's important to me now as opposed to then, for example. Her advice made it easier, because there was really only one, major thing that I wished I could go back and tell my pre-cancer self. And that was this.

Be a better advocate for your own health.

I was twenty-four when I first found the lump. It wasn't like I was actively searching for it, because at that age breast cancer was the last thing on my mind. I was young, after all, in the prime of my life. I worried about things like the fine art of balancing my pay cheque between my bills and a social life, or whether my thighs looked big in my jeans or there was enough make-up in the world to cover my latest breakout. I certainly wasn't giving any thought to dying.

I was in the shower, enjoying the exotic scent of my new coconut body scrub, when I thought I felt something. Nothing obvious, just *something*. I prodded and rubbed the area on my right breast, just to the side almost under my armpit, for a few minutes before I decided I was imagining things, because sometimes I could feel it and sometimes I couldn't. It wouldn't be anything serious, I reasoned, if I could only find it half the time.

So I dismissed it until a few weeks later when I felt it again. I went along to my GP, only my normal GP wasn't there and I was ushered in to see a twelve-year-old-looking woman with a waist-length braid who looked like she'd be more at home under a skipping rope.

'It'll be nothing. A cyst most likely,' she said, in what she imagined was a reassuring way but which actually came across as massively condescending.

'But what if it's not.'

'Then there are a myriad of other possibilities. It is highly unlikely, at your age, to be malignant.'

'Are you sure you're, you know, *qualified*?'

She'd smiled like she'd heard that a hundred

times that day already and asked me to lie down on the bed.

She couldn't feel it. I put my finger over it and she tried again. She frowned.

'If anything it feels like a slight thickening, rather than a lump. I think it's hormone-related. Where are you on your cycle?'

'I don't know, somewhere in the middle?'

'Come back and see me in a month, once you've had a period. If you can still feel it, that is.'

A month later not only could I still feel it, but it felt bigger. Harder.

My usual GP was back from her holiday, resplendent with golden tan and an air of seaside-induced breeziness. I'll never forget the way her smile slipped, and how her eyebrows almost met above her nose when she frowned.

'Oh yes, I can feel it,' she'd said. 'Let's book you in for an ultrasound.'

She saw the look of abject terror on my face.

'Just to be on the safe side.' She smiled. 'I'm sure it's nothing more than a completely benign cyst.'

It wasn't.

The lady who did the scan gave nothing away, although I searched her face for clues. I was still feeling fraudulent, like I was making a drama over nothing and sucking up appointment time that some poor woman somewhere with a *real* problem could have been using.

My breast had never seen as much action as it got over the next few weeks. I got used to flopping it out on slabs while it was squashed and photographed and scanned and poked and prodded and drawn on and had needles stuck in so the guy who did my lumpectomy would know where to cut.

'It's OK,' the oncologist said. 'We've caught it early. I'm fairly confident I can remove it all doing a lumpectomy.'

After the operation his face told a different story. He didn't get clear margins. He'd need to go in again. I signed the form that gave him permission to do a full mastectomy if needed, while inwardly I made deals with a God I had no faith in for this not to be the case.

Afterwards, good news, this time. Better. No mastectomy required, just tissue removal. The margins were clear. He'd got it all. My lymph nodes came back clear, it hadn't spread.

I had chemotherapy and radiation treatment. The skin on my breast turned red like sunburn and blistered. It hurt. It hurt like hell. My hair fell out. I moved back in with my parents, gained twenty kilos and looked like a bloated caricature of myself. The nausea was ever-present and I threw up until my teeth started to rot. The worst thing was, when I looked in the mirror I saw cancer, not me.

'But you're too young,' people would say, puzzled. 'Isn't that an older woman's disease?'

Cancer is an indiscriminate bastard.

I started on a course of Tamoxifen, a drug that decreased my chances of developing secondary cancer. It wasn't easy, the drug made me develop early menopausal symptoms and the hot flushes were horrendous. But every time I took another pill I told myself I was doing this so that I could live. Everything was going to be OK.

Until it wasn't.

Notes from Ava

(Women's Weekly September 25th)

YOU are the best advocate you could ever possibly have when it comes to your own health.

That doctor, sitting in the chair opposite you, they're human too. And as well-meaning as they generally are, they're often harried; overwhelmed by an overburdened health system and its demands on their time. Medicine is a business just like any other, with a bottom line and goals and targets that must be reached. That doctor in front of you might have had a rough night, little sleep, caring for a newborn at home or an elderly dementia parent, recently moved into the annex. They might be distracted, worrying about when they're going to have time to type up the last three patients' notes, and yours, before it all becomes a domino effect and the rest of the day goes down the gurgler. They might be thinking about what they'll have for dinner, or wondering why Brenda the receptionist gave the other staff members Christmas cards but not them. Have they done something to upset her?

Fifteen minutes, tops. That's all the time

you have to convince the doctor sitting in front of you that *something is potentially wrong*. You know this, because you know your own body, certainly far better than they, who have only just now made its acquaintance, do.

Most of the time, of course, they will be correct with their diagnosis. They have to be, it is, after all, what they go through seven years plus of training for. But sometimes, just sometimes, they're not. And it's not out of malice. They don't personally want to see you hurt or dying. But they're human, like you, and humans make mistakes. Cancer symptoms can mimic symptoms of other health issues. After all, how many of us are tired most of the time? And does anyone really have perfect bowel movements every day?

Don't be fobbed off if you are unhappy with the outcome. Seek a second opinion, a third if necessary. If that offends them, they are not the right doctor for you. (Or anyone for that matter.) Push to see a specialist; pay for the tests yourself if it comes to it. Don't be afraid to have a voice. Not all people who get ill fall into a generalised age group, or a particular gender. You're not 'too young' to have cancer. No one is.

You will never regret standing up for yourself.

But you will regret it if you don't.

16

'What the hell is that smell?'

Amanda's nose crinkles up with disgust as she steps out of the back seat of my mother's car. Even though I was in the slightly roomier front passenger seat, my legs are cramping, and as I stretch them I tell myself it's from the car journey, not the cancer.

My mother gets out of the driver's side and inhales deeply.

'Ah,' she says, 'that, my dear, is the smell of the country. A combination of cow shit and silage hay.'

'It's disgusting.' Amanda turns to me. 'You can't seriously consider having your wedding here. Not with that smell.'

'I don't know,' I say looking around. 'I think it's charming. Anyway, I'm sure you'd get used to it.'

'I wouldn't count on it,' she mutters.

A car crunches on the gravel driveway as it pulls in behind us. Nadia gingerly climbs out of the back seat, keeping one hand firmly on the door and looking around as if she has just been transported into another dimension.

'Are you sure this is the right place?' she asks.

Despite the fact she herself formed the same first impression, Amanda rolls her eyes at me. She doesn't like Nadia; I know this because she told me in no uncertain terms after our first meeting. With Amanda you get one chance to make her like you. Screw it up and that's it.

'Looks like it.' I point to a sign on the wooden gate in front of us. *Marmalade Farm*.

She gives a stiff little smile. 'How quaint.'

I'm surprised when two other cars pull into the car park and lift one hand to shield my eyes from the sun so I can see them clearer. One I recognise but can't place, until Kelly clambers out and I realise it was at Kate's house when they did the first interview.

'Hi, Ava,' Sophie calls out warmly as she exits the passenger side.

'Hi,' I squeak back, caught off guard. 'What are you guys doing here?'

She looks at Nadia, who frowns at me. 'What do you mean?' she asks. 'Have you forgotten we're doing a series of articles on your search for the perfect wedding?'

'No, of course not,' I say. 'I just didn't realise we were doing the whole shebang again.' I gesture to Kelly and Sophie. Then a thought occurs to me. If they're here to do make-up again, then that must mean . . .

'Hi, Ava.'

At the sound of his voice I squeeze my eyes shut for a moment before I open them and turn around. 'James, hi.' He looks even better than I remembered.

'I thought last time was a one-off job?' I say, trying hard not to betray how glad I am that this was not, in fact, the case.

'It was supposed to be, yes.' His manner is slightly stiff, as if he is here against his will.

'Oh?'

He frowns as if he's irritated by having to explain. 'The magazine's normal photographer is still sick so Marilyn begged me to help out again today. I've made it clear it's the last time though. This isn't my normal line of work.' He adds the last sentence disdainfully, and I wonder what exactly he means in particular. Weddings? Women's magazines? Dying women in wedding dresses?

'Oh.' And there was me hoping he'd wanted to see me again. My mother hears the flat tone in my voice and gives me a sharp look. Meanwhile Amanda is giving me bug eyes.

'James, can I have a word,' Nadia calls. 'I just want to compare notes so we're both on the same page as to the direction of the article.'

'Oh my God, it's that hot photographer again,' Amanda hisses when James leaves to join Nadia next to her car. Unlike Nadia, James made quite the first impression on both Amanda and Kate when he'd come to the house for the first article. They'd been all giggly and silly in his presence like they were sixteen-year-old school girls. He'd been nothing but professional though, almost *too* professional. He had refused to be drawn into short talk and as soon as he was satisfied he had the right photo he packed his things away hastily and left while I was getting changed. It had seemed rude, which confused me because I'm normally a good judge of character, and my first impression of him was not that.

'Is it?' I answer Amanda, feigning nonchalance.

She elbows me. 'Oh whatever, Ava, don't pretend you didn't notice last time. You couldn't take your eyes off him.'

I'm rescued by the arrival of the farm owners, a lovely couple in their fifties who, according to their messages, fled the rat race of the city to farm goats, make cheese and host weddings in the barn they had converted specifically for the purpose. The couple, Ruth and David, are as warm and welcoming in person as they were in their messages offering the barn and their services. She takes my hands and wells up with tears when we are introduced, which threatens to set my mother off too.

'Is there somewhere Ava can try on the dresses?' Sophie asks. She is carefully holding a few dress bags, maybe five or six, in one hand. They are not see-through flimsy wrap like last time. These are cream-coloured and sturdy, and the bulky size of some of them suggests to me that they are most likely . . .

'Wedding dresses?' I ask.

Her eyes widen as she nods. 'Oh my God, wait till you see them. They're gorgeous. I had so many to choose from, it was seriously hard to narrow it down, but I picked a few that I know you'll look amazing in. It's your choice though, of course, which one you decide to wear for the shoot.'

'You want *me* to wear one?' I point to my own chest.

She looks at me like I'm a bit thick. 'Well, yeah. You're the one having the wedding, remember?'

'I know that, but why?'

'Because the editor thinks it will be more interesting for the readers than just you in a pair of jeans checking out a barn. No offence.'

'None taken.'

Nadia interrupts. 'I know for you this is all about the big day itself, but we really want our readers to feel like they're also on this journey with you. We want them to understand, through the article and photos, just how much this means to you.' She waves her hands around theatrically as she speaks, using them for emphasis on the pertinent points.

She's full of shit, of course, but if it means I get to dress up I really don't care.

'Plus you get to be pampered and wear a seriously divine dress.' Kelly adds.

They all look at me expectantly.

'Is that OK with you?' Nadia asks.

I nod. 'You had me at 'pampered'.'

'I promise we won't do anything you don't feel comfortable with,' James says.

'That's a shame,' Amanda sniggers.

17

'Oh yes.' Mum claps her hands to her cheeks so soundly I'm worried she'll leave a mark. She nods her head energetically. '*Definitely* that one.'

'You said that about the last three.'

'Sorry. I can't help it. You look amazing in them all.' She turns to Sophie. 'She gets her figure from me you know.'

Sophie smiles diplomatically.

'Which one did *you* like the best,' Kelly asks. 'After all, it's your day, your decision.'

I turn back to the mirror and study the dress I am wearing. It's made of a soft material that drapes gently over my body, and even though I am much thinner than I should be, it mystically gives me a womanly appearance. Curves where there are none. Long enough for me to trip if I'm not careful, it also has a lacy top with cap sleeves. I can't stop looking at myself. It is beautiful, and I *feel* beautiful in it.

'This one,' I say.

Sophie sets about pinning the hemline to prevent accidents, while Kelly curls my hair into waves. She pins a silk flowered garland into my hair, and applies subtle make-up, gentle bronzes and golds, ever so slightly shimmering in the right light.

When they step back to admire their handiwork I wait, breath held, for the verdict. Together with Mum, Amanda and Ruth, they huddle around, shoulder to shoulder like a rugby scrum and look me up and down.

'Well?'

'You look amazing. Like one of those brides in a bridal magazine,' Amanda says.

'Have you ever read a bridal magazine?'

'Hell no. Never. Well, not willingly anyway. But you were always shoving them in our faces when we were kids. Remember whenever we went to the corner dairy for lollies you'd flick through the pages, drooling over the dresses, until the old man behind the counter yelled at us that it wasn't a library and if you weren't going to bloody pay for it, put it back on the shelf.'

'Oh yeah, I forgot about that,' I say wistfully. Any reminder of my childhood gives me nostalgia lately. 'I don't think he liked kids very much.'

'Would you, if you had to stand there waiting for them to decide which lollies to spend their ten cents on every day?'

'Good point.'

'You look absolutely stunning.' Mum smiles proudly.

Ruth, to all our surprise, starts crying. Silent tears, that trickle down her cheeks like raindrops on a window.

'I'm sorry,' she says, wiping them with her sleeve. 'It's just you remind me so much of her.'

'Who?'

'My sister. Connie. She died five years ago but it feels as if it were only yesterday.'

'I'm sorry to hear that,' Mum says.

And just like that, I know what's coming. I

hear the words rushing like waves to the seashore, their thundering crescendo building.

'She had breast cancer too,' Ruth carries on. 'Awful death it was. I watched her fade away till her body just couldn't fight it any more. That's why when I saw your story I knew we had to help if we could.'

I look down to where my feet are hidden under the dress. 'Well, thank you. I appreciate it.'

Why can I never escape it? Why do there have to be reminders everywhere I go? My diagnosis brought me access to a special club, The Cancer Club. Far more members than you would expect, you realise once you're in. It's not the cool kind of club where you sip champagne out of crystal flutes in fancy rooms, while deliciously hot young men in black and white penguin suits pass around trays of caviar and shrimp as you converse, revelling in the exclusivity of your membership. This is the kind of club that meets in a draughty Boy Scout's hall, where the tea bags are bought in bulk and taste like it, and the biscuits are stale because no one ate them last week so they were tipped back into the Tupperware container because, well, waste not, want not after all. This is a club that no one wants in on.

There is an awkward silence because no one knows what to say next. Ruth looks ready to crumble under the weight of her memories and grief. I know I should say more, but I can't. I don't want to. I *want* to forget, for however brief a moment. I only have a finite number of moments left, and I have to fill them wisely.

114

Selfish and ungrateful maybe, probably. But I can't help how I feel. I just don't have the energy in me to help anyone else cope with their grief.

I am saved by a knock on the door and James's impatient voice.

'Is Ava ready? There are clouds on the horizon, but the light is good right now. We should make a start.'

'Yes,' I call gratefully. 'I am.'

He has his camera around his neck and a small black bag hanging over one shoulder to bounce at his hip.

Mum and the others have followed us outside.

'You don't all have to come, do you?' I ask, suddenly shy. The thought of posing with all of them watching is unappealing.

'I don't,' Nadia says. 'The photos are James's business. I'll take care of the words.' She turns to Ruth. 'I'll need to see the — ' her shoulders give a light shudder — 'barn please.'

'Of course. I'll show you around.' Ruth has composed herself again. 'And afterwards we'll go inside for afternoon tea. I've baked scones and whipped up some cream, and we have a drawer full of the largest range of herbal teas in the district. Some of which we make ourselves. My echinacea and lemon is particularly delicious. Good for your health, too.'

'Do you have coffee?' Amanda asks. 'I don't drink things I can't pronounce.'

'Philistine,' Mum sighs.

Amanda shrugs. 'Can't pronounce that either.'

'There aren't any goats in the barn are there?' Sophie asks.

'Don't be silly, of course not,' Ruth answers. 'Can't have wedding guests treading in poo all the time now can we?'

'Why is it called Marmalade Farm?' Kelly asks. 'Do you make your own marmalade here too?'

'No, we don't. I can understand why you'd think that's the reason, everyone does. But it's not.' Ruth starts walking towards the path that leads up the lawn to the barn and the others follow. 'It's quite a funny story, actually.'

'Is it long?' Amanda mutters, trailing after them and rolling her eyes at me. 'I'm hungry.'

'I'm just going to take you back to the field I saw as we were coming up the driveway, for a few shots,' James says once they are gone. 'If that's OK?'

I nod, feeling absurd standing in front of him in full bridal dress and make-up.

Mum's eagle ears hear him and she stops and turns, frowning.

'I don't think that's a good idea,' she says. 'The driveway is about two kilometres long. That's too far for Ava to walk.'

'I wasn't planning on making her walk. We'll go in my car.'

'I guess that will be OK. I'll come with you.' She starts back down the path.

'No,' I say too loudly and too quickly. They both look at me, surprised. 'Sorry. I just think you should stay here with the others, Mum. You *did* say you couldn't wait to see inside the barn.'

'I can see it later. You might need help.'

'I'll be fine.'

'I don't want you wearing yourself out.'

'I won't. Besides, what are you going to do, carry me?'

'If I have to.' She has her determined face on.

I step forward to give her a hug and speak softly in her ear. 'Please don't treat me like an invalid, Mum. I'm not dead yet. I know my limits. Let me enjoy this.'

Her arms tighten around my ribs with as much pressure as she dares exert. She is worried, my mother, about hurting me. Her extreme gentleness is heart-breaking.

'I'm sorry,' she breathes back. 'I just want to protect you. Stupid I know.'

'It's not stupid. It's lovely.'

She steps back to hold me at arm's length, her eyes betraying her emotion. 'Hang on.' She scrambles in her purse. 'I need to send a photo to your father. Where's my bloody phone?'

'He'll see me when it's published, Mum.' I am conscious of James waiting, watching.

'Yes, I know that, but as your father I think he should get a sneak preview, don't you? Ah, here it is.'

She fishes her phone out of her bag and also, throwing a frown at James, her glasses. Putting them on, she peers at her phone until she finds the right icon and jabs at it a few times because no matter how many times I tell her you don't have to double click on your phone like you do on a computer, she just can't break the habit.

'Stand over by that tree,' she says.

'No. Just hurry up and take the photo.'

James clears his throat impatiently. 'Would you

117

like me to take one of you both together?'

Mum takes her glasses off quickly. 'That would be nice, thank you.' She passes him the phone. 'You just push that little camera-looking picture on the bottom. Make sure you hold it steady though or it'll be blurry. And watch you don't put your thumb in front of that little square bit there. Can't tell you how many times I've done that.'

I see James stifle a smile as I groan.

'He's a professional photographer, Mum. I think he can work a phone camera.'

'Oh yes, silly me.'

She comes to stand beside me and we hold each other's waist, heads together, and we smile as James snaps off a couple of shots.

How many photos of me in my lifetime? With my mother? My father? With anyone?

'Thank you,' Mum says, taking the phone off him and texting one off to my father. 'Are you sure you don't need me to come with you?'

I shake my head. 'Go join the others. You'll just make me feel self-conscious if you come.'

'OK.' She kisses me on the cheek. 'Look after her,' she says sternly to James.

'Of course.'

'Sorry about that,' I say once we are in the car, bouncing our way down the gravel driveway. 'She's just a bit protective.'

'It's understandable.'

'And unnecessary.'

He flicks a sideways glance at me. 'You can't blame her though.'

'No I can't. Of course not. I just feel like she's

118

putting too much pressure and guilt on herself.'

'Isn't guilt part of a mother's job description?'

I smile. 'Good point. Is your mother overprotective as well?'

'We're here.' He changes the subject abruptly, pulling the car over on to the grass shoulder and parking it under the shade of a cherry tree. I'm nervous. This is so far out of my comfort zone it's like the other side of the planet, but that's exactly why I want to do it. My mindfulness app told me the other day that we only regret the things we didn't do, not the ones we did. I haven't done enough things.

I get out of the car and follow him over to an old wooden farm gate. He climbs up and over in one smooth movement, dismounting on the other side with the agility of a cat. Then he holds out a hand.

'Need help?'

I walk to where the gate meets the fence and unlatch it, opening it to walk through. 'No thanks.'

He stares at me for a moment before starting to laugh. He does it naturally and unashamedly and I watch in delight. If I had to describe him, I'd say he's a man's man. He is physically large but not in an obvious way, just a vibrant larger-than-life kind of way. He exudes vitality, and next to him I feel almost wraithlike. Like I am fading out of this world and, as much as I try to hang on, my fingers are slipping.

Seize the day.

You only regret the things you didn't do.

'Well that just made me look a bit of an idiot,

didn't it?' he says, when he quietens back down to a chuckle.

'How old are you?' I blurt out without thinking.

His eyes widen with his surprise at the question, but he answers. 'Thirty-four. You?'

'Twenty-eight. Just. Are you married?'

'No.'

'Girlfriend?'

'Am I auditioning for something here?'

'Just answer the question.'

'No. Not any more. We broke up a few months back.'

'Sorry to hear that.' I'm not though.

'Anything else you'd like to know?' he asks. 'Only we really should get on with the photo shoot.'

'One more question.'

'OK.'

'It's a big one,' I warn. 'And you have to promise you'll answer honestly.'

He looks at me curiously. 'OK.'

'Have you ever been in love?'

I like that he doesn't answer immediately. That he respects me enough to give the question his proper consideration.

'Yes, once.'

'What was it like?'

He looks down and starts fiddling with his camera, adjusting settings or something, and I think I've gone too far. That he is trying to think of a polite way to tell me to mind my own business.

'It was both amazing and awful,' he says finally.

'Awful? Why?'

'Because when it's over, when it all goes wrong, you think you'll never survive.'

'But you did.'

'I did.'

'So is it true what they say? That it's better to have loved and lost than never have loved at all?'

'I'm not sure. And that's me being honest.'

I sigh deeply. 'Thank you.'

'Do you question all guys like this?'

'Only the cute ones.' I smile sweetly.

'OK. Come on,' he says, looking down to hide a smile. He jerks his head. 'There's some old farm equipment on the other side of the field under that big tree. I want to get a few shots there. And then over amongst the flowers.'

I'm so conscious of him walking beside me that I don't look where I'm walking and trip on some uneven ground. He quickly places a hand on my arm to steady me.

'You OK?'

'Yeah, I'm fine.'

'Here.' He takes my hand and tucks it through his arm. 'Hang on to me.'

'I *am* capable of walking still,' I say, even in the face of evidence to the contrary.

'Nevertheless I promised your mother I would return you in one piece, and I have no intention of getting on her bad side.'

I wonder if he feels how my pulse quickens at his touch.

'Lead the way then.' I smile up at him. He looks down at me and his expression is peculiar, as if he is unsure about something. I see his features harden with decisiveness and he stops suddenly, our hips bumping together.

'Wait,' he says. 'As we seem to be all about honesty today, I have a question for *you*.'

'Sounds slightly ominous. But go ahead.'

'Why are you doing this?' he asks.

I am deliberately obtuse. 'This? What, wearing a wedding dress? Posing for photos in a field?'

'No.' His face tells me he knows I understand. 'This whole wedding thing. Isn't it a little bit . . . morbid?'

My eyes widen at his choice of word and he hurries to elaborate.

'Not morbid, maybe. But you have to admit it's unusual. I understand the concept of bucket lists. And I've read about people marrying on their deathbed. But what you're doing, having a wedding celebration by yourself, doesn't that just strike you as a little bit, well, *sad*?'

'Of course it's sad. Believe me, I never planned on walking down the aisle alone, no one waiting at the end, and I'm aware that I probably sound like a total loser doing just that.'

'Then why?'

I sigh.

'Sorry.' He holds up his hands. 'You don't have to explain yourself to me or anyone. I'm not trying to upset you, just trying to understand. I find the whole idea a bit uncomfortable, if I'm honest.'

'Did you always dream of being a photographer?' I ask quietly.

He frowns at the change of subject but allows the indulgence. 'Yes.'

'When did you know, exactly, that it's what you wanted to do?'

'I don't know.'

'*Think.*'

He takes a deep breath in through his nose and then exhales slowly, his face watching mine. 'From when I was a young boy. I don't remember the exact age. My mother was an amateur photographer and she used to take me out with her on weekends. We'd explore the local forests and lakes.'

'She must be proud of you.'

'I'm sure she is. But what's that got to do with anything?'

I look at the ground, willing tears to stay away. 'I never had that moment, or epiphany. Growing up, I didn't dream of being anything. While other girls aspired to be ballet dancers, or teachers, or Olympic equestrians, I had no idea what I wanted to do with my life. The only thing I ever knew with any certainty was that I wanted to get married. I've been dreaming of my wedding for as long as I can remember.'

His face softens. 'I see.'

'And it's hard not to wonder now, whether the reason I couldn't see a career or future for myself was because maybe deep down, on some cellular level, I knew I *had* no future.'

He looks sceptical.

'I know. It sounds crazy. But believe me, when you're told you're dying, while you still *feel* and *look* healthy, it's hard not to question your whole life. Examine it for clues, signs of what was to come. Anyway. When they told me the cancer was back and that it was terminal, I figured, why not? Why not have the only thing I've ever wanted?'

'I understand.' His face doesn't quite reflect his words though.

'No, I don't think you do.' My voice grows heated. I'm not sure why it's so important to me that he understands, but it is. 'I'm not doing this to be self-indulgent, or because I want everyone to see me look pretty in a big white dress. I'm doing this because I *can*. Because it's the one thing I've always wanted, and it's the only thing left that I can have any control over.'

He gives a little nod. 'Fair enough. I can't imagine what it's like to be in your position. I shouldn't have asked.'

'No, I'm glad you did.'

'Really?'

'Yes.'

'Then can I ask one more question? Or am I pushing my luck?'

'Of course you can.'

'Why get the magazine involved? Why not keep it as something private, between you and your family?'

'I didn't get them involved. My friend, Amanda, she plastered it all over social media.'

He winces. 'Ah yes, social media. The blessing *and* curse of our times.'

'Her heart was in the right place. She just wanted to help out, financially. But for some reason the story just took off, and then the magazine got in touch, wanting to write about it. I did say no, initially. But then I was reminded by some very wise women that it could be a powerful platform to help raise awareness.'

'That's admirable.'

'Not really. I'm nervous about putting myself out there, I'm not going to lie. But if it stops even one person from going through the same thing it'll be worth it. I wasn't taken seriously at first, when I went to see a doctor. And I didn't push the issue because I figured they knew what they were doing.'

'We place a lot of trust in the medical profession. Sometimes misguidedly.' His voice sounds bitter.

'Exactly. So I figure that if, by telling my story I can help other women, especially younger ones, be better advocates for their own health, why not. Why are you looking at me like that?'

'I owe you an apology.'

'For what?'

'For misjudging you. Your intentions.'

I shrug. 'That's OK. You're probably not the only one.'

'No, it's not OK. I feel terrible.'

'Don't.' I smile. 'I'm not bothered.'

'That's because you appear to be one of those people who look for the positive in any situation.'

'Well it's not much fun dwelling on the negative, is it?'

'No. It's not.' He looks at me with better understanding. 'Thank you, for answering my questions honestly.'

'You did the same for me, it was the least I could do.'

He smiles again, and it is more open and

genuine. 'Let's get these photos, shall we?'

I screw up my nose. 'If we have to. I'm not very good at posing, sorry. Always have to fight the urge to pull a face.'

He laughs. 'Relax. I know what I'm doing. You'll be a natural by the time I'm finished with you.'

18

He is a wonder to watch as he works. The way he scans an area for optimum lighting angles and the aesthetics of the background. He seems to know instinctively what will work and what won't, and I meekly move as he tells me, sometimes imperceptibly, until he is satisfied. At first I am self-conscious and stiff, but his voice as he gives directions is calming and soon I relax, determined to enjoy the experience.

'Tilt your chin up a little,' he says from behind the lens. 'And angle your head to the right. Perfect.'

I am leaning against the trunk of the willow tree. Its bark is scratchy against my back but it doesn't hurt, and I quite enjoy sensations that remind me I'm alive. The shade from the hanging tendrils of branches is a welcome relief, especially when I am wearing a full-length gown that weighs more than it's delicate appearance would suggest. A fly buzzes around my head and I try to blow it away without moving my head.

'Stay still.'

'I'm trying.'

'Try harder.'

'Yes, *boss*.'

'Put your right foot slightly against the tree and bend your knee.'

'Why? You can't see it under the dress.'

He clicks his tongue and says mock sternly,

'Are you seriously questioning me? The professional photographer?'

'Sorry.' I do as he asked.

'I should think so.' He takes a photo and checks the screen on the back of his camera. 'Perfect.' Then he walks over and shows me the photos, flicking back and forward between the ones before he asked me to move and afterwards.

'Ah,' I say. 'I see.'

The subtle move has emphasised the contouring of the dress, and I look more relaxed, like I am truly a bride simply hanging out in a paddock as opposed to someone modelling a dress.

'Trust the master now?' he teases.

'Oh no, I never trust anyone who refers to themselves as 'master'. Far too *Fifty Shades.*'

'Fifty shades of what?'

'Seriously?'

He looks at me blankly.

'Maybe google it,' I say, flushing slightly at the thought of trying to explain the subject matter to him.

'OK.' He goes back to his position and starts taking more photos.

'So, have you done this before?' I ask.

'A photo shoot in a field?'

'Yes.'

'Not someone in bridal wear, no. But I did shoot a naked fireman with a leg up on a hay bale and a discreetly placed pitchfork once. It was for a charity calendar.'

'You're kidding.'

'I'm not.'

'You don't happen to still have copies of that photo, do you?'

His eyebrows arch over the camera.

'For my friend, Amanda.' I add hastily. 'They would make a good Christmas present.'

'I'll see what I can do,' he says, clearly amused.

'Thanks. And any, you know, outtakes as well. Just chuck them in. For Amanda.'

'Sure. For Amanda.'

'It's true,' I laugh.

'I believe you. Thousands wouldn't. OK.' He checks his camera to make sure he has the perfect shot. 'I want to get one of you lying in those wildflowers over there. You don't have allergies, do you?'

'Only to paclitaxel. And that's more of a hypersensitivity.'

'Paclitaxel?'

'Chemotherapy drug.'

'Oh. Right.' He clears his throat and swallows noisily.

Immediately, I'm regretful. I've made him uncomfortable by bringing cancer into the conversation. And it was all my own fault, this time. 'Sorry.'

'What for?'

'Bringing down the mood.'

'You don't have anything to be sorry for. It's me who should be sorry. I just don't know what to say, and it's frustrating, because I should.' He runs a hand through his hair, clearly annoyed with himself.

'It's OK.'

'It's not.'

'It is, honestly. I'm used to it and I don't blame people for avoiding the topic as much as I used to.'

His eyes study me and I shift nervously under the intensity I see in them.

'How do you do that?' he asks quietly.

'How do I do what?'

'Stay positive. Keep smiling. Joke around.'

'What's the alternative? Being bitter won't change anything. All that would do is make the time I have left miserable, and I don't want that.'

'I don't know if I could do it.'

'Sure you could. But I hope you never have to. Don't get me wrong, I have my bad days. Days where I cry or throw stuff at walls and lash out at my loved ones because my rage at the unfairness of it is so fierce inside of me that I want to hurt someone just the way I am hurting. But I try not to do that, because it's no one's fault.'

'How do you even begin to accept it?'

'I don't know. You just have to. I've soul-searched for a reason why this is happening to me. And I've drawn a blank. Because I did nothing wrong. It's not luck of the draw, or the cards that I've been dealt. It's just shit. But it is what it is, and there's nothing I can do about it.'

I've worked myself up while I've been speaking, and even though I don't want them to, hot tears well up in my eyes and threaten to burst over. I blink furiously to dispel them and James takes two quick steps to stand in front of me. He is awkward, for the briefest of moments, as he hesitates.

'Um, should I . . . do you want me to . . . ?'

Then his instincts take over and he reaches out to pull me into an embrace. It takes him by surprise just as much as it does me.

I sniff noisily into his shoulder.

'I'm sorry,' he says. 'I shouldn't have said anything.'

'You didn't, remember? I did.' He smells fresh and ever so slightly floral; and I imagine his laundry powder markets itself as sunshine in a box. But I can smell the essence of him too, and it's comforting. He is warm and he is alive and the weight of his arms around my shoulders and neck is calming. I sink in further against him and enjoy the sense of shelter he provides. His chin rests on the top of my head and I feel his breath in my hair, warm. I feel like I could stay here all day, but then reality crashes back in.

'Shit.' I pull back.

'What's wrong?'

'My make-up, have I ruined it?'

He smiles and uses one hand to tilt my head up towards him. Then he uses his thumb to rub gently underneath my eye. 'No. You still look beautiful.'

I flush and look down, unable to remember the last time someone other than my mother called me that.

'I bet you say that to all the girls.'

'Only the cute ones.' He echoes my earlier words teasingly.

'You think I'm cute?'

'Stop fishing for more compliments.'

He laughs when I look outraged. 'Come on. I

131

need to get this last shot nailed and then get you back to your mother before she sends out a search party.'

'As much as I'd like to dismiss that as a joke, I wouldn't actually put it past her.'

I follow him over to a patch of wildflowers at the other end of the field, near a fence that has a small river on the other side. If I wasn't in a bridal dress I'd be tempted to go for a wade. In fact if James wasn't here, I'd be tempted to ditch the dress completely and have a swim. The water looks waist-deep where we are but I can see a bend further down where the river widens and the water darkens with depth. It looks cold, but that doesn't scare me; I've had a thing for wild swimming ever since I was a child. My father will swim anywhere at any time, given enough water, and he's passed that love on to me. I cast a longing look and debate whether it's too deep for me to just hold the dress up, but then James interrupts my thoughts.

'OK, lie down right here I think,' he says, gesturing amongst the long grass and flowers.

'Lie down?'

'Yes.'

'There?'

'Yes.'

'On the flowers?'

'Yes. Is there a problem?'

'No, no. No problem.'

'There's a higher concentration of flowers in this spot. More colours.'

'Until I squash them,' I mumble, gingerly trying to lie amongst the long grass and flowers.

'I'm sure Ruth won't mind a few losses, for the sake of art after all. Close your eyes.'

'I do as I'm told.'

'Look pensive.'

'I'm not sure what that means.'

'Thoughtful.'

'Oh OK, I can manage that.'

There's silence for a minute or so, and I assume he is making the necessary camera adjustments. I figure there's no time like the present to practise some mindfulness, so I relax on to the earth and focus on my senses, trying not to think about creepy-crawlies in my hair or finding their way into my ears. The grass is tickly against my bare skin, but not in an entirely unpleasant way. I can smell the wildflowers around me, some I recognise as poppies and cornflowers, but most are varieties of which I have no idea. There is such a large assortment that I realise Ruth must have planted them here deliberately.

I can hear the water in the river babbling softly, and birds in the willow tree and surrounding native bush as they warble and call to each other. It's magical, it's perfection. But of course I can only enjoy it for so long before negative thoughts creep back in. There is a whole world of nature I have yet to discover. Scandinavian forests. The Alaskan wilderness. Mexican beaches. I've seen them all in movies and magazines. I yearn to touch/smell/explore them first hand.

'You OK?'

I open my eyes. James is silhouetted against

the sun, looking down at me. He has his camera to his eye and I realise he has been taking photos while I was unaware.

'Yes.' I smile. 'I'm fine.'

'Good.' He lowers the camera to cast a critical eye over me. 'There's something missing.'

He reaches down to pluck a few flowers, which he clumsily arranges into a makeshift bouquet. 'Here.' He thrusts them at me. 'Hold those.'

I close my eyes and smell the flowers he passed me. Pollen goes straight up my nose and I start sneezing violently.

'Christ, you didn't inhale a bee, did you?' he asks, concerned.

'If I did it's now in my brain,' I laugh, managing to bring myself back under control. 'Good luck explaining *that* to my mother.'

'OK, close your eyes again and hold the flowers on your chest,' he says when I have calmed down.

I give him a pointed look but do as he says, and then lie there and listen to the gentle whirr of the camera as he takes photos.

'Doesn't this look a bit weird?' I ask after a while.

'Shush, don't talk.'

'But I feel like Ophelia,' I say out of the corner of my mouth.

I hear him sigh. 'Who?'

'Ophelia, you know, in that painting.'

'What painting?'

I open my eyes, sit up and give the flowers a little shake. 'The really famous one, by John Everett Millais. Come on, you're an artist of sorts, how can you not know what I'm talking about?'

He lowers the camera and I watch his eyes widen in horror. 'Oh God. You're right. Probably not the best pose, given the circumstances. I'm so sorry. I should have realised.' He squeezes his eyes shut, angry with himself.

'Hey, don't stress, I'm not upset.'

'You should be.'

'Like I told you, life's too short. But I will remind you of your earlier 'master' comment.'

'You're right.' He gives me a hangdog expression. 'I've lost all privileges to call myself that.'

'Temporarily suspended. Not lost.'

'You're too kind. OK. Ditch the flowers,' he says. 'Just do what feels natural.'

I pull one of the flowers from the bunch, a red poppy, and tuck it behind my ear. Then I throw the others to the wind and watch as they scatter like confetti. Lying back, I put both arms behind my head and rest on them. Then I look up at the clouds in the sky and I smile.

'That's perfect,' he says softly, lifting the camera back to his face.

'What does that cloud look like to you,' I ask.

'Which one,' he answers, without looking away from his camera.

I lift one arm out and point. 'That big one over there.'

He stops to give it a quick glance. 'I don't know. A giant marshmallow?'

I roll my eyes. 'That's original. Have another look.'

'We're losing the best daylight here.'

'It'll only take you a second. Go on, indulge me.'

He sighs and stands still to give it a proper look. 'A spaceship. Like an alien one. Why, what does it look like to you?'

'A heart.'

'Seriously?' He tilts his head and looks at it quizzically.

'Not like a drawing of a heart. A real one. How it looks inside of us.'

'You have a great imagination.'

'Thanks.'

'Now do you mind if I finish doing my job?'

'Be my guest.'

And while he photographs me, I watch as the cloud, just like time, moves gently on by.

Notes from Ava

(Women's Weekly October 23rd)

Open the door. Step outside. Get in your car and drive away from the city. The concrete jungle.

Smell a forest. Hug a tree. Feed a bird. Pick mushrooms. Dance in the rain. Build a snowman. Dive into a big pile of colourful autumn leaves. Swim naked in the ocean; swim anywhere you can, anytime you get the chance. If you can't swim, learn. Walk barefoot through a paddock of wildflowers. Forage for fruit. Swing on a rope swing. Climb a mountain. Kayak across a lake.

Make a snow angel. Ride a bike along a country lane. Sail a yacht across the Pacific. Grow your own vegetables. Build a sand-castle. Study the night sky, and then sleep under the stars. Climb a tree. Cook over a campfire.

Watch the sun rise.

And then watch it set.

Breathe in the splendour that is nature and never, ever take it for granted. Enjoy every moment of it, for those of us who no longer can.

19

By the time James is satisfied he has the perfect picture the sky has started to change colour, and that dream-like time between day and nightfall is upon us. When the sky goes hazy with the satisfaction of another day well done, Breathtaking in its stealth, the moment day becomes dusk is a hard moment to catch; I know because I've tried. It steals over you like sleep, one moment it's not there, the next it is all around you.

Even before I was sick, if you'd asked me for my favourite part of the day I'd have said this, sundown. It's when the world really seems to come alive, and anything, even magic, seems possible.

'We'd better head back,' James says, bent over while he packs his camera and gear into his bag.

'I suppose so.'

He flicks me a puzzled look. 'You don't sound very enthusiastic. I thought you'd be worried about all the fun you're missing out on.'

'No, that doesn't bother me.' I lift my dress hem up and twirl around in a lazy circle. 'I love this time of day, don't you?'

He zips up his bag and straightens up, watching me with an unreadable expression. 'Sunset?'

I nod and murmur in agreement.

'It's something special, for sure.'

'You must have seen some amazing ones on your travels.'

'I have.'

I smile at him wistfully. 'I'm jealous.'

He smiles back sadly but doesn't answer.

I walk to the fence, grip the top wire and lean over to look at the river. The surface of the water reflects the colour of the sky. 'It's just so peaceful out here.'

'The countryside generally is.' I didn't hear him move but he has walked to stand beside me.

I wish fervently that I could pause this moment. Everything. The colours, the smells and the sounds. I want to freeze it in time and enjoy it for longer because I know that all too soon it will be over. The sun will go, the sky will darken, the birds will fall silent. I will be back in my room, tucked up in my bed, and this will be nothing but a memory. The problem is, memories don't do moments justice. They are weak versions in our heads, a poor playback. Moments play out in technicolour; memories are insipid in comparison. Nevertheless, I tilt my head to the sky and close my eyes, trying to capture this moment in my head, so I can bring it back when I am most in need of it.

But then I think . . .

. . . I don't want to waste time trying to remember it. I am *here*. This is *now*.

I am *living* it.

I open my eyes.

'Turn around,' I tell James.

'Sorry?'

'Turn around and close your eyes.'

'Why?'

'Please?' I ask imploringly.

139

He frowns, but nods. 'OK. But as long as you're not up to anything that's going to get me in trouble.'

'I wouldn't dream of it.'

When he turns his back to me I twist my arms behind my back and unzip the dress carefully, shivering as I lower it down my body and the cool breeze seizes the opportunity to caress my skin. Goosebumps spring up and I give a delighted laugh.

This is what I'm talking about.

Wearing only my knickers and a strapless bra, I drape the dress over a nearby log, keeping a cautious eye on James the whole time.

'No peeking,' I remind him, when he turns his head ever so slightly.

'I'm trying not to, but I'm a curious guy by nature.' I hear him shuffle in the grass. 'Telling me not to look at something is like telling someone not to push a big red button,' he complains.

I scuttle back to the fence and, as elegantly as I can, climb over, grateful that no one is around to watch.

'Let me guess,' I huff as I swing my leg over and drop triumphantly to the other side. 'You'd push the big red button.'

'Every time,' he confirms.

'Well you'll just have to be patient a little longer.'

'Why? What are you doing?'

I study the bank for the easiest route down into the water. It's only a metre or two but it's steep, luckily there are reeds and long grass growing on the banks that I can use as handholds. 'Don't worry. I'm not going to stick a pitchfork in your back.'

'The thought hadn't crossed my mind.'

'Really? I think I've seen too many scary movies. It's the first thing I'd worry about if someone I barely knew told me to turn around while we were alone in a field.'

'Well it's not like you had a pitchfork hidden in a pocket on that dress, is it?'

'Good point.' I grab a fistful of grass and slide down on my bottom as far as I can, tantalisingly close to the water.

'OK,' James says firmly. 'You've had your fun, you've got three seconds and then I'm turning around. One . . . '

'No,' I squeal.

'Two . . . '

I take a breath, let go of the grass and slide the rest of the way, landing with a small splash. The water is deeper than I thought and I go under, but I surface again in seconds, alternating between swearing like a sailor because of the cold and laughing with delight.

'Three,' James calls. I can no longer see him but I hear him exclaim in bewilderment. 'Ava? Where are you?'

'Down here.'

'Where?'

'In the water.'

I hear him swear and then the twang of the wires as he scales the fence. His face peers down at me.

'What are you doing?'

'What does it look like?'

'I know what it looks like, but why?'

'Why not?' I do a little dolphin dive, careful not to flash too much above the surface of the water. When I emerge he is watching me, bemused.

'Why don't you come in? The water's fabulous.'

'Liar. It looks freezing.'

'Oh I'm sorry, I had you mistaken for a big brave man.'

'Hey, I'm brave. I've been in war zones and disaster areas I'll have you know.'

'But a little old river is just too much, eh?' I roll my eyes and start swimming away from him, towards the bend where the river widens.

'Where are you going?'

'Exploring.'

'On your own?'

I flip back around and tilt my head, treading water. 'Unless you feel like coming with me.'

He is torn, I can tell by his facial expression. Finally, with a shake of his head, he lifts his T-shirt off. 'I must be crazy,' he mumbles.

'If this is crazy then lock me up and throw away the key.'

'I might have to next time — your mother's going to kill me.' He puts his hands on the bands of his shorts and then gives me a pointed look. 'Turn around.'

Thirty seconds later I hear a splash and then a few expletives.

'Bracing, isn't it?' I say mildly.

'Bracing? It's bloody arctic.'

'Don't be so dramatic. You'll soon get used to it.'

'Before my — manly parts — freeze off or after?'

I laugh at the forlorn expression on his face. 'Come on.' Then I turn and paddle languidly upriver, trusting that he's following.

'Aren't you worried about eels?' he calls.

'Not really. They're like sharks. More scared of us than we are of them. Or is that spiders?'

'I swear something just touched my toe.'

'It's OK. Toes aren't important in your career.'

He snorts. 'I'm quite attached to them all the same.'

I turn over on to my back and sweep my arms and legs in wide circles, enjoying the sensation of the water as my body moves easily through it. 'Come on. Aren't you enjoying this?' I ask. 'Not even one little bit?'

He does a few brisk strokes and comes up beside me. This close I can see water droplets on his beautiful tanned skin. His eyes, in the fading light, are luminous and vibrant. He is, hands down, the best-looking man I have ever had the pleasure of being half naked in the company of.

'Maybe a little bit,' he admits.

'When was the last time you went swimming?'

He has to think about it, which tells me that it's been too long.

'I can't remember,' he says finally. 'A couple of years, maybe? Yes, three years. It was in the sea off Mexico.'

'Work?'

'No. Holiday.'

He doesn't elaborate so I take a guess that it was with his now ex-girlfriend.

'What was it like?'

'The same as any sea, really. Wet. Full of fish. Waves.'

'Mexico, you idiot.'

'Hey, that's Master idiot to you.' He frowns teasingly. 'Mexico was nice. Very hot most of the time, and colourful. Friendly people. Delicious food. Cold beer.'

'Like in the movies, then.'

'Yes. And no. You don't see the poverty in the movies. The crime that's infiltrated right through to the top of the police force. And then there's the racism. Sometimes, in some countries and to some people, you get the sense human life isn't worth very much.'

'That's sad.'

'It is.'

We have reached the bend in the river and I was right, it deepens to where I can't touch the bottom. A large willow tree grows on the bank, its long branches trailing in the water. Against the brilliant orange glow in the sky it makes for a stunning sight. The air is perfumed with the smell of honeysuckle that grows wild on the hill the other side of the river. The only sounds are the rustle of the willow leaves, and our breathing.

'OK,' James says softly. 'I admit it. This is nice.'

'So you're glad you joined me.'

'Yes. I'm glad I joined you.'

'And I'm not crazy.'

He shrugs. 'Jury's still out on that one.'

I splash water towards him and he laughs and dodges it.

'You have the most amazing smile,' he says. 'Anyone ever tell you that?'

'Not that I can remember.'

'That's a shame. You should have been told every day.' He gives me a penetrating look and I swallow nervously. No one's ever looked at me the way he is currently looking at me, and I feel out of my depth in more ways than one.

'Everyone will be wondering where we are,' I say, heading towards the sandy bank that, unlike where we entered the river, slopes gently back up to the paddock.

'Yes. You're probably right.'

He sounds disappointed, which is how I feel.

'My dress is somewhere that way.' I point.

'So it is.'

'Be a gentleman and go and get it?'

'No. I'm not leaving you here alone. But I will promise not to look on the walk back.'

'I guess it's nothing a bikini wouldn't show anyway.' I stand up and hear him give a sharp intake of breath. I squeeze my eyes shut for a moment and hope desperately that it's not because of my scars and the fact I am too thin. Then I realise I have bigger things to worry about. The swim has depleted my energy, and once back on land my legs start to wobble, my muscles weak from everything I have been through. He is beside me in an instant, his arms steadying.

'Are you OK?' he asks, concerned.

I nod. 'Just tired. I'm sorry.'

'I shouldn't have let you swim.'

'You couldn't have stopped me,' I say defiantly. 'And I don't regret it at all. It was wonderful.'

'Do you always get your own way?'

'Usually.'

'Well, so do I.' And before I realise what he is doing he has scooped up my legs with his right arm, and I am in his arms. My arms involuntarily curl around his neck, my hands entwining.

'Hey,' I protest.

'What?'

'Aren't you taking this bridal shoot thing a bit far?'

'Just be quiet and relax, will you?' he murmurs. 'I've got you.'

'Do I have a choice?'

'No.'

So I do as he says, and rest my head against his shoulder, closing my eyes wearily as he strides across the field in search of our clothes. I have never been held in a man's arms like this before.

This is a memory that will never fade, I am sure of it.

20

Three days later I get an email from James with a few of the photos attached.

Thought you'd like a preview. The photos came up great, but with you as a subject that's hardly surprising. Enjoy x

I click on the first attachment and when it opens I slouch back into my chair, speechless. Is that really me?

The photos are just like the ones I'd always admired in the bridal magazines, except instead of some wafer-thin model pouting sultrily into the lens, it's me. In one, I'm under the shade of the big willow tree, my back slightly to the camera, my face looking over my shoulder and off into the distance. The dress is lightly blowing in the breeze, my hair doing the same.

In another, I am lying amongst the wildflowers, my face bathed in sunlight, eyes closed, a knowing little smile on my face. My hair is fanned out around me, one arm slung casually above my head.

I can hardly believe it's me. I look the most beautiful I have ever looked.

I immediately forward the email to everyone on my contact list of course, and for the rest of the afternoon enjoy the ping of replies as my friends and family admire the photos. My mother replies to say she's going to get one blown up and put on canvas, which is a bit over the top but does make me feel good. I can't stop looking at them. It is me, but the best version of me I have ever seen. The thought that even once I am gone, these images will still be here, is a good one.

I never wrote a bucket list. I never even considered it after the first diagnosis, because I was going to beat it. That was all I would allow myself to think. Positive. Writing a bucket list would be like admitting there was a chance otherwise, and I refused to do that. Even when I was at my sickest, the treatment wreaking havoc on my physical body, taking me to what I imagined was the very brink of death, I couldn't do it. I wouldn't do it.

Now, with the cancer back and the outcome inevitable, I still can't do it. There are things I wish I'd had the opportunity to do, sure. Given a life untouched by cancer. But as simple as it may be, I want to spend the time I have left with my loved ones. I want to give them memories of me to last their lifetime. I don't want them to forget me. It's an irrational fear because I know they won't, but that's the thing I fear most. Being forgotten.

21

There was a lady in my first support group who I was particularly drawn to. I'm not sure why. She was in a different phase of life, a few years older than me, married and with young children.

Maybe it was her attitude, her determination not to take things so seriously. She would roll her eyes at inappropriate times, like when someone was being overly weepy and self-pitying, and I would get the giggles and have to stifle them, usually failing and drawing the silent ire of the support group leader, Irene.

The lady, Lisa, would say things like, 'Christ on a bike, if the cancer doesn't kill us, these rock-hard muffins will.' Then she'd tap one on the edge of the table for emphasis, and I'd be set off giggling again.

'Do you think they reuse the same tea bags every week?' she'd whisper to me. 'This tastes like weak piss.'

I found myself sitting next to her each week, attracted into her orbit of no nonsense. Asked about her cancer she'd reel off the facts in a clinical manner. Both breasts were gone, and good riddance to them, the traitorous pair. Reconstruction? No. Not needed. Her husband adored her with or without tits, and she didn't need to fill a shirt to feel like a woman. She intended on getting a chest tattoo instead, once the scars healed enough. A big lion's head to represent the warrior she was, and when she described it to the group I could tell she enjoyed the horrified reaction from some of the more traditionally minded women.

She was only here because her doctor was worried she wasn't taking it seriously enough.

'Why would I give it the satisfaction?' she said, waving a hand in irritation. 'Cancer gets too much airtime as it is. I refuse to give it more.'

She was a breath of fresh air in a room stale with the fear of death.

Then one week she wasn't there. Nor the next, nor the one after that. I hoped it meant she was in the clear, that she'd done what she kept saying she was going to do and kicked cancer to the kerb, leaving it, and us, behind in her rear-view mirror.

Then one day I walked in and she was back, slouched low in a chair, shoulders hunched, eyes on the floor. I don't think I hid my shock very well at the sight of her, and when she looked up at me, the no-nonsense determination was gone, replaced by fear and disbelief.

'The bastard came back,' she told me, shaking her head. 'It bloody came back.'

She died in the middle of April, as the first leaves were turning colour on the trees. I went to her funeral and sat at the back of the church, weeping at the sight of the small heads in the front row, lined up like ducklings beside their father so heavy with grief he nearly slipped to the floor. I watched the slide-show of photos of Lisa and her life and I thought: If this thing is ruthless enough to tear a mother away from her children, what hope is there for the rest of us? And it made me angry.

People speak of fate, destiny. How can this be mine? To have my life boil down to this, the one fact that people will most remember about me: She Died of Cancer.

Sure, they will also say, '*Oh Ava Green, yes she was nice, lovely girl. Good at quizzes. Quite pretty too, when she bothered to do her hair and slap on a bit of make-up. A generally happy girl, she was.*' But they will also, *always*, end by saying, '*She died of cancer. Very sad. Terrible tragedy.*'

I don't want to be remembered only for that, and it's *not* a tragedy, because that implies some sense of random bad luck. That I stood on a crack in the pavement when I should have jumped over it. Spilt salt or broke a mirror. No. I didn't bring this on myself. It has been brewing inside me since I was a cluster of cells floating in my mother's uterus. It was always there, lurking within, just waiting to take over.

22

'OK, now you're just officially stalking me.'

I say it with one hand on my hip, looking at James pointedly. He is standing by the reception desk of the small motel I have checked into myself around half an hour before.

He turns around, room key in hand, and looks at me sheepishly. 'Hi, Ava.'

'I thought you said last time was the *last* time?'

He nods. 'I vaguely recall saying something like that, yes.'

'So? Another favour for Marilyn?'

He coughs. 'Not this time, no. Actually I was still here, between assignments, and when she happened to mention that you were heading to Lake Tarawera for a shoot I volunteered. Always wanted to see this part of the country.'

'Really.'

'Yes.'

'You volunteered because you wanted to see 'this part of the country'.'

'Yes.'

'No other reason?'

'What do you want me to say, that I was so desperate to see you again I pestered her until she let me have this job?'

'That would be a little more flattering, sure.'

He laughs. 'You can believe what you want.'

'I will. Anyway, regardless of why you're here, can I just say how lovely it is to see you again?'

He nods in agreement. 'It's nice to see you too. My toe is still sore by the way.'

'Your toe?' I frown.

'The eel bite? From when we swam in the river? I'm extremely lucky it didn't go septic.' He lifts up one foot, shaking off his sandal, and points to a small red mark on the top of his big toe. He looks so pitiful I can't help but laugh.

'What's so funny?'

'Nothing.' I attempt to straighten my face into a serious expression. 'I apologise unreservedly for your wound, however it was inflicted.'

'What do you mean, 'however it was inflicted'? It was an eel. A giant one, like a mutant or something.'

I peer at his toe. 'Are you sure you didn't just stub it on a rock? Or a stick? It doesn't really look like a bite as such.'

He slips his foot back into his sandal. 'Doctor now, are you?'

'James, darling, what are you doing here?'

Nadia, emerging from the restaurant holding a bottle of bubbly wine, interrupts us. She is much more in her element here than she was at the farm. Luxury boutique accommodation. We are all booked in for the night — Sophie and Kelly, Nadia and I. And now, I'm assuming, James is as well.

'Fishing,' he answers her with a straight face. 'Heard there are some pretty big trout in the lake. Much friendlier than eels.' The last bit is of course for my benefit.

She blinks. 'Oh really? What a coincidence,

we're here doing an article on another potential wedding venue for Ava. You remember Ava?'

'Vaguely, yes.'

'Sorry, who are you again?' I ask. 'Are you the valet?'

Nadia looks back and forward between James and me, clearly confused. James takes pity on her.

'I'm here to take the photos,' he says. 'And of course I remember Ava.'

'Oh lovely,' Nadia coos. 'You're so much better than Steven, our normal guy. I mean don't get me wrong, he's nice enough, but he can be a bit too avant-garde, if you know what I mean. His work has a time and place, but with a wedding you really do need to be a bit more traditional.'

'Well, I'm just happy that you're happy,' James says.

Nadia checks her watch. 'Why don't you check in and then meet the rest of us on the lawn for drinks. Say six?'

'Sounds great.'

'Wonderful.' She looks at me. 'Are you up for drinks Ava? I understand if you'd rather just rest in your room. Big day tomorrow.'

'I wouldn't miss it for the world.'

'Splendid.' She air-kisses me on both cheeks and heads towards the staircase.

'Need help with your bags?' I ask James.

'Even if I did, I wouldn't ask you.'

'I'm stronger than I look.'

He smiles. 'The answer is still no.'

'Suit yourself.'

He looks around the foyer and then at me. 'No

154

entourage this time?'

'Entoura — oh, you mean my mother and Amanda?'

He nods.

'No. Not this time. I mean, my mother wanted to come but she's in rehearsals for her latest play and I didn't want her to miss out on my account.'

'Your mother's an actress?' He picks up his bags and starts walking across to the staircase.

I follow him, pulling a face. 'In a loose manner of speaking. She's part of an amateur dramatic club at the local theatre behind the supermarket.'

'Oh I see.'

'They put on shows two or three times a year, depending on how much sponsorship they can get. Right now they're rehearsing *The Rocky Horror Picture Show*.'

'I'll have to get along one night and check it out.'

'You really shouldn't.'

'Why not? Which part is your mother playing? The young, naive Janet Weiss?'

'I wish. No she's Dr Frank-N-Furter.'

'Isn't that normally played by a guy?'

'Normally, yes. But they have more women than men in the group and as Fred Burrows broke his hip gardening, my mother is taking his place.'

'So she's a — ' He squints as he tries to work it out.

'A woman playing the part of a man, pretending to be a woman. Yes. In fishnet stockings no less.'

He tries hard to stifle his smile. 'Sounds . . . interesting.'

''Interesting' is one word for it,' I concede.

We reach the bottom of the stairs and turn to face each other.

'So.'

'So.'

'I guess I'll see you on the lawn at six?'

'You will.'

'Excellent.'

He steps up. So do I. We climb to the top of the stairs together. At the top, he looks at me and does a fake double take.

'Fancy seeing you here.'

'My room is that way.' I point over his right shoulder.

He checks his key and compares it to the sign in front of us. 'I'm the other direction.'

'Pity.'

'Sorry?'

'Nothing.'

★   ★   ★

When I walk out on to the beautifully manicured lawn a little after six, I don't see James at first. Nadia and the girls are standing over by the bar, and Sophie waves when she sees me. I head their way and am presented with a pale green cocktail.

'Cheers,' they giggle in unison, clearly on their way to being three sheets to the wind.

I hold the glass and look at its contents suspiciously. 'What's this?'

'Margarita.'

'No thanks. I'm not really much of a drinker.'

'You can have one, surely.' Sophie says. 'They're so refreshing.'

I take a sip. She's right. I taste lime and the unmistakable aftertaste of alcohol that immediately gives me a warm glow. It's the kind of drink that goes down too easily, so I resolve to drink it slowly and make it last. Nadia is deep in conversation with a grey-haired man in a suit and acknowledges my presence with a curt nod, before resuming her conversation.

'No James?' I ask as nonchalantly as I can, taking another sip.

'He's over there.' Kelly downs the rest of her drink in one and points with her empty glass. She and Sophie are giddy with the excitement that only a night in a hotel with a bar on a work expense account can bring, and it makes me wistful. She picks up the drinks menu. 'Which one shall we try now?' I back away slowly, leaving them tossing up their choices, and wander across the lawn that slopes gently down towards the shore of the lake. James is standing a metre or so back, staring out across the water. I pause for a moment, unsure whether to intrude or leave him to his thoughts, but then he senses my presence and turns.

'Evening.' His face softens into a smile.

'Care for some company? Or would you rather be alone.'

'I spend far too much time alone. Some company would be very welcome.'

I walk to stand beside him. The lake smells earthy, very different to the sea that I am used to.

Small mosquitoes hover above the surface. Behind the lake, the volcanic mountain Tarawera looms intimidatingly against the pale sky. Although it has been dormant for quite some time, it hasn't lost any of its menace and I shiver under its shadow.

'Impressive, isn't it?' James says quietly. 'Nature. I'm constantly in awe of it.'

'It's kind of spooky,' I admit.

'Spooky?'

'Yeah, you know. Thinking about all the death and destruction it caused when it blew up and obliterated everything in its path. Those natural pink and white terraces that used to be in the lake looked amazing. I'd have loved to swim in them. Such a waste that they were destroyed in the eruption.'

'That's nature for you. Unpredictable. Did you know that some say they're still there, the terraces, just buried in the bottom of the lake under mud and ash.'

'No, I didn't, but I hope that's the case. Better that than they were completely destroyed.'

'There's an amazing walk you can take up the mountain, quite breathtaking scenery and view for miles. And once at the top, you can run down into the crater. It's a little scary because it's loose scoria rock, so one wrong step and you'll end up rolling down and losing some skin in the process. But that's half the fun.'

I look at him through narrowed eyes. 'I thought you hadn't been to this area of the country before.'

He freezes like a deer in headlights. 'Sorry?'

'Dinner time, guys,' Sophie interrupts cheerfully, saving him.

'Oh good, I'm starving.' He clears his throat and gestures for me to walk in front. 'Ladies first.'

The meal, served in an elegant dining room with relaxed lighting, is nice, but a bit pretentious for my usual tastes. They serve us twelve courses, tiny ones.

At one point James leans across the table to whisper loudly, 'They can't be serious. Where's the rest of the food? This is just a snack right? A taster?'

I bite my bottom lip to stop myself from laughing out loud at his outraged expression.

'Here, have mine.' I start to push my plate across the table to him. We've just been served poached crayfish with pickled melon, marinated cherry tomatoes, Greek basil and feta. It looks pretty on the plate, all arranged artistically and with edible flowers, but I'm not a huge crayfish fan.

'I couldn't,' he says, although his face looking at my plate longingly.

'Suit yourself.' I pull the plate back. 'I'll offer it to Nadia.'

Nadia has been devouring everything set in front of her with all the gusto of a food critic.

'No, wait.' His voice is loud and sharp, and the people seated at nearby tables turn to see what the commotion is. He smiles apologetically at them until they lose interest and then gestures to my plate. 'Go on then. Slide it over.'

Despite his misgivings, he is satisfied enough

at the end of the meal, or at least I assume he is by the way he leans back in his chair and smiles contentedly.

'Everything OK here?' the waitress asks, collecting his final plate. She has been flirting with him all evening, holding his gaze longer than necessary, pressing herself into his shoulder when she leans over to pick up his plates. I want to resent her, because she is everything that I am not, but I can't. She is young and beautiful and *healthy*. Why shouldn't she flirt with an attractive man?

'That,' he declares, wiping the edges of his mouth, 'was superb. My compliments to the chef.'

She giggles, coquettish. 'I'll pass that information on.'

'Thanks — ' he peers at her name badge — 'Kimberly.'

At his use of her name she becomes emboldened and bends down to whisper something in his ear. I see his eyebrows shoot up and he clears his throat, his cheeks slightly flushed, before he smiles up at her and mumbles something that I can't hear. I feel instantly deflated. James is free to do whatever he wants with whomever he pleases, but it is yet another painful reminder of something I have lost: potential.

The potential for love. That giddy, delirious feeling when you meet someone new who you're attracted to. Who is attracted to you too, so a flirtatious dance begins as you get to know each other, slowly, offering up titbits of information, enough to whet their appetite, but withholding enough of yourself to keep the allure alive. It might only last a month, it might last for ever. But that feeling keeps whole industries alive, and it's one I crave, more now that I can no longer have it.

I realise I have allowed myself to be swept up in a stupid little daydream about James. To believe that the potential for magic was there, between us, and I feel completely ridiculous now that I think about it. He has been nothing but friendly and kind in return, but then anyone would, given the circumstances, and he is, of course, much too polite to draw attention to my inappropriateness.

'Excuse me.' I push back my chair and stand abruptly.

Nadia breaks off her conversation with the grey-haired man, Bill, who she had invited to join us. 'Are you OK, Ava? I thought after this we might head to the bar for a nightcap.'

'I'm fine, just tired. I should really get some sleep so I don't look a complete fright tomorrow. I hope you all enjoy the rest of your evening.'

I can't help but look at James when I say the last sentence, and he frowns, puzzled by my curt tone. He starts to stand.

'I'll walk you to your room.'

'No, thank you. There's no need. I'm pretty sure I can find it by myself.'

I walk away before he can answer.

23

In the foyer, I hesitate. To my left are the stairs leading up to my room, and sanctuary from my mortification. But the thought of being there by myself, feeling the way I am feeling, is unappealing. So I head straight instead, towards the doors that allow me to slip out into the night, under a cloak of darkness that goes some way towards hiding how absurd I feel.

What was I thinking? I wasn't. That was the problem. And now here I am, feeling pitifully sorry for myself but with only myself to blame.

With the sun gone the temperature has dropped, and the breeze blowing in off the lake is brisk and invigorating. A degree or two warmer and I'd have been tempted to swim. To cleanse off my foolishness and bring me back to my senses. But the black water is more sinister than inviting, and our earlier discussion about the mountain keeps my feet planted firmly on the shore.

I try to always trust my instincts. More so since my diagnosis. They are the deeper work of something we are yet to understand, and I believe people should listen to them more than they do. But they can be confusing, too. The same instincts that are telling me to stay out of the water also told me James was one of the good guys. And yet the way he smiled at the waitress when she whispered in his ear, it seemed like he was agreeing to something I wouldn't have expected of him. I hope I'm wrong, but I also know I can't blame him if I'm not.

Walking along the lawn, away from the lights of the foyer and the restaurant, I trip on something and hop around on one foot, swearing blue words into the inky darkness. As my eyes adjust, I realise there is a life-size chessboard paved into the lawn and I caught my foot on the edge of one tile. On top are chess pieces that come up to my knees. I play around with them for a while, but I've never understood the game and quickly lose interest. Turning, I decide I should probably do what I said I would and get some sleep so I am prepared for tomorrow, but then I see some white wooden loungers, four of them, with full-length cushions on top. They look tempting, and I lower myself gently down on to one and stretch out. It is surprisingly comfortable. Overhead, the stars litter the sky like glitter on a child's art project; haphazard and random, and completely impossible to ignore. It reminds me of the roof in my bedroom growing up, and I remember how I'd always wanted to sleep under the stars but never had. Tonight, I decide, is as good a time as any.

It seems only five minutes later I am awoken by a quiet voice and a torch in my face.

'There you are.'

Disorientated, I forget where I am and try to roll over, almost falling. A hand firmly grips my arm, steadying me. 'Careful.'

'James?'

'Yes.'

'What are you doing here?'

'I could ask you the same thing.'

'You gave me a fright.'

'I'm sorry. But, in my defence, you gave me one too. You left dinner so suddenly I was worried you might be unwell. Then there was no answer when I knocked on your door.'

'How did you know I wasn't just asleep? And can you please get that torchlight out of my eyes?'

'Of course. Sorry.' He switches it off and we are plunged back into darkness. For a moment I am completely blind, unable to make out anything. I realise that all the internal lights in the hotel have been turned off, apart from a dim one in the reception area.

'I didn't know,' he continues. 'But I was worried when you didn't answer, so I bribed the night concierge into opening your door.'

I blink in the direction I last saw him standing. 'You what?'

'I didn't really have much choice.' His voice is now on my other side and I jump. He moved stealthily, like a cat. 'It was that or wake Nadia and have her call the police.'

'Oh my God. Do you always overreact?'

'Do you always fall sleep outside when you have a perfectly good hotel room *inside?*'

He has a point I suppose. Still, I am petulant. 'Why were you even looking for me?'

'Like I said, you left dinner very quickly. I was worried.'

I lean back against the lounger and stare up at the stars. 'I would have thought you'd have been too busy to worry about me.'

I hear him sit down on the lounger next to mine. 'What's that supposed to mean?'

'Nothing.'

'Doesn't sound like nothing.'

'I just thought that maybe, you know, you and Kimberly might be busy.' I say her name in a silly voice. He doesn't answer immediately, and I squeeze my eyes shut, aware I sound like a jealous girlfriend. When he does answer his tone is amused.

'You thought Kimberly and I would be busy doing what, exactly?'

'You know.'

'Nope. No idea.'

'God, do I have to spell it out to you? She's a gorgeous young woman. You're a . . . reasonably attractive, young*ish* man. You connect the dots and do the math.'

He laughs, loudly, like he did that day in the field.

'Young*ish*?'

'Yes.'

'OK. So let me get this straight. You thought I was somewhere, senselessly shagging the hot young waitress that I met about, oh I don't know, three hours ago? By that math I'd say you put two and two together and came up with five.'

I hate that he uses the word 'hot' to describe her; it is another reminder of everything I am not. Before cancer I was often described as pretty, but never hot. At least to my knowledge. Now I stand no chance. Next to her, I am like a pale shrivelled-up worm, left too long in the sun.

'I saw her flirting with you.' I scowl. 'And you're only human, male at that. You can't blame me for jumping to conclusions.'

'I can actually. Yes, she offered to show me around her staff quarters, which may or may not have been a euphemism for something else. And to be honest she seems perfectly nice. But just because I'm a man doesn't mean I have sex with anyone offering it. I do have *some* morals.'

I smile in the dark, but make a harrumph noise. 'I wouldn't know. I barely know you.'

'I know. But I'd like that to change.' His tone is quiet and serious, and I feel a thrill run through me at his words. I don't know what to say, so I just sit quietly. He sighs and. shuffles around, stretching his legs out on the lounger and resting his head on his arms above his head, his fingers laced together.

'What are you doing?' I ask.

'What does it look like I'm doing? I'm keeping you company.'

'You don't have to do that.'

'I know I don't. I want to.'

'Why would you want to sleep out here when you have a perfectly good hotel room *inside*?' I echo his earlier words teasingly.

'I don't know. I guess I prefer the company.'

We lie on our individual loungers, so close I can hear him breathing, and look up at the night sky.

'There's the Southern Cross,' I say after a while.

'So it is.' He chuckles. 'I almost had that tattooed on my shoulder once. Thought it was a

166

good way to show the world what a proud Antipodean boy I am.'

'Seriously?'

'I was drunk. It seemed a good idea at the time.'

'So what stopped you?'

'I don't really want to say.'

'Why not?'

'It's embarrassing.'

'OK, well now you have to tell me, it's only fair.'

'How do you figure that?'

'I've already embarrassed myself tonight by jumping to conclusions. If you tell me it might help me feel better.'

He sighs. 'I was in the chair, the guy had the needle poised and ready, and then I saw a picture on the wall that I, in my drunken wisdom, decided was much cooler, so I got that instead.'

I wait. He is silent.

'So?' I prompt. 'What did you get?'

'I don't want to say.'

'Oh come on. You can't tell half a story. Those kinds of people are so annoying. Just tell me.'

He sighs again exaggeratedly. 'Fine. Homer.'

'Sorry, Homer?'

'Simpson. Homer Simpson.'

I stifle a laugh. 'You got Homer Simpson tattooed on your shoulder?'

'Yes. Holding a can of Duff beer.'

'Why? I mean, seriously?' I laugh outright then. 'How could you think Homer was cooler than the Southern Cross?'

'Like I said, I was drunk. And in my inebriated state, I thought Homer was a good representation of the way I should view life.'

'Which is?'

'Fearlessly, I suppose. Although stupidly could be another way of saying it. I don't know if you've ever watched an episode, but I have. A fair few, in my younger days. He never lets anything stop him from doing what he wants, or going where he chooses. And somehow, no matter what scrape he gets himself into, it always works out OK in the end.' He says it emotively, rousingly, as if he's giving a motivational speech.

'I'm sorry, but that's the stupidest thing I've ever heard.'

'Ah well, it was worth a try.'

'He's a fictional cartoon character who walks around scratching his nuts and saying 'Doh!' all the time. I mean he's funny, sure. But inspirational?'

'Hey, you're not saying anything I haven't already said to myself. I plead youth and too much alcohol.'

'I can't believe I didn't notice it when we were swimming.'

'Yeah,' he chuckles sheepishly, 'that was on purpose. As I said, it's up on my back, top of my right shoulder. I kind of kept that side away from you as much as possible and anyway, you were so enchanted with the sunset you weren't really looking at me.'

'Huh.' I muse.

'What.'

'Well, it just goes to show, doesn't it?'

'Show what?'

'That you just never can tell about some people. You seem like this professional, straight-up, serious kind of guy. And now I find out you're partial to the devil's brew and a bit of ink. You're like Popeye.'

'I don't like spinach.'

'OK, apart from that. Look, there's a satellite.' I point to the eastern side of the sky where a light is slowly making its way overhead.

'So it is. Do you really think alcohol is the devil's brew?'

'No. I'm fond of the odd tipple myself. More so before the diagnosis.'

I wince. There it is.

'What about you?' he asks.

'What about me?'

'Any shameful secrets you'd care to share?'

'No.'

'No, you have none, or no, you don't want to share.'

'The first option. I'm pretty tame. No wild youth to speak of.'

'You're still young,' he teases, and then he realises what he has said. 'Shit. I'm sorry, Ava, that was thoughtless.'

'It's OK, honestly.'

'I think you're pretty admirable, you know. What you're doing. And brave.'

I feel warmth at his words. So he didn't describe me as 'hot'. This was better. I'd take it.

24

After a busy few weeks and three more articles run, the number of likes on the page Amanda set up almost doubles, and I receive so many messages of support and offers of help that I decide, sadly, that I can no longer reply to them all. I want to, but there are so many it would take up valuable time that I just can't afford. Instead, Amanda does a communal post to tell everyone that I appreciate their messages and their thoughts.

A date has been set, and a venue chosen.

After much deliberation and facing truths I found hard to face, I picked a date in mid-January. Apart from some pain, manageable still, I feel OK. But I have no idea how long that will last, and I don't want to be wheeled down the aisle in a wheelchair, or worse, be unable to participate at all. January gives us two months to plan everything. Plus, it will be the height of summer. My favourite season, and more chance of a fine day.

As well as the barn at Marmalade Farm, and the luxury boutique accommodation at Taupo, we also checked out a vineyard in the Hawkes Bay, a converted woolshed in Wanaka, and a retreat nestled amongst native bush on the Coromandel peninsula. They were all incredible venues that any bride would dream of being married at. Nadia tries her hardest to convince me to choose the luxury resort, Mum likes the serenity of the retreat and Amanda likes the idea of a plentiful supply of alcohol on hand at the vineyard.

But none of them feel right. It might have been different if I were actually getting married, but I'm not, and they just aren't me. Nadia has more lined up to visit for magazine articles but I am tired, so I say no. Tired of car trips and nights in motels. I *want* to enjoy them, and I try, the scenery in this country is breathtaking after all, but my body aches if it is in one position for too long, and I develop locational insomnia, unable to sleep under unfamiliar ceilings. I don't feel on the verge of death, but I don't know what the verge of death feels like, and I'm terrified of dying in a bed strangers will sleep in after me.

So I break Nadia's heart and I choose the one place that I can't stop thinking of and dreaming of when I am away from it. She comes to the house to get the story for the latest issue, and I break it to her gently.

'I've decided to have my wedding day on the beach, next to the ocean,' I tell her.

'The beach.' She grimaces slightly, as if she's having to re-imagine her outfit choice.

'Yes.'

'Fiji?' she asks hopefully.

'What? No.'

'Rarotonga?'

'No.'

'Somewhere else equally as tropical and where they serve cocktails with little umbrellas?

Preferably at the end of a short plane ride?'

'No. Right here.' I point off Kate's deck.

She sighs. 'I was afraid you were going to say that.'

'What's wrong with it?'

'It's not big enough for a start.'

'It's not a wide stretch of beach, no,' I admit. 'But it's plenty big enough for my family and friends.'

'And what about everyone else?'

'Who else?'

'Well. You're making this thing public, right? So many readers want to come along and show their support.'

'Woah.' I hold up my hands. 'Just stop right there. This is *not* open to the public, no. This is a very private day, just for my friends and family. And you and whoever else you need to do the story, but that's it. I never agreed to anything else.'

'I just assumed it was implied.'

'You know what they say about assuming,' Amanda, who is sunning herself in one of the deck chairs, pipes up. 'Means you're an ass.'

'That's not quite how the saying goes,' I say quickly as Nadia frowns. 'Anyway, that's irrelevant. Sorry, Nadia. But it's my decision and this is what I want.'

'It's up to you, of course it is. This is your day. I just think it's a shame that the people who are following your journey can't be a part of it.'

'If they care as much as you say they do, they'll understand,' Amanda says firmly. 'Like

172

you say, it's Ava's day. She needs to feel comfortable and she wouldn't with a bunch of strangers around, as well meaning as they may be.'

I throw Amanda a grateful look. She knows me so well.

'Of course,' Nadia agrees.

She means well, I'm sure of it. She just sometimes forgets to take her journalist hat off in the search for a good story.

★   ★   ★

That night, I get a message from James. I haven't seen or heard from him since the night we slept under the stars beside Lake Taupo, but he's never been far from my thoughts. I keep remembering what it was like to wake up to a dawn sky and him asleep on the lounger next to me. Studying his face, I felt like something had shifted between us, and the whole morning while he shot photos of me on the jetty and around the lake, it was as if we were both on the verge of saying something. But neither of us did, and he left before I checked out.

When a photographer called Steven turned up at the next article shoot, the one at the vineyard, I'd been disappointed.

'No James?' I'd asked Sophie nonchalantly as she adjusted the waistline on the beautiful ivory dress I was wearing for that article.

She'd given me a shrewd smile, even with pins clenched between her teeth. 'He's overseas on some assignment for *National Geographic.*'

'Wow. Impressive.'

'He's very good at what he does. Very in demand.'

'Far too good to be taking photos of me, that's for sure.'

'He enjoyed it, actually. Said you were a star pupil.'

'Really?' I felt ridiculously proud at her words, but sad that I might not see him again.

So when my phone beeps and I see his name pop up with an instant message, I'm surprised. I am outside on the deck enjoying the belated birthday present Kate bought me, even though, as I'd pointed out, she'd already given me a bottle of perfume on my actual birthday.

She'd shrugged. 'Call it an early present for next year then.'

Her present was a swing seat, a wide three-seater that I could lie down on and watch the stars, or just sit and swing and watch the ocean and the clouds. Both pastimes I found particularly soothing.

His message says,
Hi, Ava.

I message him straight back:
Hi! Where in the world are you? I hear you're off on an adventurous photo expedition.

James:
Not so glamourous, I was in Burma covering the Rohingya situation. Back home now though.

Ava:
Oh sorry! Hope I didn't upset you with my flippancy. You must have seen some pretty sad stuff.

James:
It wasn't fun, that's for sure. I'm not upset though. In fact, funny you should say that. I wrote and deleted my first message to you about six times. I don't know whether to ask how you are, or whether that's a stupid question. I don't want to upset you.

Ava:
It's not stupid. I'd rather you ask than not. Shows you're thinking about me.

James:
Actually, I haven't stopped thinking about you.

I freeze. My heart doesn't.

Ava:
Why?

James:
Truthfully, I don't know.

Ava:
Oh. Well, thanks for being honest

James:
You made me promise to, remember? OK.

So the reason I'm messaging . . . do you want to meet? I was thinking dinner?

Ava:
Are you asking me out on a date?

I hold my breath and watch as the three grey dots that indicate he is typing something blink at me for an inordinately long amount of time. They blink while the moon rises further overhead; while shooting stars flash across the sky; and somewhere in the universe whole solar systems implode. They blink as the tide gently recedes into the distance and the earth tilts on its axis.

James:
I think so.

Ava:
You know I'm dying, right?

James:
Yes.

Ava:
Did my mother put you up to this?

James:
No, absolutely not

Ava:
Are you asking me out of pity?

James:
No! I'm asking because I enjoy your company.

Ava:
In that case I'd love to.

James:
Really?

Ava:
Of course. Name a time and place. My calendar is wide open. For the next few months at least.

James:
I'll pick you up. Tomorrow night. Six o'clock.

Ava:
I shall be waiting.

James:
Good night, Ava.

Ava:
Good night, James.

25

'Not quite what you were expecting, is it?'

'No.'

He looks crestfallen. 'I'm sorry.'

'It's *better* than I was expecting.'

His face brightens again. 'Really?'

'Let's face it, when it comes to dining out in this town, the options are limited. And while I do enjoy both the Indian cuisine at the Maharaja *and* the Thai at the Lemongrass, sometimes you just can't beat good old fish 'n' chips.'

We are walking along the grassy beachfront in town, having just ordered and collected our dinner from Erik's takeaways. Even though James is carrying the newspaper-wrapped bundle, I can smell the food, and it's making my stomach rumble.

'You forgot about the pizza palace,' James reminds me.

'Oops. Don't tell Leonardo. He gets upset easily.'

'Emotional people, the Italians.'

'You're telling me. I remember when Italy were knocked out of the soccer World Cup. He didn't open the restaurant for a week. Just sat in his courtyard out the back drinking wine and weeping. Rose from the drycleaner's next door heard him.'

He arches his eyebrows. 'And promptly told everyone?'

'Of course. You know what small towns are like.'

'I'm beginning to learn, yes.'

'Where did you grow up? I know it wasn't around here, because there's no way we wouldn't have crossed paths before now. Also you have a certain . . . ' I wave my hands around as I try to think of the right word; I fail . . . 'city air, about you.' I say lamely.

'City air?'

'You know, suave and cultured. Like you visit museums and art galleries and dine at restaurants with more than one fork on the table.'

He laughs. 'In that case, guilty as charged. Born and bred city boy, I'm afraid. But before you completely write me off, I don't really enjoy living in the city. Too frantic for me. I much prefer the pace out here.'

'You've redeemed yourself slightly then.'

'That's why I bought a small place out here four years ago. Initially as a holiday home, somewhere to escape the rat race for mini breaks. But the more time I spend here the more I like the idea of making this a permanent base.'

'It gets under your skin, doesn't it?'

'Small town life?'

'Yes. There's a real sense of community here. We look out for one another.'

'I've noticed.'

As we walk, the sun sinks lower and the world takes on a gentle hue: muted, softer. Occasionally joggers pass by us on the path, smiling a greeting as we shuffle to one side to let them

179

past. Two old men are camped out on deckchairs on the sand, rods in the water, beers in hand. I can hear the laughter and shrieks of children at the playground near the main jetty, fifty metres or so behind us. Their voices carry easily in the still air and bring a smile to my face. There is a general sense of calm and serenity. I immediately feel regret for all the nights I have wasted, sitting inside watching *Friends* reruns at this precise time, instead of being out here enjoying the refined elegance of dusk.

'So,' James continues. 'How good are the locals at accepting outsiders? Do I have a chance, do you think?'

'Mm.' I pretend to think about it. 'That depends.'

'On what?'

'Whether you mind everybody knowing your business.'

He shrugs. 'I have nothing to hide.'

'Then you'll be fine. Just lend a hand when you're asked, accept a drink when it's offered, and stay out of the feud between the Mayor and my mother.'

'Your mother has a feud with the Mayor?'

'Going on ten years now.'

'Sounds interesting.'

'It's really not, but if you insist on knowing I'll explain it all, at a later date. Right now I just want to know if you intend on eating that food tonight or if we're just taking it for a walk.'

He holds up the paper-wrapped bundle. 'Oh I'm sorry, are you hungry?'

'Starving. And *this* close to going feral and

ripping it out of your hands.'

'I really am intrigued by this story about your mother and the Mayor though. What if, in my ignorance, I make a faux pas and incur her wrath?'

I sigh. 'Look. Just promise her you'll vote for the opposition come election time, whether you intend to or not, and everything will be just fine.'

'OK.' He smiles. 'We can eat now. How about here?' He points to a picnic table under the shade of a large pohutukawa tree.

'Here will do just fine.' My stomach rumbles audibly. He laughs and places the food down, teasingly unwrapping it slowly. I sit on the side that faces out over the ocean and shuffle over as he sits beside me instead of opposite. I eagerly reach for a piece of golden battered fish and yelp when he smacks my hand away lightly.

'Wait,' he scolds. 'I haven't said grace yet.'

'Oh.' Chastened, I cross my hands and put them in my lap, looking down at them. I'm not sure whether to close my eyes or not, because I wasn't raised religious and the only grace my father ever paused long enough to say was 'Smells good, love.' I risk a sideways peek at James and he has his eyes shut, so I close mine as well.

'Father, Son, and the Holy Ghost,' he says solemnly. 'Whoever eats fastest, gets the most.'

It takes a second for me to understand what he's just said, and when I do I my eyes fly open. He has picked up the piece of fish that I'd been going for, the biggest piece, and has already taken a bite.

'Hey,' I protest, smacking him on the arm. 'No fair.'

He shrugs. 'You snooze you lose.'

'And there I was thinking you were a gentleman.'

'I don't know what gave you that idea.'

I adopt a pitiful expression.

'Oh don't look at me like that. I'll feel bad.'

'That's the point.' I sniff and blink a few times.

He sighs. 'Here. If it means that much to you.' He proffers out what's left of the piece of fish.

I screw my face up at it. 'I don't want your leftovers.'

'Suit yourself.' He throws the rest into his mouth and chews, his eyes alight with amusement. 'Aren't you eating?'

Ten minutes later, there are only the scrappy, hard and small chips left, which James throws to the seagulls. I rub my finger on the greasy white paper a few times and lick it, and he gives me a questioning look.

'I like the salt.'

'You know it's bad for you, right.'

I shrug. 'Everything in moderation.'

'So what are your other weaknesses?' He rolls up the paper into a little ball and looks around for a rubbish bin.

'Is it boring if I say chocolate and wine?'

'Not if it's true.'

I get gingerly to my feet. My lower back has started to ache, but I'm not ready to call it a night yet.

He balls the newspaper up a bit tighter and does a basketball throw towards the rubbish bin.

It misses and lands on the ground.

'Pathetic,' I say, shaking my head.

'Why do you think I'm a photographer and not an NBA player.'

'So you can check out nude firemen?'

He snorts as he bends to pick up the paper, putting it carefully into the rubbish bin this time. Then he gives me a pointed look. ''There are other things I'd much rather check out.'

Is he flirting? I'm so out of practice I'm unsure, but it feels like it. As good as it feels though, it's also confusing, and I must betray my uncertainty on my face because his eyes narrow knowingly.

'I'm sorry,' he apologises. 'The last thing I want to do is make you feel uncomfortable.'

I shake my head. 'You don't.'

We gaze intently at each other for a whisker of time, before his eyes drop to the ground and he swallows hard. He looks vulnerable, achingly so, and I want to step forward and try to wrap him in my arms, all of him, even though he is almost twice the size I am, and make him feel better.

'Do you want me to be honest?' he asks softly, looking at my face again.

I nod. 'Always.'

'I'm not sure why I'm here.' He shrugs his shoulders. 'I mean, not *here*, here,' he clarifies. 'I invited you after all. It's the motives behind the invitation I'm a little confused about.'

'Motives?'

'I'm not making much sense, am I?'

'Not really.'

'Shall we go for a walk? Burn off some of the ninety million calories we just consumed.'

'*You* consumed, you mean. I was lucky to get a few chips.'

I joke to try to relax him, but there is a stiff set to his shoulder as he walks next to me that suggests he is still mulling over our brief conversation.

'Cold?' he asks, when I shiver.

'No.' I shake my head. 'Just someone walking over my grave.'

He doesn't smile. 'I've never understood that saying.'

'Me neither,' I admit. 'It's just one of those things you say without thinking. Like 'Bless you', when someone sneezes.'

He stops walking suddenly, but it takes me a moment to realise, so I stop a couple of steps ahead of him and turn, puzzled as to why he has stopped.

'I don't want to hurt you,' he says earnestly. 'Or upset you in any way.'

'You haven't.'

'I know. I mean in the future. You know, if there was a . . . if we were to . . . '

'OK.' I step back towards him, realising that whatever it is he is trying to say will need to be coaxed out of him. 'Take a deep breath.'

He frowns. 'I don't need — '

'*Take a deep breath.*'

He sucks in air quickly, his eyes big as he waits for my permission to exhale again.

'And release.'

He blows out noisily.

184

'Better?'

'Not really.'

'Then you didn't do it properly.' I move to his side and place a hand on his chest, at the bottom of where I think his diaphragm would be. I pretend I don't hear his sharp intake of breath as I touch him. 'Right, breathe in again,' I tell him. 'A proper, big breath. Right down to here.' I apply mild pressure to his chest. He turns his head to look down at me as he follows my instructions, and the expression in his eyes almost robs me of my own breath. I quickly look back at his chest and tell him sternly to breathe deeper.

'You're something special, Ava, you know that?' he says quietly after he exhales. 'I've never met anyone else like you.'

'A worldly traveller such as yourself?' I chuckle nervously. 'I find that hard to believe.'

'It's true,' he insists. 'I wouldn't say it otherwise.'

'You're pretty spectacular yourself. You know, for a city guy.'

I fall back on humour because I don't know what else to say, or do. The way he's making me feel is new to me.

'Ava,' he says. 'Look at me.'

I can't. I'm scared of seeing something in his eyes that reflects what I'm feeling. I'm more scared though that I won't see it. My phone rings with a text alert and, relieved, I fumble in my back pocket, pulling it out to check the screen.

'Kate,' I tell him. 'Asking where I am.'

'You didn't tell your friends you were coming out with me?'

'And have to endure the million questions beforehand and the post-mortem afterwards? No. I didn't tell them.'

'What if I was an axe murderer?'

'Are you?'

'No.'

'Didn't think so. Anyway, my mother would have avenged me in ways worse than anything you could have ever done.'

He shudders as he laughs. 'I don't doubt that for a second.'

I quickly reply to Kate, simply saying I'm out with a friend and will be home soon. She texts back at the speed of light, as I knew she would.

Friend? What friend?

I don't reply this time, instead putting the phone on silent and sliding it back into my pocket. 'Sorry.'

'It's OK. It's good that you have people who care so much about you.'

The ache in my back is becoming more urgent, and as much as I don't want to leave him, I know that I will suffer if I don't get home and take pain relief and the weight off it now. The sun has almost disappeared over the horizon, its majestic colours spread across the sky in one last, triumphant hurrah. On cue, the street lights flicker on around us. The children have gone home, as have the fishermen. Soon, the first stars will appear in the sky.

'I should get you home,' James says, reading my mind.

'Yes, I'm sorry.'

'Don't be. Never be. You have nothing to be sorry for. Come on.' He reaches out and picks up my hand, tucking it through his arm like he did in the field that day. We walk like that, our hips occasionally bumping, back along the promenade to his car, the last one left in the car park outside the surf club.

'This was nice,' I say once we are both inside the car and he is reaching to put the key in the ignition.

He pauses to look at me. 'Really?'

'Yes. I've enjoyed myself.' I look down at my hands in my lap shyly. 'I hope you did too.'

'It was OK, I suppose.'

I look at him sharply, feeling stricken. He is smiling, teasing.

'I'm kidding.' He laughs. 'Sorry. Yes, I've had a wonderful night.' He rubs his hand through his hair roughly. 'Um, so I was wondering, what are you doing this weekend?'

'This weekend?' I think quickly. I have my standard Sunday night meal date at my parents' house, and a vague agreement with Kate to go curtain shopping. 'Nothing that can't be cancelled.'

'Good.' He smiles broadly. 'That's good. I'll pick you up Saturday morning. Pack an overnight bag.'

'Overnight?' My voice comes out higher-pitched than I intend.

'Don't worry,' he reassures. 'I'm a gentleman,

remember. I'll book two rooms. Your virtue will remain intact.'

'Oh.' I try not to sound disappointed. 'That's good then.'

26

'You can't be serious.'

'Why not?'

'Well for one, you barely know the guy. He could be an axe murderer for all you know.'

I pause from folding a T-shirt neatly to pack in my small suitcase and stare at Kate. 'Does he *look* like an axe murderer to you?'

'Not really,' she admits. 'But what does an axe murderer actually look like? Hm?'

'I think it's brilliant,' declares Amanda from where she is draped across the wicker chair in the corner of my bedroom. The morning sun is beaming through the blinds behind her, giving her an angelic halo effect that she doesn't deserve. 'He's gorgeous.'

The three of us pause to picture James and adopt similar dreamy expressions.

'As gorgeous as he is,' Kate says sternly, shaking herself out of her reverie, 'we still don't know the first thing about him.'

'Kate.' I put the last item of clothing in the case and zip it carefully, then walk to stand in front of where she is perched on the end of my bed. 'I love you for being so protective. I really do. And I know your concern is coming from a caring place.'

She smiles.

'But seriously,' I continue, 'if you try and ruin this for me I will kill you with an axe myself. Understood?'

Amanda snorts with laughter while Kate gapes at me like a fish. She nods slowly.

'Thank you.' I smile sweetly.

'Where's he taking you?' Amanda asks.

'No idea. He didn't say.'

'You didn't ask?'

'I was just too excited by the invitation to even think about it.'

'So is it, like, a date?'

'Again, no idea.' I shrug. 'The sensible side of me thinks, no way, absolutely not. Why would he be interested in me when I'm, you know?'

Amanda pulls a sympathetic face. I sit down on the bed and Kate turns so I am facing them both.

'But then there's the way he looks at me. I've never been looked at like that before.'

'Like how?'

'Like . . . ' I try to think of the words to explain it. 'Like he thinks I'm the most interesting thing in the entire universe. Like he's completely fascinated by me, and we could be standing in the middle of the Playboy Mansion and he'd *still* only have eyes for me.'

Kate and Amanda exchange an open-eyed look.

'Wow,' says Kate.

'I know. It's hard to explain. I'm not really doing it justice.'

'Look, Ava.' Kate shuffles over to pick up my hands and look earnestly in my eyes. 'If that's the case, if he is developing feelings for you, you need to stop and think about where this is going. It's only going to end in hurt, for you both. But especially him. I know you like him, but can you really start something knowing what the future holds?'

My shoulders sag. She's right, of course.

'Besides, I think you already have so much going on that you need to focus your energies on. Your health, of course, and the wedding.'

'I don't agree,' Amanda interjects loudly. 'I say fuck it, don't think about the future. Just make the most of the moment and if you enjoy his company as much as you say you do, then do whatever it is that makes you feel good and happy. It's a hell of a cliche but it's one you know all too well. Life is short. Don't play it safe. Live wild.'

'That kind of thinking is not fair on either Ava or James,' Kate tells her sharply. 'It'll only end in hurt.' She squeezes my hand gently. 'You have us. We love you. Do you really need anything else right now?'

I smile softly and squeeze her hand back. 'You know I love you guys. And I'm so grateful to have you in my life, because I need you more than I ever have before. But this is different. This ... feeling I get when I'm with James, it's something I haven't felt in a long time, if ever. I never expected this to happen, but he makes me feel alive. And I need that right now.'

She sighs. 'I guess I can understand that.'

'I don't want to hurt him though.'

'He's a big boy. He can take care of himself,' Amanda scoffs.

We all jump at a loud knock on the front door of the house.

191

'He's here.' Kate gets up, stating the obvious. 'It's not too late to change your mind.' She gives me a pointed look. 'For his sake as much as your own.'

I feel a brief surge of panic inside. What am I doing? Why did I think this was a good idea?

'Ava,' Amanda says gently. I look at her familiar, comforting face. It grounds me, and the panic begins to recede. 'You don't know what he wants, or where he's taking you. For all we know you could be worrying about something, or nothing at all. Don't overthink it. Just follow your instincts like you've always told us to do.'

I nod. 'OK.'

Standing up, I take a deep breath, then I walk to the front door and open it. When I see him, I know what to do.

'Hey.' He smiles. 'You ready?'

I step outside, aware that Kate and Amanda are lurking inside, within earshot but out of sight.

I stop in front of him. 'I'm sorry, but this isn't going to work.'

He frowns. 'Sorry?'

I smile. 'I forgot my case. I can't go anywhere without that now, can I?'

27

We are all dying. Every day, a little bit more.

When I was younger I watched a movie with Kate and Amanda, about a group of six teenage friends who, while giddy under the influence of beer and marijuana and caught up in the delirium that is living life as a teenager, went to see a fortune-teller in a spooky booth at a fairground at midnight. She saw them each individually, and gave them all the chance to decide if they wanted to know the date they would die. They all, apart from one girl, chose to find out.

The next day, unsure if it was all just a bad dream and determined to find the old witch and give her a piece of their minds, they went back. But (cue ghostly, unnerving music) the fair was GONE.

So they carried on living their lives with this fear hanging over their heads. Was she legit? Did she really have some kind of crystal ball that showed her the future? Or was she simply an opportunist out to make a quick buck and who got off on scaring the living daylights out of kids. A few years later, unable to cope with the insanity and determined to prove her wrong, one of the boys committed suicide. The fact he did this on a date which was *not* the date the fortune-teller gave him should have gone some way towards calming the minds of the others.

But no, alas, as we found out, they never told each other what date they were given. (Cue mild hysteria.) I can't remember much of the rest of it. It was pretty rubbish cinematography and the actors D grade enough that I never saw any of them in anything else.

Afterwards, in the dark as we lay in our sleeping bags on the lounge floor we talked about what we'd do in the same situation. Kate and I were adamant we wouldn't find out, that we'd want to remain oblivious. Amanda was the opposite. She'd want to know, she insisted, so she could make sure she did everything she wanted to do before her time was up. She wanted to go out in a blaze of glory, she said. Drunk, in love and owing a fortune.

Her words made me wonder whether, given the knowledge they were given, the kids in the film lived life differently to how they would have done if they'd remained blissfully unaware. Whether it influenced the choices they made, and altered their path.

I torment myself sometimes with thoughts of what my life might now be like had I not been given the initial diagnosis. Would I be married? A mother? A high-flying executive? Maybe I'd have been bitten by the travel bug, and would have been right this minute sipping the froth off a cold beer in an Irish pub somewhere in the middle of nowhere, my filthy, well-used backpack at my feet and *joie de vivre* in my heart because really, *this* was the life.

But what really torments me, is that really, deep, *deep* down in my heart, I know that in all probability not much would have changed. I'd probably still have been in the same flat, working the same job, watching the same TV shows and drinking far too much soft drink than health departments currently recommend.

I don't know the date I will die, or what time of the day it will happen. I don't know the location, or the exact means (I'm hoping I will be on so much medication I won't be aware of the end when it comes, because to think otherwise terrifies me).

But this I do know.

I know it will most likely be some time in the next year, more if I'm lucky and the doctor was having an off day with his estimations. I know it *won't* be in fifty, or sixty, years' time, like it *should* have been.

And I know that I don't want to just sit around and wait to die, but that is exactly what I have been doing. I don't know why James has come into my life now, or whether he gets that same fluttery feeling in his stomach that I do when I think about him. But I don't want to question it. I don't want to overthink it, or dwell on 'what could have been'. I just want to *feel* it, and never *stop* feeling it until the moment I cease breathing. And then, well then I can only hope that it goes on, somewhere, somehow.

28

'What's that?'

'What does it look like?'

'A helicopter.'

'Ten points to you.' James slams the boot of his truck shut and grins at me.

'Ha ha.' I pull a dry face. 'Funny. But seriously, what's it doing there?'

'I think the other car park was full.'

'James . . . ' My voice is low, warning.

'OK, OK. Ava.' He steps forward and gestures with a flourish. 'Your chariot awaits.'

'Are you serious?'

He nods.

'We're getting on that thing?' I point to it.

'Yes.'

I gaze at it, wide eyed. I've never been up this close to a helicopter before, and it's *huge*. 'Bloody hell,' I say.

James, who had started to walk towards the machine, freezes and turns, his face worried.

'What? What does that mean? Is that a good 'bloody hell'? Or a 'There's no way in hell you're getting me on that thing,' kind of 'bloody hell'.'

'I'm not sure.'

'Have you ever been on one before?'

I shake my head.

'Well there's always a first time for everything,' he says hopefully. 'Right?'

I look at the blade things above the helicopter.

They are moving up and down slightly in the breeze and look ever so flimsy. How do they hold this thing up in the air? A man wearing aviator sunglasses like Tom Cruise in *Top Gun* is walking around the helicopter with a clipboard, checking things and making notes. Unlike Tom Cruise, he is as bald as a boiled egg, and is wearing a T-shirt stretched thinly over a paunch that says 'Trust me! I'm a flyboy!' James walks back to stand in front of me.

'Seriously though, Ava. If you don't want to do this, that's OK. I'm not going to pressure you into anything you don't want to do. Say the word and we can go somewhere else, somewhere that doesn't involve flying. It's not for everyone after all, and if you're scared that's perfectly understandable.'

His words give me the push I need. 'No,' I say. 'I'm not scared. OK, maybe a little. But I want to do it.'

His face relaxes again. 'Are you sure?'

'Positive.'

'Ready for an adventure?'

'I was born ready.'

He smiles. 'OK. I'm just going into the office to sort out the paperwork. I'll be back soon.'

I nearly chicken out when he's in the office talking to the woman behind the counter. The thought of being high in the air inside the metal contraption sitting before me is terrifying, to say the least. But I trust him. And his use of the word 'adventure' has sparked my imagination. I have no idea where we're going, and whether I enjoy the ride there remains to be seen, but I'm determined to make the most of this opportunity that I have been offered.

James comes back outside, beaming. 'We're all good to go.'

'Really? You're sure they don't need like a passport, or something? Because I didn't bring mine.' I pull a face. 'Aw, we can't go, what a shame.'

'We're not leaving the country, Ava. You don't need a passport.'

'Oh.'

He smiles reassuringly. 'Last chance to change your mind.'

I take a deep breath and hold it for six seconds, then exhale feeling calmer. Not as calm as a whiskey would have made me feel, but I was pretty sure helicopters didn't serve in-flight drinks, so it would have to do. 'No. Let's do this.'

He takes my hand and leads me over to where the pilot is holding open the door.

'Hey, Toby,' James greets him warmly.

'James,' Toby crows. 'Good to see you again, man. How've you been?'

'Oh you know, can't complain.' They do some kind of guy handshake where they bump fists a few times, wiggle fingers and end with butting shoulders. I try to stifle my laughter but fail.

'What?' James asks defensively.

'Nothing.'

He turns back to Toby. 'How's life treating you?'

'Yeah good, thanks. Wife's about to have our second child in a few weeks. Another girl to twist Daddy around her little finger.'

James laughs and I watch him fondly. I'm beginning to realise he is friendly like this with everyone, that he is genuinely interested in people and really listens when they talk. It makes me feel warm inside.

'OK.' Toby consults his clipboard. 'Wind's picking up over the ranges so we need to get this show on the road. You guys get in and buckle up while I load your bags.'

My nerves pick up again as I step up into the helicopter, running my eyes around appraisingly.

'Take the window seat,' James says. 'I don't want you to miss the view.'

We are in a row of four seats behind the pilot's seat. I take the seat James is pointing to and he helps me fasten the seat belts and tighten them until he is satisfied. Toby closes the door and checks it's securely locked into place, then climbs into his own seat and puts his headphones on. He gestures over his shoulder and James picks up headsets hanging in front of us.

'Put this on,' he says.

'Why?'

'To help cover the noise of the blades,' he explains. 'Also so we can all communicate once we're in the air.'

'You've done this before once or twice I take it,' I say, doing as I'm told. Instantly, the world is muffled. Toby gives us the thumbs-up and James gives one back. It's not long before the helicopter is going, and I'm amazed by how loud it is, even with the headphones. James gives me a questioning look and I smile to show I am OK.

He reaches over and picks up my hand off my lap, and as I look down at his long fingers wrapped around my own, I feel a delicious sensation inside.

I can't help it, I close my eyes while we lift off. I try to keep them open but the sight of the ground rushing away makes me feel queasy, so I close my eyes and tighten my grip on James's hand instead. He gives me a reassuring squeeze. It calms me. Besides, surely fate isn't so ironic as to take a dying girl and kill her prematurely in a helicopter crash.

Toby pushes a button in front of him and I hear a click in my headphone, followed by his mechanical voice in my ear.

'You guys OK back there?'

'Yeah we're good, thanks,' James tells him. He looks at me for confirmation. I nod.

'Where are we going?' I ask.

'Wait and see.'

'Never heard of it. Is it far?'

'Not long to go, another ten minutes and you'll see for yourself.' Toby's voice crackles.

James is so close I can see flecks of brown in his green eyes and the fine lines that crease his skin when he smiles, which he does every time he looks at me. It's contagious, so I smile back before turning to look out the window. We are low-flying over a forest, a carpet of green that stretches as far as I can see. Undulating hills and ranges shape the land, and if I look really hard, in the distance I can see the blue line that is the ocean.

'You guys been together long?' Toby asks.

'Oh we're not a couple like that,' I splutter, while James looks amused.

Toby's eyebrows arch in surprise. 'Oh. Sorry. I just thought . . . '

I turn my head to look out of the window, embarrassed. Is it that transparent? That I like James? Because I *do* like him. I like him more and more every moment I am with him. He makes me forget everything and just focus on the moment we are in.

'We'll be landing in a minute,' Toby says. 'Everybody still belted in?'

'Yes,' James confirms.

'Good. Might get a little dicey as we go over this hill,' Toby warns, and he's barely finished saying the words before the helicopter drops a few feet, taking my stomach with it. Involuntarily, I clutch James's arm and pull myself close. He puts an arm around me and in spite of my fear I'm struck by how right it feels to be so close to him. It's like I have been searching for this sense of belonging my entire life, and now I've found it. Here, with him. And the cruelty that it has happened now, when I am dying, is almost too much to bear.

James sees the tear that trickles down my cheek and wipes it away with a thumb, his skin rough and scratchy. Then he taps my shoulder and points out of the window.

I gasp. We have made it over the top of the hill and below us, nestled amongst miles and miles of native forest, are a series of tree houses, with a clear area of grass to one side which includes gardens, a pool and the helicopter landing pad. It is the kind of thing you see in romantic movies.

'What is this place?' I ask in wonder. 'I had no idea this even existed.'

'That's the beauty of it,' James answers. 'Not many people do.'

Toby gently lands the helicopter on the helipad and we wait until the blades stop spinning to dismount. A woman is standing a few metres away, in a white shirt with black vest and skirt. Her hair is pulled into a tidy bun and her make-up is artfully applied. She is immaculate, and I feel like a hobo next to her.

'Mr Gable,' she says warmly, stepping forward. 'Welcome back, sir, it's a pleasure to have you staying with us again.'

Immediately I feel my stomach clench. He's been here before? Who with? But it's not my place to be jealous so I force a smile.

'Thank you, Mary,' he says, then he looks down at me to explain. 'I shot photos here for an article about the most exclusive accommodations in the country.'

My smile relaxes. He was here for work. I look around while he and Mary talk. We are under a canopy of trees, tall ones, that stretch high into the sky, filtering the sunlight. There are wooden steps leading up to what I can only describe as tree houses, built on platforms around the larger trees. There are four smaller ones and two large ones, and the small ones are connected to the larger ones by wooden platforms and bridges.

'It was a wonderful article.' Mary agrees. 'You did the place justice, for which we're grateful. Anything you need while you're here, please let us know.' She gestures to a man nearby who nods and collects our bags off Toby.

'Thank you,' James says. 'Right now, I think we could just do with a rest.'

I know he means me, that I need a rest, but he is being polite by including himself in the statement and I don't care because I'm grateful. I *am* tired. I was so nervous last night I barely slept, and it's catching up to me. Also my body hasn't taken kindly to the vibrations of the helicopter and I'm feeling a little nauseous. Even though this place is begging to be explored, I want nothing more than to curl up on a bed and close my eyes for a while. I need to get some strength back.

'Of course.' She smiles. 'Follow me.'

She leads us to the only building on the ground, a wooden lodge. Inside, there is a reception area and some rooms behind doors that I assume are offices, and a door that says STAFF ONLY. Mary leads us towards a set of metallic elevator doors.

'You have an elevator?' I ask. 'In the forest?'

She nods. 'Two, actually. We are an exclusive, hidden resort, and although we cater mostly to the famous and wealthy, some of them are of course elderly or have mobility issues. We make it comfortable and accessible for them all.'

'This place is insane,' I hiss quietly to James as we wait for the doors to open.

'Is that a good thing or a bad thing?'

'Good. Definitely good.'

'Wait until you see what's at the top.'

The elevator makes a *ding* noise, and the

doors open. Mary steps to the side and gestures for us to go in first. I am about to step forward when her words connect with my brain.

'Stop,' I say, sharper than intended. Both James and Mary look at me quizzically. 'You said the elevators are for the elderly and the infirm.'

Mary nods, but the fleeting glance she shoots at James answers my questions. I take his hand and pull him away, out of Mary's immediate earshot.

'I know your heart is in the right place, and that you were no doubt thinking of me and my health when you organised this. But please, I don't want to be treated like an invalid. At least, not until I am one. I just want to be normal.'

His face softens, although his eyes are sad. It's a look I've seen a million times, and it never gets any easier. When I see the sadness in the eyes of someone whose heart is breaking because I am dying, it breaks *my* heart. And I feel guilty, which is nonsense because none of this is my fault. But still, I hate to be the cause of hurt in anyone, let alone anyone I care deeply about.

'OK.' He nods. Then he turns to Mary and speaks loudly. 'Mary, change of plans. We're taking the steps.'

'Are you sure?'

'Yes.'

Her eyebrows arch but to her credit she says nothing, even though my cynical mind tells me she's probably worried about insurance or lawsuit issues should I fall and break my neck. She leads us up the widest set of steps, the ones that lead to the larger of the tree houses.

'This is the restaurant,' she indicates with a hand. 'Closed now but you'll be seeing it tonight. Your rooms are this way.'

I notice the guy with our bags has been waiting for us outside the doors of our rooms. They are adjacent to each other, and connected by a platform, but still separate rooms. Just as James promised. He opens the door and I step inside. Immediately my mouth drops open. Larger than it appears from the outside, the room is crafted entirely from different kinds of wood and natural materials. Built around the existing tree trunk, there are two large branches that come up through the floor and disappear out the roof, giving the appearance that the tree has grown around the house and not vice versa. One side is floor-to-ceiling glass doors, which open out on to a deck with a view over the forest and the ranges. The bed in the centre of the room is the biggest bed I have ever seen, with four posts on the corners and frothy white mosquito nets, which I assume means I can sleep with the doors open if I like and remain uneaten. The linen is crisp, white and luxurious.

I gape at James. 'I'm sleeping here? Are you serious?'

James grins, delighted by my reaction. 'It's all yours,' he confirms. 'But you haven't seen the best bit yet.'

He strides over past the bed behind a screened area and I follow him. There are more glass doors and he pushes them open effortlessly.

'Ta da,' he says.

Behind him, set into the deck, is a large spa

bath. At the sight of it, all thoughts of sleep disappear in an instant. I have the water running before the man with the bags has even left the room. James lingers to watch on indulgently as I run the bath water.

'You look very smug,' I tell him as I check the labels on the little bottles that are lined up on the marble vanity. I could be wrong, but I'm fairly sure the brand is one that retails only in exclusive boutiques.

'Do I?'

'Yes. But that's OK. You deserve to. I can't believe this place.' I unscrew the lid on the bath gel bottle and sniff it gingerly. It smells of extravagance and indulgence. I pour the whole lot into the bath and the water immediately starts frothing up into bubbles.

'I knew you'd like this place,' James says. 'And you've barely seen half of what it has to offer.'

'Honestly, I could just stay in this room and be perfectly happy.' I sigh. 'This bath, that bed. Is there a minibar?'

He laughs. 'I believe so, yes.'

'Then I'm all set.'

'Well, I hope you do leave the room at some point,' he says. 'I'd quite like to spend some time with you, if you can spare it.'

I pretend to consider it. 'I suppose I should,' I say eventually. 'As you've gone to so much effort and everything.'

'How about — ' he consults his watch — 'I pick you up at seven o'clock for dinner. Four hours. Is that enough time for you to enjoy this?' He gestures towards the bath, where the bubbles are threatening to overspill.

'It will have to do.'

'I can make it eight if you prefer.'

'I'm kidding. If I sat in there for four hours you'd be dining with a wrinkly old prune.'

'I'll see you at seven then.'

'You will.'

'Enjoy your bath.'

'I'm sure I will.'

He opens the door and steps out into the hall. Before the door can close I call his name, and he catches it, pushing it open again.

'Yes?'

'Thank you.' I smile. 'For bringing me here.'

'You deserve it,' he says softly.

'I'm still not sure though, exactly *why* we're here?'

'All will be revealed in good time, Ava,' he says mysteriously, winking. Then he laughs. 'Well, tomorrow anyway. For now, just relax. Enjoy the moment. I'll see you soon.'

He lets go of the door and it closes behind him. I stare at it for a minute, wondering what he meant by, 'all will be revealed'. Then I realise that wondering about it won't bring me any closer to the answer, so I do what he says. I strip off, climb in the bath, and I enjoy the hell out of the moment.

29

Seven o'clock on the dot there is a knock on my door. I am ready and waiting, and have been for the last half an hour. An hour in the bath and then a nap has given me strength back, and I feel renewed and ready to face the evening. Standing up, I straighten down the skirt on my dress nervously, take a deep breath and then open the door.

'Hey.' He smiles, and takes my breath away. 'You look amazing.'

I look down, suddenly coy under his appraising eye. 'Thank you.'

'How was your bath?'

'Wonderful.' I sigh, dreamily. ' 'The jets of water massage *everywhere*. Oh my God, my whole body thoroughly enjoyed it.' My words catch up to my ears and, realising how they could be misconstrued, I blush. 'I mean . . . not like . . . just my . . . Ugh. You can stop smirking now.' I give up, realising I'm just making it worse.

'Smirking? Me?' He adopts a radiantly innocent expression. 'I have no idea what you're talking about.'

'Let's try this again.' I close the door.

He knocks.

I open it.

'Evening,' he says. 'You're looking very beautiful. Enjoy your bath?'

'Yes, thank you. It was very relaxing.'

'I bet it was.'

I give him a sharp look but he just stares innocently back at me. Then he holds out his arm. 'Shall we?'

I accept it. 'If you mean let's eat, then yes. Please. I'm starving.'

'Good. I've asked the chef to prepare his best dishes.'

'You know the chef personally?' I ask as we walk along the wooden walkways that connect the buildings. In the four hours since we have arrived it has started to darken, and lights now guide our way along.

He nods. 'I know all the staff. Not well, but on a friendly enough basis. When I'm on assignment somewhere like this, I like to get to know the people behind the scenes. It gives you a better sense of the place.'

'You take your work very seriously, don't you?'

'It's not work when you're passionate about it.'

'I suppose not. You're lucky, finding that thing in life that makes you happy. Your parents must be proud.'

He stiffens slightly, then comes to a stop. 'We're here.' He opens the door we saw earlier that Mary casually indicated was the restaurant, and gestures for me to enter. I do, but stop just inside the door to exclaim softly. That simple word 'restaurant' doesn't come close to doing justice to what I'm looking at. Not at all. I feel a little nudge on my back as James pushes me out of the doorway so he can enter and stand beside me.

'Well?' His face is excited, like he is a parent showing a child their new puppy.

'You know how I said my room was the most amazing thing I've ever seen?'

'Yes.'

'I think it just got beaten.'

The dining room, because with only the one table in the centre it deserves a more intimate title than restaurant, at least in my opinion, is alight with the cosy glow of fairy lights woven around small branches and a large tree trunk, and candles placed strategically (and carefully) around the room to create a welcoming and romantic ambience. The table is large and natural wood, the chairs the same. In the centre is a large arrangement of flowers, and I'm pleased to note it's an eclectic assortment of colours and types, because a prim and proper bouquet just would not have suited this room at all. Everything is designed to blend into and enhance the natural environment, and it works perfectly. The other side of the room, like in my bedroom, is floor-to-ceiling glass doors. These ones are open to the air, and the breeze that wafts in carries with it an anticipatory air. Outside stretches a canopy of green, and a sky the colour of ripe apricots. I feel like I am on a movie set.

'I've officially run out of words,' I admit finally. 'Everything I can think of to describe this place is woeful and inadequate.'

'That's exactly the reaction I was hoping for.'

I turn to face him. 'Thank you. Again. It's perfect. Everything is perfect.'

'Everything?' A smile tugs at his lips. The first part of him I remember being enamoured by. Not that long ago, yet I feel I have known him much longer. Something in the way I am looking at him makes his expression turn serious. He opens his mouth to say something but is interrupted.

'Welcome to Treetops.' The young man who carried our bags earlier is lingering by the table. He had come into the room unnoticed. 'Are you ready to dine?'

James closes his mouth, a fleeting look of disappointment flashing across his face. Then he relaxes and nods.

'Yes. Thank you, Craig, we are.'

Craig pulls out my seat and I sit, trying not to feel self-conscious that someone is waiting on me but secretly enjoying the experience all the same. James sits at the other end of the table. It's only three or four metres long, but he seems far away and I get the urge to giggle and break into a song from *Beauty and the Beast* because it reminds me of a scene in the movie. James casts an expert eye over the wine menu and orders a bottle of red, after checking that I'm happy with his choice, and Craig disappears through a discreet door to fetch it.

'I hope you don't mind,' James says from his end of the table. 'But they don't do a menu here, just a selection of courses they bring out. If there's something you don't like you don't have to eat it. The chef here isn't one of those precious ones who take offence easily.'

'Pardon?' I answer mischievously, cupping a

hand to my ear. 'I'm sorry I can't hear you from all the way down here.'

He laughs. 'You're right. This is a bit ridiculous, isn't it?'

He pushes back his chair and, with one scrape, gathers all his cutlery into his napkin. He then dumps it noisily on to the table to my right, and goes back to fetch his chair.

'There,' he huffs, once he's dragged it into place. He sits down and beams at me. 'That's better. Hear me now?'

'Loud and clear.'

If Craig is surprised with the new seating arrangement he doesn't show it, barely blinking as he emerges from the back with a bottle of wine that James declares is, 'a particularly good vintage'.

Craig pours some in a glass and James swirls it around his mouth, his face thoughtful. Finally, he swallows and nods. 'First rate drop, that is,' he says. 'The top notes of cherry and plum are particularly noteworthy, and the depth of the smoky oak balances it out perfectly.'

When Craig leaves, James leans over.

'How did I sound?'

'Impressive.'

'Like I knew what I was talking about?'

'Definitely.'

'Good.' He flicks out his napkin and places it on his lap. 'Don't tell him, but I don't know the first thing about wine. I looked up their wine menu when I was back in my room and googled the different brands. Everything I just said came straight off a website.'

I snort back laughter. 'You mean you're not really a wine connoisseur?'

'Well, I can tell the difference between red and white, but that's about as far as it goes.'

'I feel so betrayed.'

'I'm sorry.' He adopts an abandoned puppy look. 'I just wanted to appear knowledgeable.'

'I'm only kidding. I think it's funny. And very sweet that you went to all that effort just to impress Craig.'

He gives me an intense look. 'I wasn't trying to impress Craig.'

I swallow hard and pick up the wine to take a sip. It doesn't taste any different to the cheap stuff Kate buys.

'Do you like it?' James asks.

'It's OK. To be honest all wines taste pretty much the same to me.' I take another sip.

'At ninety-six dollars a bottle, I would expect it to taste like gold.'

I nearly spit out my mouthful, but manage to swallow it instead, my eyes watering. 'Sorry, how much?'

'Ninety-six dollars a bottle.'

'Are you serious?' I look at my glass incredulously. 'I've had cars cost less than that.'

'You have?'

'No of course not. But that's a ridiculous amount of money to pay. Just crazy.'

'Oh I agree, one hundred per cent.'

I hadn't given a thought until now about how much this weekend must be costing him. But if a bottle of wine costs almost a hundred dollars, I shudder to think how much the meal or even the room must be costing.

'Just so we're clear,' I say, 'I want to pay for half. Of everything, the accommodation, helicopter ride. Everything.'

He picks up his own glass to take a sip. 'Just so we're clear,' he says after he swallows. 'No.'

'No?'

'No.'

'What do you mean, no?'

'No, you're not paying for anything. You are my guest. I invited you here.'

'But this place must be costing you a fortune. I can't let you spend so much money on me.'

He shrugs. 'I got mates' rates, because of the article.'

I narrow my eyes, unable to be sure whether he's telling the truth or not.

He puts his glass down and leans forward to look at me earnestly.

'I don't want you to worry about it. In fact, I don't want you to give money a second thought. Which is my fault, I shouldn't have mentioned the price of the wine.'

'But — '

'No,' he interrupts. 'No buts. Ava, I wanted to do this for you. Please don't worry about anything. I just want you to enjoy it.'

I exhale softly. It's clear he is not going to change his mind.

He senses my acceptance and smiles. 'Thank you.'

'OK. I'll drop the subject of money. On one condition.'

'What's that?'

'I can have a beer instead.'

'You don't like the wine?'

I shrug. 'It's just not really me.'

His smiles widens so his teeth gleam in the candle-light. 'Deal.'

When Craig appears through the door a moment later to lay our first course on the table — seasoned scallops in their shell — James hands him back the remaining wine in the bottle. Sensing a complaint is on the cards, Craig immediately looks defensive.

'Something wrong with the wine, sir?'

'No, not at all. We've just decided we'd rather have a beer each, thanks.'

'A beer, sir?' Craig hesitates, unsure.

'Yes, whatever you have on tap will be fine. And don't worry,' James reassures him, 'I'll still pay for the wine.'

'Should I just . . . tip it down the sink?' His face baulks at the very thought.

'God no. At that price someone should enjoy it. Why don't you and the chef finish off the rest.'

'Oh no, we're not allowed to drink while working.'

James shrugs. 'Then take it back to your room after you knock off. It's yours to do whatever you want with. I'm gifting it to you. Enjoy.'

Craig gives a small smile and nods. 'In that case, thank you, sir. Enjoy your starters.' He backs out of the room holding the bottle carefully.

I smile at James.

'What?'

'That was nice of you.'

'I'm a nice guy.'

'Yes. You are.'

I watch him eat his scallops with gusto, the juices running down his chin before he dabs at them with a serviette, murmuring his delight as he eats. He is incredible. Not only is he the most ridiculously good-looking man I have ever met and been attracted to, but he is kind, and generous, and just a really good, all-round person.

I really like him. As in, *like*, like. The realisation hits like a ton of bricks and I feel my whole body clench with it. Why? Why now? He has come into my life with the most lousiest of timing, and he is making me crave desperately for things that I can never have.

I push back my chair and stand. 'Excuse me, I need some air.'

'Are you OK?'

But I can't answer him, only nod as I walk quickly towards the open doors and the deck outside. Grasping tightly on to the railing, I squeeze my eyes and will myself to hold it together. The last thing I want to do is make a scene of myself, and make him feel uncomfortable. He has done such a nice thing, bringing me here. I don't want to make things awkward.

'Ava? What's wrong?'

He has come to stand beside me, and I have a strong urge to turn and bury myself in his arms. I remember how it felt when he carried me across the paddock, and I long for that feeling again. Instead, I force on a smile and loosen my grip on the railing, relaxing against it.

'Nothing. Nothing is wrong. I'm sorry, I just got a little light-headed. Maybe the wine was a bit much.'

'You had two small sips.'

'I've always been a cheap drunk.'

He relaxes against the railing too, and we watch as the tip of the sun disappears behind the hill in the distance, although its colour lingers across the sky.

'I want you to know that you can talk to me about anything,' he says. 'I won't always have answers, or necessarily have the right words to say. But I'm here, if you need to talk.'

I swallow hard. 'Thanks.'

He looks straight ahead and it seems to take an effort to say his next words. 'I may not know what it's like to be terminally ill . . . '

'Which is a good thing.'

'Yes. But I do know what it's like to watch someone you love die.'

I turn my face sideways to look at him, but he keeps staring straight ahead.

'Who?'

'My mother.'

'When.'

'Nearly twenty years ago. I was fourteen.'

I lay a hand gently on his arm. 'I'm so sorry.'

'Thanks.'

'Was it . . . ?' I hold my breath, scared of the answer.

'Cancer? Yes. Pancreatic. She put off going to the doctor for a long time even though she didn't feel right. She never said anything to my father or me though, only mentioned it afterwards. She always put our needs first. Then she was brushed off time and time again, so by the time she was officially diagnosed it was all through her and she went downhill quickly. She died just under six weeks later.'

'Oh my God. James, that's terrible.' My heart breaks to see the depth of sadness and grief on his face, and I feel a deep, bone-numbing sadness for what he must have been through, losing his mum so young and so horribly. 'What was she like?' I ask, then add quickly, 'I mean, only if you want to talk about her. I understand if you don't.'

'She was great,' he answers wistfully. 'The best mother I could have asked for. You would have liked her.' He turns his whole body so he is facing me. 'She had the same optimism and joy for life that I see in you.'

'I wish I could have met her.'

We are standing so close I can hear him breathing. It quickens, and I wonder if he is feeling as nervous as I am. He leans forward, bending his head and I realise he is about to kiss me.

There is a polite cough. 'Excuse me, sir, are you ready for the next course?'

James squeezes his eyes shut and shakes his head sardonically. 'This guy has the lousiest timing,' he whispers.

'No arguments here.'

30

The early sun on my face wakes me. Last night, I fell asleep with the doors wide open, the Milky Way my nightlight. Rolling over in bed, I stretch gingerly, open one eye and smile. It wasn't all a dream. I really am here, in this tree house, having the most wonderful experience of my life.

After making myself a cup of green tea with lemon, I wander out to the deck to watch the sunrise. There is a hanging egg chair and a couple of lounge chairs, and although I like the idea of curling into the egg chair, I worry I may have difficulty getting back out, so I choose the lounge chair, curling up on the cream-coloured cushions.

The leafy foliage of the forest is rustling gently in the morning breeze, the musky smell of nature heavy in the air. There is no other sound apart from birdsong as the dawn chorus stirs. I close my eyes and reminisce on the night before and how perfect it was. After we could eat no more, we sat on the veranda in front of the dining room, discussing everything and nothing under a sky so beautiful I couldn't take my eyes off it. Tucked up here, away from civilisation, there was no light pollution to ruin the view or hide the sheer magnitude of stars. It was just breathtaking. He told me more about his mother, although he was reticent to discuss his life in the aftermath of her death. I wanted to sit with him and talk all night, but he insisted we both turn in, separately, just after eleven. He said we needed our sleep for the day ahead, but wouldn't tell me why. I thought the curiosity would keep me awake but I slept easily and quickly. A full stomach, a comfortable bed and fresh country air will do that to you.

When my tea is long gone and the cup has cooled, I wander back inside and check my phone. It is only just after six-thirty, so I decide to have another spa bath. May as well get as much use out of it as I can while I'm here, I figure. I have been in it for half an hour, reading one of the books off the shelf in the room — left by a previous guest, I think, judging by the well-loved state of it — when there is a knock on the door. Immediately I feel delirious and light-headed. *James.* I wrap a towel around myself and walk as quickly as I can to the door, pausing before I open it to take a deep breath and compose myself. Then I open it, a wide smile on my face.

'Good mor — Oh.'

It's not him. My smile slips slightly.

'Good morning.' Mary smiles. 'I hope you slept well?'

'Yes. I did, thank you. The bed is very comfortable.'

'Good. Mr Gable wanted me to pass on a message to you.'

My heart quickens at her words, but with fear this time. 'A message? Why? Where is he?'

'I'm afraid I don't know anything other than I am to give you this.' She passes me an envelope.

'Thank you.' I take it, desperate to open it and find out what is going on, but I wait, impatiently, until she has started to walk away. Then I rip open the back of the envelope, letting it drop to the floor as I unfold the piece of paper within. There is handwriting scrawled across it, James's I assume, although I've never seen his before. The letters are large and brisk, no nonsense. Like him.

Dear Ava,
    I know I'm probably driving you a little crazy with all the surprises by now, but bear with me; because I have one more. When you are ready, go to reception. They'll tell you what to do from there.
    James xx

An hour later I am as ready as I'll ever be, and, even if I do say so myself, looking pretty damn good. Because I have no idea what he has planned, I have chosen a dress I feel is midway between casual and dressy. A soft bluey-grey maxi, it is long and ruffled in layers. I feel feminine and do a little twirl in front of the mirror. Over the top I wear a three-quarter-sleeved cropped denim jacket. My hair, I let dry naturally. There's not much I can do with it myself anyway since it grew back after the chemo, it is too wild and strong-willed.

    I apply my make-up, being more generous with the bronzer than usual. It makes me look like I have just returned from a week in the Caribbean. Tanned. Healthier. Radiant. A flick of eyeliner, two layers of mascara and I am done. Natural, but subtly enhanced. It isn't anywhere near as glamorous as I look under Kelly's skilled hands, but it is me, and it will do. I run some serum through my hair to tame any frizz the humidity might bring and I am good to go.

Walking slowly down the steps outside, I have to resist the urge to wave regally, because I feel rather like Cinderella making her royal way down the grand staircase. Craig is waiting at the bottom. He smiles when he sees me.

'Wow. You look absolutely stunning, Miss Green.'

'Thanks, but please, call me Ava. You're making me feel old.' I check to make sure Mary isn't within earshot and lower my voice conspiratorially. 'How was the wine?'

'Delicious, thank you.'

'Well I'm glad it wasn't wasted and that someone enjoyed it.'

'Oh we did, very much so.'

I hear a crackling, voice, distorted and look around puzzled. 'Who was that?'

He unclips a walkie-talkie from his waist belt. 'That was Heath, our caretaker guy. He also does maintenance and other jobs as required.' He holds the walkie-talkie up to his mouth. 'Hey, Heath, you ready yet? We're out front.'

We both watch it expectantly. There's no answer. Craig pushes the button again. 'Heath, are you there?'

Finally, we hear a crackle as the reply comes back. 'Roger. Heath here. You didn't say 'over and out'.'

Craig rolls his eyes and pushes the button. 'If I stop talking just assume I'm finished.'

Crackle. 'You have to say 'over and out'. It's proper walkie-talkie protocol.'

'Sorry about this,' Craig apologises to me. 'He can be a bit over the top about some stuff. Too long out here in the wilderness, I think. Can you just excuse me one moment?' He turns his back to me and pushes the button, speaking in a hushed, exasperated voice. 'Yeah, in *a cop show maybe*. Just get around here will you.'

Silence.

Craig sighs and pushes the button again. 'Oh my God, dude. You're so annoying. Hurry up. The guest is waiting. OVER AND OUT.'

Crackle. Then in a smug voice, 'Roger. Be there in two. Over and out.'

Craig turns back around. 'He's on his way.'

'So I heard.'

'Don't worry, he's a good driver.'

'Driver?'

A 4WD pulls up behind me, its tyres kicking up dirt. The driver gets out and runs around to open the passenger door. I reel back a little. He is huge. Massive, but not in a fat way. More in a The Rock, Dwayne Johnson kind of way. 'Welcome aboard, Miss Green.'

I look from the vehicle to him and back again. 'Ava, please,' I say automatically. 'I'm sorry, you want me to get in there?'

He nods.

'Why?'

He looks at Craig for help, who steps forward. 'It's all been organised by Ja — Mr Gable.'

'And just where is Mr Gable?'

'Hop in and I'll take you to him.'

Climbing into a vehicle clearly used for maintenance and grounds work while wearing a beautiful dress that you want to keep clean for as long as possible is no easy feat. I spend a good three minutes trying to figure out where to put my hands and feet so I'm touching as little of the vehicle as possible, and in the end Craig helps by holding up my dress, while averting his eyes for modesty purposes, while I boost myself up and on to the seat that Heath has covered with a towel.

'I take it your celebrity guests aren't treated to this mode of transport?' I say, eyebrows arched.

'Oh no. This is special one-off favour for Ja — Mr Gable. Have fun.' Craig grins, slamming the door and standing well back.

'Buckle up,' says Heath, who is back in the driver's seat. 'This might get a little bumpy.'

He's not wrong. The following journey takes forty-five long minutes, thirty of which are technically driven on what could be called gravel roads, but which are littered with potholes and rocks the size of my head that must be dodged. The last fifteen we are in open paddocks. Heath has to stop every few minutes to open gates, drive through them, and then get out and shut them again. In one paddock we startle a herd of animals who blink at us vacantly through long shaggy brown hair as we drive slowly through to the other side.

'What are they?' I ask Heath. 'I mean, I'm assuming they're some kind of . . . cow?' I say the last word uncertainly. I've never seen animals like these before.

'Highland cattle. Scottish breed.'

'They're so fluffy.'

'They are.'

'Oh there's a baby one, oh how cute is that.' I clap my hands together in delight. Heath arches an eyebrow as if he's now seen and heard it all. A thought occurs to me and I blanch.

'I didn't eat one of those last night, did I?'

'No,' he reassures me. 'This land isn't part of the resort. These cattle are farmed by the owner of this station, but as long as we leave it as we find it we're allowed to use it for access.'

I look sideways at him. 'Access to what?'

He nods, looking directly ahead. 'To that, your destination.'

I turn my head to where he is looking just as the truck crests a last little hill. My hands fly to my mouth as I give a sharp little intake of breath. 'Oh!'

Just below us, carved into the land by time and nature, is a basin, with a sharp cliff rising steeply behind it. In the bottom of the basin is a round little lake. It is a rich and lustrous green like the forest and immediately I want to dive into its depths and feel the water on my skin. The lake, the fern-covered cliffs, the little pebbly beach where the ripples sweep up on; it is all majestic and captivating, and yet it pales in comparison to the star of the show that is demanding my attention.

'Pretty neat huh?' Heath says beside me. 'A hidden gem.'

Cascading off the cliffs is a waterfall. White, turbulent waters tumbling from a stream on the top, thirty metres down to the small lake below. It throws up spray where it hits the lake, and fleeting rainbows burn bright before fading away.

I am so caught up in the wonder of it I don't see James approach my door, so when it opens I scream and jump, clutching my chest.

'Sorry, it's just me,' he says soothingly. 'I didn't mean to give you a fright.'

'James, what are you . . . how did you find this . . . where are we . . . ?'

'You like it?'

'What do you think?'

'I knew you'd appreciate it.'

'It's . . . stunning,' I say, floundering for words. 'How did you know it was here?'

He holds out his hand to help me down from the truck. When I step on to the ground and straighten up he looks me up and down and his grip on my hand tightens.

'When I was first here,' he explains, 'Heath showed me this place and I've never been able to forget it. The staff come here in the summer to relax and cool off.'

'They're lucky. It's just beautiful.'

'It is,' he agrees. 'But you're more beautiful. In fact, you look even more beautiful than I remember.'

'You only saw me last night,' I joke, flushing underneath his intense look. He doesn't laugh back, just stares at me intently.

Finally, he breaks away to turn and sweep a hand around the view. 'Ever since I left this place

I've wanted to come back with my camera and try and capture it. And I thought, why not photograph you here too?'

My heart drops, as does my face.

'What's wrong?' he asks. 'You don't like the idea?'

I shake my head and look down, shrugging disappointedly. 'No, I do. I just . . . I didn't realise all of this, the weekend, was all for the magazine.'

He steps forward and puts one hand on my shoulder, the other cupping my chin and gently nudging it upwards so I am looking into his face. 'No,' he says firmly. 'You've got it wrong. This is not for an article for the magazine. This is for *you*. It's all for you. Everything. Ever since that day in the field, when we swam in the stream together, I've wanted to share this place with you. I can't explain why, it's just an urge I've felt.'

I swallow hard. 'Well, thank you. For sharing it with me.'

He takes a deep breath. 'Ava. I want to photograph you here, in this place, for your family. So they'll have it once you're . . . ' His voice chokes and he doesn't finish the sentence. He takes a deep breath. 'And for me. But only if you want me to. Only if you'll let me.'

I can't trust myself to speak so I nod and he exhales a sigh of relief and finally starts to smile.

31

Jacket removed, I am standing on a small outcrop of land that looms out over the small lake. This close, the sound of the water on its journey over rock is loud and almost musical in its rhythm. Heath has departed, with the promise to be back in a few hours. Before he left he unloaded a picnic basket and blanket, which he has left under the shade of a large native tree. James is checking his equipment, which he had set up before I arrived. Apparently mine was not Heath's first trip out here today.

'Sorry,' James calls. 'Won't be too much longer, I promise. I wanted to have this all ready when you got here but I got caught up exploring the place again.'

'Can't blame you for that.'

He has more camera equipment this time. A tripod is set up, with his camera perched on top. A portable small table is nearby with an open laptop on the top. Cables connect the laptop to the camera. He clicks off a few shots and checks them on his screen. 'OK, we're good to go. Wait, can you move to the right a little?'

I peer down. 'Not unless you want to photograph me swimming in this dress.'

'As artistic as that sounds, I'm trying to keep you out of the water until *after* I've taken my photos. I know how much you like swimming. Do you think you can wait until I have the perfect shot at least?'

'I'll try. Can't promise though. I don't like to make promises I might not be able to keep. And there's no such thing as perfect.'

He straightens up. 'OK. Pretend I'm not here and just move around as much as you can in that spot. Whatever feels natural. Slowly though, I want to capture as many organic moments as I can.'

I look down at the water. Up close, it is even greener than it looked from the top of the hill. It swirls and eddies languorously, hinting at the hidden depths below. Another moment, another memory. What happens when I am gone? Do my memories cease to exist along with me? If so, does that wipe the moment from the memory of the world? There must be some endless, universal memory bank of moments. There has to be. Otherwise we are all just fleeting blips on a machine, gone in seconds, forgotten, no trace left behind. In a hundred years' time, who will know I stood here, on this spot. Life is gone all too soon, the years go too fast. We fool ourselves into believing we are important, and we place too much emphasis on the wrong things. But therein lies the cruel irony. It takes learning your time is up to appreciate the things, or people, who do actually deserve your time.

In the end, none of it matters. We all meet the same fate eventually, we just approach it through different means and at different times.

I squeeze my eyes shut but the tears spill over anyway. I would give anything, *anything*, for more time. More time with the knowledge I now have. Oh what a life I would live. I wouldn't spend fifty years of days in an office, surrounded by four walls, or fifty years of nights in a dingy little flat, surrounded by a different set of walls. No. I'd live a million sunrises in a million places.

I don't hear James approach until he is behind me.

'Ava?'

I exhale slowly, trembling, trying to hide the pain I am in. 'Did you get your perfect photo?'

'No. There's something missing.'

I wipe my eyes. 'Oh. What's that?'

'Me.'

I turn around. The pain I feel is reflected in his eyes when he looks at me. He is breathing hard, his face tortured. When he says my name it is more of a question. 'Ava.'

We meet roughly as our bodies collide like stars. His hands curl into my hair as my own find his hips. His face stops millimetres away, his eyes questioning. Then his expression changes as he finds his answer in mine, and he pulls me in hungrily, kissing me like I have never been kissed before. He moans softly, his lips firmly against mine as we try desperately to be as close to each other as we can. It's not enough. It could never be enough. The waterfall thunders in the background as I start pushing his jacket open, trying to free his arms. He shrugs it off, and I furiously set to work on his shirt buttons, all without breaking apart from our kiss.

I've never wanted anyone more in my life. I never even knew this feeling existed. Not like this, so raw and animalistic that I feel like snarling with my frustration. How could I have nearly died without experiencing this? When love and lust combine to ignite something so spectacularly brilliant that it quietens all else, and two people come together to burn brightly in the here and now.

I react to him with a passionate savagery I didn't know I was capable of, ripping open his shirt because unbuttoning it is taking too long. But then,

. . . cold air and confusion as he disengages from our kiss. I blink at him, feeling uncertain and bereft.

'James?'

'Are you sure about this?' he asks, his voice slurred with his own longing.

'I've never been surer about anything in my life.'

'I don't want to hurt you.'

I take his hand and place it on my chest, over my heart. 'I would rather feel this and be hurt than die without feeling anything. Please. I want you — '

The last word is cut off as his lips find mine again, and never has anything felt more right. I squeal as his arms go around me and he lifts me up easily, then I wrap my legs around his waist and hold his face in my hands, peppering him with kisses as he moans and carries me down off the little outcrop and over to the picnic blanket. He lowers me down reluctantly and then hops around, cursing as he tries to kick his shoes and jeans off. I fumble behind my back for the zip on the dress but I am all thumbs and it remains elusive.

'Turn around.'

I do as I am told, shivering as his fingers brush against my skin. He gently lowers the zip, while nuzzling into my neck.

'God, you smell so good,' he says huskily. His hands wrap around me, over my stomach, as I tilt my head to kiss him. Then I feel him unhook my bra and he turns me easily so that we are skin against skin.

'Wait,' I say, pushing him slightly away to cover myself protectively with my arms.

He pulls back. 'What is it, what's wrong.'

'I haven't been with anyone. Not since, you know.' I hate the vulnerability in my voice, but I can't help it nor can I hide it. I am terrified that he will be repulsed by me.

'Do you trust me?' he asks softly.

I nod.

He reaches out and gently lowers my arms to my sides. My first instinct is to close my eyes, that I won't want to see his face when he sees the damage wrought upon my body. But my heart tells me I have to do this. If I truly trust him as I say I do, it will be OK. His eyes hold mine until he is sure I am comfortable, and then he lowers them, slowly. Down past my collarbone where they linger on the jagged scar from where the chemotherapy port was placed under my skin to administer the drugs directly into my veins. He holds out a finger and touches it lightly.

'Does it hurt?'

I shake my head. 'Not any more.'

'Are you OK with this?'

232

I take a shallow breath and nod.

His eyes follow the contours of my skin down. I am too thin, and the bones of my chest protrude more than they should. He traces them lightly. Then with one last look to make sure I am OK, he looks directly at my breasts. I hold my breath.

I couldn't look at myself for the longest time, neither during nor after treatment. In fact, I actively avoided it, turning my head when the nurses changed the dressings, and removing the mirror from my bedroom so I couldn't accidentally catch a glimpse when getting dressed. I didn't want to see or know what my new 'normal' was. As far as I was concerned, nothing would ever be normal again. When I finally did muster up the courage, I cried for two days, only pausing when I was so physically tired I slept. Then I would wake and remember, and I would cry some more. My breasts before the cancer weren't the kind of breasts that grace magazine covers. They most likely wouldn't have inspired any ancient carvers into chiselling a statue in their honour. But they were mine. And according to ex-boyfriends they were pretty nice to look at. Average size, C cup. The right one slightly bigger than the left. After the surgery this changed, and lefty become the superior. Righty was misshapen now, and slightly floppy. There were two scars, a big one that ran right from under my armpit and down the outside, and another vertical one that circumvented my nipple and left it permanently pointing to the side after it healed. The skin was puckered and dry like a deflated party balloon, and bright red from the radiation treatment. Sometimes I wished they'd just done the mastectomy from the get-go, then I could have had reconstruction surgery and maybe boosted myself a size or two in compensation. But they didn't, and I hadn't, and it was all moot now anyway because the cancer was stubborn, and had decided to inhabit other parts of my body as well.

So it is understandable that I am nervous, but when James looks at me, I don't see pity, or revulsion. I see his eyes widen. I hear his breath quicken. And then his hands are on my breasts, gently, with all the care in the world. And in that moment I feel like a woman again.

'You're so beautiful Ava,' he says, and I hear nothing but honesty in his voice.

All my anxiety fades away, and I reach for him. It has been too long, and I can't wait any longer. He lowers me down on to the blanket and soon we are joined together, moving in sync, our breath mingling as our hearts beat against each other.

I find love that day. There, beside a waterfall so powerful it has changed the shape of the land, I receive the ultimate reminder of life.

32

'So . . . ' I have my head in my hand, leaning up on one elbow. James is lying on his back beside me, his hands underneath his head, eyes closed but with a smile playing around his lips.

'So.'

'That was . . . '

'Impressive? Epic? Ground-shaking?'

'Oh yes, definitely. All of the above.'

He opens his eyes and reaches up a hand to tuck my hair behind my ear. 'You're so beautiful, Ava.'

'So you keep saying.'

'Because it's true. I remember the first time I saw you, on the beach, with your dress hoisted up around your legs as you paddled in the water. I could barely take my eyes off you then. There was just something so intriguing about you.'

'I felt the same way about you.'

'Really?'

I nod. Lowering my head, I kiss his lips lightly, my whole body tensing at the touch.

'Your lips were the first thing I noticed about you,' I murmur. 'That and how insanely good-looking you are, of course.'

'Of course.' He pulls my head down firmly and kisses me, with a hunger that can never be satiated. Abruptly, I push him away, climbing to my feet. I stand too quickly and immediately stumble, dizzy. Thankfully he doesn't notice.

'Where are you going?'

Steadying myself, I walk away from him, towards the water. Turning my head, I call back over my shoulder. 'Exploring. You coming?'

'Not this again,' he complains, light-heartedly.

I don't hear him until he is right behind me, and then it is too late and he scoops me up easily, laughing.

'Put me down,' I squeal, aware that if anyone were watching they would catch an eyeful more than they bargained for. But there's no one of course, not for miles. He walks quickly down to the water and wades right in. We both exclaim at the temperature, and I tighten my grip.

'If you say so,' he says, and drops me.

I emerge from beneath the surface, spluttering. 'Oh my God that's cold.' But as cold as it is, it also feels sensational; both refreshing and cleansing on my body.

'I know a way that we can warm each other up.'

'Why, sir,' I say coyly, paddling slowly away from him with broad strokes. 'You have a very wicked glint in your eye.'

'Do I? Maybe that's because I'm thinking some very wicked thoughts. Now get back here.'

'Catch me if you can,' I call, laughing and swimming away from him, towards the waterfall. But he is taller, of course, with much longer arms and legs, and he soon catches me, one of his arms snaking around my waist to pull me back against him.

'I win,' he says triumphantly.

'And now.' I wrap my arms around his neck

and my legs around his waist, shifting until he is inside of me and we are joined again, marvelling at the intense waves of pleasure that sweep through my entire body. 'You can claim your prize.'

Afterwards, when we are exhausted from our lovemaking but reluctant to let the moment end, we drift on our backs, the spray from the waterfall dancing around us like whimsical wraiths. I try to relax and just enjoy it, but my thoughts turn to death, as they always do now. How close I came to dying without seeing this place, or making love with James. I would have died without knowing that I'd missed out of course. But now that it has happened, and even though I wouldn't change what we have done for anything in the world, I *know* what I will miss out on. A lifetime of these moments with him. Waking up next to him every morning, going to sleep in his arms every night. Making love for a million days in a million ways and places, never tiring of him, always craving him. I have seen a glimpse of the future, but it won't be mine. James and I, we have been as close as is physically possible, but it is not enough. I want more. I want to join with him so tightly that I become a part of him, anchored to him and this earth. Allowed to stay, because in order for them to take me they would have to take him also, and it is not his time, nor his story.

Life is pain. It is also joy, but with the good must also come the bad. I don't pretend to know why, I can't even say I understand it. If there is a God — and if there is then he's doing a fairly lousy job as far as I'm concerned — then there must also be an opposite. A Yin to his Yang. A black to his white. And maybe that guy, *he's* the one who points his sharp finger at the board game and says, 'That girl, she's too happy. Can't have that, quick, throw a disease her way.' Then he clicks his fingers and toddles off to eat souls for lunch.

I am somebody's pawn in the game of life. Disposable.

But here, now, in James's arms and in his eyes, I have become someone's whole world. And I have to figure out a way to let that be enough.

33

'You were very quiet on the trip back. Are you sure you're OK?'

James holds my hand as I step down from the helicopter, involuntarily ducking even though the blades are well above my head.

'I'm fine.' I smile to reassure him, as we walk back past the safety line, into the shadows of the office. The sky is grey and moody today and it has started to drizzle. 'Just feeling a little melancholic.'

'No regrets?'

'No. Well, maybe one.'

'Really?' He immediately looks worried.

'Yes.' I step closer and snuggle into his chest, warm and safe and secure. He wraps his arms tightly around me. I tilt my head to look up at him. 'I wish the weekend hadn't ended so soon. That we could stay there longer.'

He relaxes, exhales. 'God, you had me worried then.'

'Don't worry. I will never regret a second of time spent with you.'

'Me neither.' He bends his head and kisses me softly.

We hear a throat being cleared and turn our heads to where Toby is nearby, watching us. 'I thought you guys said you weren't a couple?'

'Oh right.' James smiles sheepishly. 'Yeah, so that situation has kind of changed.'

'Yes, I can see that.' He smirks knowingly.

I know James is worried, I can feel it in the air between us. But I just can't shake the heaviness that has settled on my heart. I told him beside the lake that I would rather feel this and be hurt, than die without feeling anything, but it's so much harder than I thought it would be. I know what I'm leaving behind now. For the first time, I have a clearer idea of the kind of future I could have had. *And it's just not fair.* Tears trickle down my cheeks as I watch the rain-sodden landscape flash by the car window.

'Talk to me, Ava,' he says softly. 'I want to help you, if I can.'

I sniff noisily, wiping the tears with my sleeve, and turn my face to him. 'You can't. No one can. That's the problem.'

His hands clench the steering wheel and his knuckles turn white. 'Do you wish you'd never met me?'

'Oh God no. James, no, don't even think like that. You've made me the happiest I've ever been. I've felt more alive in the last few days with you than I've ever felt in my life. I just wish I'd met you sooner, that things could be different.'

He indicates and pulls the car over on to the gravel shoulder of the road. Then he turns the key in the ignition off and we are left with the sound of silence.

'If it helps,' he says finally, 'I don't know what I'm doing either.'

'Do you wish you'd never met me?' I echo his question, scared of the answer.

He twists in his seat and shakes his head emphatically. 'No. Of course not. Never. It's just, I don't know how I'm supposed to feel. On the one hand, I'm having all these wonderful, incredible feelings. And I just want to shout about it from the rooftops, you know?'

I nod.

'But at the same time, I feel like I can't. I can't celebrate this, whatever *this* is. As if to be happy right now would be wrong. But yet it feels so right.' He buries his face in his hands. 'I'm sorry, I'm not very eloquent.'

I reach over and touch the back of his neck. 'I understand perfectly.'

'Before I messaged you that night, I was so conflicted. And now I'm even more so. I just don't know if I can go through it again, the pain of losing someone I care so much about. But it's nothing compared to what you are going through, and I feel ashamed for even worrying about myself.'

I have gone as still as a stone, fixated on his words.

'Say something,' he says.

'You care about me?'

'What?'

'You said you aren't sure whether you can go through the pain of losing someone you care about again. Does that mean — ' I take a deep breath to try to even out my voice — 'that you care about me?'

He blinks, confused. 'Isn't it obvious?'

I shrug my shoulders.

He gets out of the car and I watch him come

around the front, cutting through the headlights that are still beaming into the ominously dark day. The rain is starting to get heavier and it feels as if a thunderstorm is brewing. He opens my door and the cold air and rain hit.

'Shift over,' he says.

'What?'

'Move.'

I move over as far as I can and he hops in beside me, so we are squished into the one seat.

'OK, this went better in my head,' he admits. 'Come here.' He half pulls and I half climb on to his lap, straddling his legs. He puts his hands aside my face and pulls me forward until we are resting forehead to forehead, his eyes staring intensely into mine.

'Ava Green, although I suspect you're being deliberately obtuse in an attempt to force me to profess my feelings out loud . . . ' he narrows his eyes at me, but his expression is teasing . . . 'I'll allow it. Because yes, I *do* care about you. I care about you a whole lot. When I'm with you I feel things I've never felt before, and although I'm reluctant to put any labels on it, or us, know this: I think you're astonishingly, remarkably, wonderful. I don't want to stop now. I want more. More you. I want to know everything there is to know about you.'

I choke back a sob, caught somewhere between tears of despair and the dizzying heights of happiness.

He smiles and I feel the heat from his lips so close to mine. 'Now, does that answer your question?'

I answer him with a kiss instead of words, crushing my lips into his ferociously, overwhelmed with the depth of emotion that his declaration has aroused. I lift his T-shirt up, our kiss breaking apart only long enough for me to lift it off over his head. He drops his hands to my hips, pulling me in against him hard.

'Oh, Ava,' he groans. 'You're driving me crazy, you know that.'

I kiss his neck, his ears, the tip of his nose, grinding myself into him. 'The feeling — ' *kiss* — 'is mutual.'

An hour later, I awaken with a start at the sound of a knock on the driver's side window.

'James,' I whisper, shaking him. 'Someone's out there.'

'Mm?' he murmurs sleepily.

The knock comes again.

'James,' I say more urgently. We are stretched out in the back seat, naked, with James's jacket laid on us for warmth. The windows are fogged up with condensation, thankfully, and the rain, which was loud and soothing on the roof of the car as we drifted off to sleep, has let up, although the sky has darkened.

'Are you OK?' a male voice calls. 'Do you need some help?'

At the sound of the man's voice, James finally wakes up. He sits up and rubs his eyes. 'Who's out there?' he asks me.

'How should I know?' I sit up too, reaching into the front with one arm to see if I can locate any of my discarded items of clothing. My fingers connect with some soft material and I

243

drag it back, triumphant, but it is only James's T-shirt.

'Thanks,' he says, taking it and pulling it over his head.

'You'd better answer him quick before he calls the police or roadside assistance or something,' I mutter as the man knocks again.

James grins at the panicked look on my face.

'Just a minute,' he calls out loudly to the man outside.

'You're enjoying this, aren't you?' I scowl.

'Having you, naked, in the back seat of my car? Hell yes I'm enjoying it.'

'It's not funny,' I protest, smacking his arm lightly. 'I'm pretty vulnerable here in case you hadn't noticed.'

'All right. Hang on.'

James climbs through the space between the front seats and after fumbling around, passes back my clothing. He waits until I am dressed before he pushes the button to wind down his window. Nothing happens, and he looks confused for a moment before realisation hits and he swears, reaching for the key in the ignition. He gives it a few turns on and off and nothing happens.

'I think I might have left the headlights on,' he says sheepishly.

'You think?'

'OK yes, I definitely left the headlights on.' He sighs and opens the door.

'What's up, mate,' the man outside says. 'You broken down or something?' The man is elderly and is wearing the unofficial uniform of farmers

244

across the country: short stubby shorts — despite the weather — black gumboots and a black thermal short-sleeved top.

'Kind of,' James admits. 'I think the battery's flat.'

'How'd that happen?'

'Well, we stopped, you see, to, um, to check directions on my phone. Because we thought we might have been lost.'

'No cell phone coverage here, mate.'

'No, no, there wasn't, as we discovered. So, uh, we thought we'd just wait, and have a nap, and see if anyone would come along that we could ask. But I forgot to turn the headlights off, and well, now here we are. So if you could just give us a jumpstart we'll be on our — '

'You had a nap.'

'Yes.'

'Both of you.'

'Yes.'

'With the headlights on.'

'Er, yes.'

'I might be old, mate, but I wasn't born yesterday.' The farmer walks off back to his truck chuckling to himself. 'A nap.'

James squints as he thinks. 'Do we tell him that what he just said doesn't actually make any sense?'

'No, you do not.' I flick my hand at him. 'You get out and you help him get this car going again so we can get out of here before you say anything even more embarrassing. Understood?'

'Loud and clear.'

The farmer comes back with the jumper leads

and he and James busy themselves underneath the bonnet. I slide down in my seat, embarrassed that he knows what we have been up to, and pretend to look at my phone even though he's quite right and there is no service here. In no time at all James climbs back inside and the two of them start their engines.

'Oh thank God,' I say as James's car purrs to life. 'Can we get out of here now? Please?'

'What's the rush?'

'I can't look him in the eye knowing he knows what we were up to,' I say, mortified.

'Relax, he's a farmer. He's probably seen it all before.'

'Yes, but I hope to God he didn't see *my* all.'

James grins and I smack him lightly on the chest.

'OK, OK,' he laughs. 'I'll just go help him disconnect and say thanks and we'll be on our way.'

'Thank you.'

★ ★ ★

We drive the rest of the way home in silence, both seemingly lost in our thoughts. I don't know about him, but even if I wanted to say something I don't have the words. These past few days have been like a dream; or like something out of a movie or novel. If he wasn't sitting in the car beside me I could fool myself into thinking it was.

He pulls into my driveway and turns the car off. 'Headlights off,' he says, exaggerating the movement and I muster a smile.

'So.'

'So.'

'Now what?' he asks.

'What do you mean?'

He rubs his eyes and I realise he is tired too.

'I don't know where we go from here,' he admits. 'All I know is that your time is . . . limited. And I don't want to steal any of that time away from your friends and your family, but I can't bear the thought of missing even a second of whatever we'll be lucky enough to have.'

I snort. 'Lucky? There's no luck here. If we were lucky we'd have fifty years to be having this conversation. But we don't.'

He looks down at his hands. 'No. I'm sorry. Wrong choice of word.'

I sigh and reach over to place my fingers on his. 'No, I'm sorry. It's just sometimes I let the bitterness get to me.'

'That's understandable.'

'But pointless. James, this is a tough conversation to have, and I'm really tired. We both have a lot to process after the weekend. Would you mind if I call you tomorrow?'

'Of course. That sounds good. No wait, damn.' He slaps his hand against the steering wheel. 'I got so caught up in our little bubble I've lost track of my days. I have to go away tomorrow, for work. But I'll be back in a week.'

'A week?' I feel completely bereft at the thought of not seeing him for that long.

'I know. Should I cancel?'

'No.' I shake my head firmly. 'Of course not.

Your work is important.'

'So are you.'

'And I'll be here waiting when you get back.'

The front door of Kate's house opens and she waves. I wave back.

'You promise?' he asks softly.

I nod, because I don't trust my words. And because I don't like to make promises I might not be able to keep.

Notes from Ava

(Women's Weekly December 4th)

When I was eight, Brian Thompson gave me a flower. One of those white and yellow daisies that grow willy-nilly along fences and roadsides. Until then he'd never been particularly nice to me, so, suspecting it was some kind of trap, I refused to accept it. He got angry and threw it at me in a huff, storming back across the playground to hide underneath the slide. You couldn't blame me for being suspicious; until that point Brian was just another hot sweaty body on the classroom mat, who occasionally pulled my pigtails and called me 'Purple Pants', due to an unfortunate case of indecent exposure when I fell off the swing one day.

The next day, his best friend Nick was given the task of telling me that, in actual fact, Brian was deeply in love with me, and was wondering if I would like to be his girlfriend? (Tick YES on this note if so.)

Enthralled by the fact I was the first girl in our class who had been asked to be a 'girlfriend', and completely clueless as to exactly what this entailed, I ticked yes. And waited excitedly to see what would happen.

Nothing happened. He still ignored me on the whole, and called me Purple Pants, but he did let me sit beside him in the back row of the mat, a spot previously reserved for boys only.

A week later, Nick delivered another note. It wasn't working out. I was dumped, effective immediately. The note wasn't in those actual words, of course, but the meaning was the same. Any air of mystique or street cred I had developed was gone, in a puff of childhood innocence. Lisa Ryan was the new girlfriend. I was alone once more.

I cried. My mother threatened to go around and cave in his kneecaps, but my father convinced her that grievous bodily harm on an eight-year-old was probably not an effective lesson to teach me.

'You just have to ride the pain out, honey,' he said sadly. 'I promise you that you will get over it someday.'

And I did, of course. After all I was eight. I bounced back fairly quickly, although I promised myself I would never let another boy into my heart again. Ah, the sweet innocence of youth.

Love hurts. It really does. When it ends, it has the ability to take you to levels of emotional pain that leave you curled in a ball on the floor, gasping for breath, convinced your heart is about to take its last beat from the sheer agony and sorrow of it. You convince yourself that you will never be the same person ever again, that it has scarred you and altered you through to the very core of your soul. You drink too much, weep, and beg futilely for just one . . . more . . . chance.

But, over time, the pain lessens. It never completely goes away because you were right, it *does* leave a scar. A song, a smell, a familiar face in the street; all have the power to bring those crushing feelings back. But you keep putting one foot in front of the other, you keep taking that next breath, and eventually you realise you got through a day without crying, then a week. A month. You begin to smile again. Notice the good things in life. In time, you tentatively open yourself up to new people, to the possibility of new love.

You will never forget a lost love. This inexplicable thing that is love is too powerful for that. But you must never let it make you bitter. Never let it mark you so badly that you close off that part of you. Self-protection might keep your heart safe, but will you truly be alive?

Love has no past, and no future. Love just is.

I promise you, when you are on your deathbed, those painful times will no longer have the power to hurt you. You will only remember the good, the beautiful, the spectacular. You will only remember how it felt to be loved, and to love another.

Yes, love hurts.

But love also heals.

Xxx

34

I sleep all night and most of the next day after my weekend away with James, getting up only when my bladder insists upon it. As I have lost my appetite even for water, this isn't too often. This is a level of fatigue that is new to me. It's as if I expended all my energy with James, and now I am depleted, drained. The batteries are well and truly flat.

Occasionally, I rise close enough to the surface to hear muffled, worried voices outside my door.

'Do you think she's OK? Should we call her doctor?'

'I don't have his number, do you?'

'No.'

'Oh. Wait, I know what we should do.'

'What?'

'Call her mum.'

'Good idea. Then it's out of our hands.'

'Where do you think James took her that made her so bloody tired?'

'I'd say it's more a case of *what* did James do to her, judging by the way she kissed him when he left. She looked like she was stuck permanently to his face, like an octopus. I thought we'd have to get the salt out to try and prise her off. Or does that only work on leeches?'

'You shouldn't have been watching,' Kate admonishes.

'I know, but I don't think they noticed.'

Their voices grow fainter as they walk back down the hallway towards the kitchen.

The last thing I want them to do is call my mother and worry her, but I am too tired to call out in protest. So the next time I wake she is there, on the chair in the corner of the room, reading a book. When I roll over, she tucks her bookmark inside the pages and places the book down on my drawers.

'Hey, sleepyhead.' Her voice is cheerful, but with some effort behind it. She crosses the room to sit carefully on the side of my bed. 'How are you feeling?'

'Tired.'

'Any pain?'

'No,' I lie. My whole body hurts, but there is a pain in my shoulder and lower back that stands out, and I am scared. I knew this was coming; it was always going to get worse. What if I'm not strong enough to cope with it?

'You're lying,' she says. 'I need to know if it's worse than usual. You don't have to put up with pain, they have ways of managing it.'

I close my eyes. 'Good night, Mum.'

'When you wake up we're talking about this,' she warns. 'The girls have made up a bed for me on the couch. I'm not going anywhere.'

★ ★ ★

I wake up, choking and disorientated. Something is in my throat. I am wet, my hair, my face, the bed around me. I try to call out but can only gargle. I'm dying. I always thought I would know when it was my time. But I didn't know, and I'm not ready. I have only just found James, and I have my wedding to attend. I don't want to die, not here, not now. With effort, I roll over and push with my legs until I am teetering on the edge of the bed. I can't breathe. Everything is going black. I fall.

Blink.

There's a bright light above me. It must be the one people speak of, the one I'm supposed to go towards. No one told me how I am supposed to do that though.

'Shit, what the hell. Ava! Ava, wake up.'

Someone, Kate, is cradling my head, slapping my cheek.

'What's happening?' Amanda, sleepy.

'I don't know. I just heard a thump and came to check. Turned the light on and found her on the floor. She fell out of bed, I think, but something's wrong, she's making an awful sound.'

Blink.

'What is it? What's going . . . Oh no, oh, Ava.' I feel a rush of air as my mother drops to the floor beside me. 'She's choking. Roll her over, into the recovery position. No, like this, grab her leg, *her left leg*. Straighten it out and hold her. Keep her like that while I call for an ambulance.' My mother's voice is trembling with her fear. 'Don't you dare do this, girl, not yet.'

Blink.

'Fuck, she's vomited *everywhere*.'

'Hello? Ambulance please, it's my daughter, something's wrong. You have to hurry.'

'I just fucking stood in it, oh God, I'm going to be sick.'

'Shut up, Amanda!'

'Sorry! Sorry. I'm just scared OK. Is she . . . dying?'

'I don't know. How should I know?'

'Number 1156, the one with the blue letterbox. There's a driveway down to the house. *Hurry.*'

'She doesn't look good.'

'No shit.'

'Ava?'

Hands brushing my hair from my face. 'That's it, girl, just keep breathing. Help is coming.'

'Stay with us, Ava. Please.'

Blink.

I know that noise. That steady hiss and click. I've heard it enough times. Oxygen. Air. Life. I open my eyes, but everything is blurry. There's a metallic scraping noise, like a chair being pushed back.

'She's awake. Get her mother, quick. She just ducked out to stretch her legs in the corridor. Ava?'

My father's shape swims into view, looming. I can't focus on him, like he's inside one of those kaleidoscope toys. Changing colours, shapes. Changing faces.

'You're in hospital, love. Don't try to talk, you're all hooked up to the machine.'

I close my eyes.

The slapping sound of my mother's shoes on

the linoleum, her panting.

'Is she conscious?'

'She was. For a moment, she looked right at me.'

'Oh.'

'I'm sorry, love.'

'It's OK. She needs her sleep. She'll wake up again soon.'

Blink.

Hiss, click. I don't like the feel of the oxygen being pushed into my nose so I reach up, fumbling, and pull it out.

'Oh no you don't, miss.' My mother's firm voice. 'That stays in until the doctor says otherwise, understood?' The straps are hooked behind my ears again, the plastic tubes reinserted into my nostrils.

'Pretty sure you don't work here,' I mumble weakly.

'I don't care,' my mother says. 'You've given me enough of a scare already. We're following the doctor's instructions.'

'I'm sorry.'

'No, I'm sorry,' she sighs. 'I knew something wasn't right. I should have called the doctor.'

'What's wrong with me? Apart from the obvious.'

She looks at Dad. 'What did he say it was called again?'

'Hypercalcemia. You have too much calcium in your blood.' He clears his throat. 'When the cancer spread to your bones it caused them to slowly break apart, releasing calcium into your blood.'

'Great. This cancer thing just keeps on giving, doesn't it.' I can't help the bitterness that seeps through my voice. Sometimes you can only be positive for so long before it slips.

Mum smiles weakly and reaches up to gently brush the hair off my forehead.

'So what do we do?' I ask, and watch as they exchange a look. I know that look. It's the look people have when they have bad news to impart. 'Tell me.'

'There is no fixing it,' my father says resignedly. 'All they can do is treat the symptoms.'

I rub my eyes, wishing I could go to sleep and wake up and have all this be nothing but a bad dream. Have I not been through enough?

It's natural, when faced with your own mortality, to question why. Why me? Why? One innocuous word, three letters. Worth a measly score of six points on a Scrabble board.

I wasn't raised religious. I've stepped foot in a church once, after my diagnosis, curious to see what one looked like. It wasn't that impressive. I'd been expecting stonemasonry and stained-glass windows. I got wooden bench seats and a bulletin board with a handwritten notice saying Terry the Budgie was missing, had anyone seen him? Any spiritual insights I'd been hoping for were not forthcoming. I left disappointed, but reaffirmed in my belief that what was happening to me was through no lack of belief on my part.

Still, I couldn't help but wonder why. What did

I do to deserve it? Why me and not the girl who lived in the flat next door to mine. She seemed a friendly enough sort; we waved to each other in the driveway and once I fed her cat for her when she went away to Fiji for a week. Why not her? Not that I would wish it on anyone else, because I wouldn't do that even if I hated someone.

But who picks? Or is it just some great, big, universal random lottery draw?

I roll over in bed and pull the rough hospital sheet up over my head, like I did when I was small and scared of the dark. I'm still scared of the dark. Perpetually. Only now it's an endlessly dark tunnel that looms before me. Infinite darkness.

'I'm tired,' I mumble.

'OK, love.' Mum's voice is tight, strained. This is hard on her, on them both. 'You sleep. We'll pop home and shower and be back later. Do you need anything?'

'No.'

Blink.

When I wake it is with a cry. Disorientated, I was dreaming that I was swimming in the ocean. Pleasant at first, but then I noticed the shore getting further and further away as I drifted out. No matter how hard I swam I couldn't get back in, until the land was just a tiny sliver of green in the distance. I could sense the incredible depth of the water beneath me, the vast open space of nothing but waves around me. I was nothing, a speck, insignificant. Slipping under.

'No!' I flail in the bed, the sheet is still over my head and I can't breathe.

'Hey, it's OK, I'm here.' The sheet is ripped off and arms slip around me, pulling me in. A voice makes a shushing sound in my ear. It is soothing like the sound of rain and I feel myself start to calm.

'James?'

'Yes. It's me. I'm so sorry I took so long. I came as quickly as I could.'

'Who called you?'

'Amanda.'

'She shouldn't have.'

'I'm glad she did.'

'You were working and this is all a fuss about nothing. I'm OK.'

I say it as much for my benefit as his.

'Of course, I know you are.' His voice lacks the conviction of his words. 'But I'm still grateful she called.'

I nestle my face into his chest and breathe in the familiar smell of him. 'Me too. But don't tell her I said so.'

'Oh, Ava. I felt so powerless, being so far away and hearing that you were so unwell.'

'I'm sorry.'

I feel his arms tighten around me. 'Don't be sorry. It's not your fault. I was worried it was mine, taking you away for the weekend and wearing you out. Did I push you too hard?'

'No, no. It's not your fault. It's just one of the crummy things that can happen when you have cancer. It could have happened anywhere, at any time.'

He exhales and I realise that he has been blaming himself.

'You gave me such a fright,' he says.

'I gave myself a fright,' I admit. 'Don't tell my mother, but I thought it was it for me. The end. Saw bright lights and everything. Of course, that was just Kate coming in and turning the light on.' I start to cry softly as he rocks me.

'I'm sorry. I should never have left you. I won't do it again.'

I pull back and look up at him. Even though he looks tired and his skin is the funny kind of grey colour wrought by a long flight inside a metal tube with recycled air, he still looks amazing. 'What do you mean?'

He arches his eyebrows and tilts his head. 'How do you feel about a new flatmate?'

'Are you serious?'

He nods. 'Completely. I've already spoken to Amanda and Kate about it, and they're happy for me to move in as long as it's what you want.' He mistakes my lack of response for hesitation, and his next words come out in a rush. 'I'm not proposing I move all my furniture in of course, nothing like that. I'll keep my place. I just meant I'll move in for now, you know. And I can sleep in the spare room if it's too much, too fast. I'd completely understand and won't be offended, I promise. I don't want to impose, and I want you to say no if that's how you feel, no pressure from me. I just thought that maybe, you know, seeing as . . . '

I silence him with a kiss, my lips pressed tightly against his. When I pull away he blinks.

'Is that a . . . ?'

'Yes.' I laugh through tears. 'Of course it's a yes.'

A smile slowly dawns across his face. 'You're sure?'

'I'm sure. I can't think of anything I want more.' I smile. 'Well, apart from a cure for cancer of course.'

'Of course.' He grimaces. 'So, we're really bunking up together?'

'Looks like it.'

'And you're really sure? I honestly would understand if it's too soon, we haven't known each other all that long really.'

'Yes, I'm sure. Are you?'

'Of course.'

'James.' I shuffle over to the side of the bed and he sits on the edge, leaning back against the upright back part. I lay my head on his shoulder and he puts an arm around me. 'I need to be sure you've really thought about this,' I tell him. 'You know that what's coming, it's not going to be easy.'

I hear him swallow. 'I know.'

'You have to be absolutely certain about this. You're going to see things you won't want to see, and I'm worried that it's going to bring back a lot of painful memories for you.'

He tightens his grip around me. 'I'm scared. I'm not going to lie. But I'm not going to let my fear stop me from being with you. I meant everything that I said that day in the car.'

I exhale, relieved. 'OK. Then we're really doing this.'

He kisses the top of my head in response.

This moving in together, it's happening so quickly, no doubt about it. In a different time and under normal circumstances, if a guy suggested moving in together so soon after we'd started seeing each other I'd have run for the hills, probably. But these *aren't* normal circumstances; far from it. And this feels right.

'There is probably one thing you should know first though, before you make your final decision,' I say solemnly.

'Oh? What's that?'

'I have to sleep on the left side of the bed. And I've been known to hog the sheets.'

He laughs. 'I think I can live with that. I snore, by the way.'

I suck air between my teeth, shaking my head. 'I suppose *I* can live with that. You know with three girls in the house, you'll need to make sure you always put the toilet seat down.'

'Duly noted. Oh and I hope you don't mind, but I have a pet lizard. Well, he's a Komodo dragon actually. Likes to sit by the bed at night and watch me sleep. Name's Rocky. Don't worry he's quite harmless. I mean, he's bitten me once but it only needed three stiches. And it was my fault, I forgot to feed him that night.'

I pull away to stare at him wide-eyed. 'Are you serious?'

He keeps a straight face for about two seconds then bursts into laughter. 'No. I'm kidding. You should see your face, I wish I had my camera.'

I smack him lightly on his bicep. 'Oh my God, you had me so worried then.'

'Sorry.'

He pulls me back in for a kiss, which deepens into something more desperate until I remember where we are and pull away, my breathing shaky. 'I just want to get out of here now.'

'Have they said how long?'

'Not to me. But I've been pretty out of it.'

'Want me to see if I can rustle up a doctor? Find out what's going on?'

'Yes, please.'

He gets up but before he can take a step I grab at his jersey and he turns, his face questioning.

I take a deep breath, summoning up all the courage I have to say what I need to say. I don't like feeling vulnerable, but he has been honest with me, and now it's my turn to be honest with him. 'When we were in the car, and you told me you care about me, I didn't say it back but I want you to know that I do. So much that it takes my breath away sometimes. And I know that the timing couldn't have been any worse, or the circumstances any lousier, because I don't know how much longer I'll be around and I can't promise you the future you deserve.' My eyes spill over with tears and he opens his mouth to speak but I hold up a hand to stop him. 'Wait. I have to finish this. I can't promise you that I'll be an amazing kind of girlfriend, because I most probably won't. It's only going to get worse and I'm only going to get sicker. And I mean really sick. It won't be glamorous and you'll most likely be revolted at some point or other. And if you want to call it a day at any point, I'll understand. I really will. And I won't hold it against you. You can get out any time you like, OK. I need you to know that.'

He bends down and presses his lips firmly against my forehead and it's only when I feel his tears on my skin that I realise he is crying too. Then he whispers, so softly it is like the breath of a new-born child.

'I'm not going anywhere.'

35

I go home a little over a week later, once they have brought my symptoms under control and updated my medicine regime. With no fanfare, I slip quietly out through the hospital doors with James on one side and my mother on the other, my dad bringing up the rear under the weight of my bag and a ragtag assortment of floral arrangements sent by well-wishers. While I appreciate their efforts, I wish they wouldn't send flowers. Watching them brown, shrivel up and die is a daily reminder I don't need. My father must sense this because somewhere on the journey home between the hospital, the chemist and the grocery store, they disappear.

My parents have spent the last week getting to know James. To their credit, they've kept the usual interrogation a new boyfriend might expect to a minimum. This is not a typical relationship. There is only one thing they really need to know when it boils down to it.

Does he make you happy?

Yes. Deliriously so.

Welcome to the family, James.

I am so enthused about James moving in with me that it's only when I walk into my bedroom and the smell of disinfectant and bleach hits that I remember the details of that night. All the feelings of fear that I felt come rushing back, leaving me curled up on a bed with brand-new sheets and duvet, crying hot tears because I know that I am well and truly screwed. That nothing is fair, and my so-called life is winding down. I am heading rapidly towards The End of My Days. And there's not a damn thing I can do about it.

James curls his body around mine and we stay like that, for hours, while the others keep a discreet distance somewhere else in the house and pretend they can't hear my gut-wrenching sobs through the walls. At some point, exhausted, I sleep. When I wake, James is gone, and the space where he was has cooled. I go in search, needing him with a ferocity that is unfair to him. He is my life jacket to cling to, my anchor in a storm. As unreasonable as it is, I don't want to be without him at my side.

They are all in the lounge with the French doors open wide. I can feel the heat as soon as I walk into the room. Summer is well and truly upon us. I go to where James is sitting on a La-Z-Boy and drape myself across him, despite the heat. The prospect of death has made me needy.

'How are you feeling?' Mum asks, getting to her feet. 'I'll get you a glass of water.'

'I'm OK.' I shrug, because I don't have the words to describe how I feel, and even if I did they don't need to hear them. 'I'm not thirsty.'

'Too bad, you're drinking it.' She returns with a glass of water and passes it over, giving me a pointed look. 'Unless you fancy ending up back in hospital connected to a drip because you're dehydrated?'

Meekly, I take the water and force myself to drink it.

'Good girl.'

I notice for the first time that the couch is not in its normal position, that it is further out from the wall than it used to be.

'Why's the couch moved?' I ask.

Kate and Amanda exchange a look.

'Shall we show her?' Kate asks.

Amanda shrugs. 'I don't see why not. Now is as good a time as any.'

'Show me what?'

'While you were in hospital we had a mail delivery.'

'What kind of mail delivery?'

Together they push the couch along, revealing a massive pile of packages. Some are wrapped in normal postal bags. Some are in colourful paper. Others are even in Christmas gift paper.

'Woah,' I say. 'Who are they for?'

'You.'

'Seriously?'

'Well they all have your name on the front,' Amanda explains. 'Though that's about it. The guy who delivered it all said they'd been getting mail addressed to 'Ava from the *Women's Weekly*' for a while. They finally managed to convince the magazine to pass on your address and, well, here it all is.'

I stare at the small mountain of gifts in wonder. 'Who are they all from?'

'Why don't you open them and find out,' Dad suggests.

'I can't.'

'Why not?'

'It would be wrong, wouldn't it?'

Mum sighs. 'Ava, I love you. But sometimes you make about as much sense as a screen door on a submarine.'

'Gee thanks, Mum.'

'Why would it be wrong to open these presents? They're all for you.'

'But I don't know the people they're from. It's not my birthday. I haven't done anything to deserve being sent gifts.'

'I know it's hard to understand, but people feel like they *know* you, through the magazine articles and your column. Apparently, their readership circulation is the highest it's been in years.'

'I'm glad someone is profiting from my death.'

The joke, as such, falls flat. 'Sorry. Anyway, what's the deal with the Christmas paper?'

'Well there is only just over three weeks until Christmas,' James answers.

I stare at him. 'There is?'

He nods.

'Wow. That came around quick.'

'December always passes by in a blur,' Mum says. 'It's the same every year. You think you have all the time in the world to be all festive and make the cake and do all the preparation that needs to be done but before you know it, the day itself is here.'

This Christmas is different though, and we all know it. My last Christmas. There is an echoing silence around the room as we all think about the same thing. Amanda, predictably and thankfully, breaks it.

She clears her throat. 'If you don't want to open them, I'm happy to.'

'Amanda,' Kate scolds.

'What? I'm just saying. It's a shame for them all to go to waste. People wanted Ava to have these things, whatever they are.'

I realise she's right. I have to stop thinking about myself sometimes, and think about the intention behind the actions of others.

'How about we all open some?' I suggest. 'Make an afternoon of it.'

So we do just that. We sit in a circle around the presents and we open them. Kate methodically insists on recording each present and who it is from, if there is a name. Some are anonymous gifts. There are things for the wedding. Some brand new, some second-hand, and some handmade; like a delicate lacy veil, clearly antique and lovingly looked after.

'It's exquisite,' Mum gasps as she opens it. She lifts up the card and reads aloud.

Dear Ava,
    My name is Lois Pearl, and this was my wedding veil sixty-five years ago when I married my husband, Jack. It was hand-made by my mother and grandmother, and I can still remember how proud I felt wearing it, and how like a princess it made me feel. Jack passed away forty years ago. He never really recovered from injuries he sustained in the Second World War. We had a fine marriage while it lasted, a happy

one. Together we raised six children and I am now a proud grandmother to nineteen, and great-grandmother to four. Life hasn't always been easy, and I've done my fair share of complaining over the years. But when I read your story I was reminded how lucky I am, and how grateful I should be. I want to thank you for that, and I want you to have my veil. It shouldn't sit in a box in a cupboard in the dark, the way it has. But I'll understand if you don't want to wear it, I know it's not exactly modern! Either way, when you're finished please gift it on. All my love, Lois.

'Oh isn't that just beautiful.' Mum sniffs through her tears.

'It smells like mothballs,' Amanda says.

We drink wine — even me, although I'm not supposed to.

'You told me to keep up my fluids,' I say to Mum when she protests.

'That's not what I meant and you know it, but go on then. I suppose a small one won't hurt.'

There are books. Fiction ones, self-help books about spirituality and mindfulness, and even a couple of Bibles. Like the flowers, the intention behind them is good. But they are another reminder. I won't have time to read them. Not all. I know that I probably won't even read one, if I'm being honest. Whilst I have been an avid reader all my life, now that time is at a premium I'd rather spend it making my own memories than reading about the memories and moments of others.

I am also gifted an assortment of knick-knacks. The kind you can buy in any good stationery shop. The ones that are designed to spur you on to greater things, or at the very least to remind you to embrace the day with a smile. Fridge magnets, coffee cups, cushions. Candles that smell like tropical islands. Aprons with inspirational quotes.

There are two wedding dresses, both too big. Four pairs of shoes, a tiara, six necklaces, three bracelets and fourteen lacy garters. There is even, rather inappropriately, a set of scarlet red lingerie.

'Are those . . . ' Amanda snatches them from me to look closer and then howls with laughter. 'Crotch-less knickers,' she bellows. 'Oh. My. God.'

I snatch them back. 'Shut up.'

James smirks until my father frowns at him, then he pretends to be suddenly fixated on something outside the window.

When we have finished, we have a pile of perfectly wonderful gifts, but I don't need any of them.

'Donate them.' I say emphatically when Kate tentatively asks where we're going to keep it all.

'Where?'

'I don't know. Women's refuge? If anyone is in need of something nice for Christmas, it'll be those women.'

'Oh that's a lovely idea.' Mum smiles. 'Are you sure though, that there's nothing you want to keep?'

271

I survey the pile again and pick up the veil. I know I won't wear it, it doesn't go with the picture I have in my head of how I want to look on the day. But I don't want it to go to just anyone. 'Just this. I'll find a new home for this.'

'That's it? Are you sure?'

I nod. 'I'm sure. I'm grateful for each and every present. And the thoughts that came with them. But I don't need any of this. I'd rather it all went to people who will appreciate it.'

'Ava Green, you have a heart of gold,' Mum says. 'You get that from me, you know.'

Notes from Ava

(Women's Weekly December 18th)

Spend less on possessions. Yes, it's a message you've heard before. Countless times. But before you roll your eyes and turn the page, hear it one more time from me, the dying girl.

I am facing my last Christmas here on earth. My last Christmas Eve, last Christmas morning. I started thinking about all the Christmases gone by, not that many, admittedly. Not near enough. And do you know what? There is only one gift I remember receiving, and that was a doll when I was about four years old. That's it. And I don't even really remember what it looked like, just how it smelt when I removed it from its packaging. I can't even

272

remember what I got *last* Christmas. How bad is that?

We spend time and money investing in the 'perfect' gifts for our loved ones, and most of them are discarded or forgotten about by New Year. That 'perfect' gift, the one that was going to change their life? Yeah it's sitting in a cupboard or drawer somewhere. They'll find it again, in a few months or a year, and they'll scratch their head and think, Now where did this come from again?

It's meaningless. Most of it anyway. Of course there are exceptions.

What I *do* remember from all those Christmases is all the fun times we had. My family. Putting out the cookies for Santa and the carrots for the reindeer on Christmas Eve. Trying to stay awake and craning to hear any sound of hooves on the roof. Christmas Day itself, the jollity and merriness of the day as we played and ate and drank and watched the Queen's message, trying to mimic her prim and proper tone and falling about in fits of laughter when my father nailed it the most accurately. Pulling crackers, running through the sprinkler, lolling on the sofa after eating too much, then an hour later getting up to forage for food once more.

It's the experiences that make us rich. The time we spend with our family and our friends, *that* is the perfect gift, and it is all we need. Don't get sucked in by endless adverts screaming BOXING DAY SALE, BARGAINS GALORE, LIMITED TIME ONLY. Just don't. Call a friend instead. Take them out for a beer, ask them how they are and really listen to their answer.

You can't take possessions with you when you go, and while you're here, they just weigh you down. Declutter and you'll feel lighter, freer, less trapped. I will leave this earth with just the shirt on my back, and I'm OK with that, in so far as I can be. I am rich because I am loved. Show your loved ones how much you love them by investing your time, not your money. They'll remember it, I promise.

36

My last Christmas on this earth is a fairly low-key affair. Energy wise I am lacking, fatigue since the hospital is an ever-present ghost, weighing down my movements so I am sluggish. Even if I wasn't tired though, there is nothing I want to do more than sit around my parents' house and spend the day enveloped in their love and the love of my friends. And James, of course. Always James. He doesn't leave my side. I don't ask him about his work, instinctively knowing he is turning down jobs to be with me and selfishly happy that he is doing so.

We decided against giving each other gifts this year, because really, what was the point. I am still getting packages in the mail almost daily from people up and down the country. While well meaning and appreciated, they are all opened and then gifted on.

I have an urgent need to make memories, not just for me, although I am starting to fixate more on what will happen to my memories after I am gone. But for my loved ones left behind. I am determined to gift them with enough memories to get them through the hard times ahead. My mother isn't coping well with the thought of this being my last Christmas, so James and I become vagabonds for the holiday period, moving between houses. We deliberately spend most nights at hers, giving her the priceless gift that is time with her daughter. When we need a break or time alone together, we go back to Kate's, where we can make love without worrying that my parents might hear through the walls. My bedroom is at the opposite end of the house to Kate's master and Amanda's room, so we are free to be as vocal as the occasion requires.

Determined to give my parents and James a Christmas to remember, we do everything Christmassy that I can think of, including a three-hour round trip to a Christmas tree farm so that we can have the perfectly shaped tree. When we get it home, it is so tall my father has to cut a foot off the bottom, and its girth is such that my mother has to make an emergency trip to the shop for more tinsel and another set of fairy lights, as the ones we have barely stretch to cover the artificial stick we normally drag out every year let alone the monstrosity I have chosen to fill our lounge with for my final year. It is all worth it though because it is perfect. The sight of the tree lit up and the smell of the pine is so evocative of happier times that I decide, if I have to be buried, then I want to be buried in a pine box. I write this down but don't tell anyone, not yet, because I don't want to upset anybody else with the vision this conjures.

In a rare, late-night splurge, I buy everyone matching Christmas jumpers even though it is thirty degrees outside and the asphalt is melting on the road, and we all pose in front of the tree for photos, with the fire lit for effect in the background. Afterwards my mother's face stays beetroot red for the remainder of the day, of which she spends most of it with her head in the fridge, ostensibly planning the menu for Christmas Day itself. It occurs to me that I most likely won't live to see another winter, therefore another open fire, so I sit and I watch it until it burns away to nothing but smouldering ashes.

We go to Carols by Candlelight in the park on a Friday night, where the sound of a thousand people singing 'Silent Night' into an early evening sky has me weeping buckets. I set my mother and Kate off crying too and everyone in our vicinity looks at us strangely, until they realise it is me, and then they are sympathetic. I lose count of how many people stop by to 'Wish us well,' and to let me know I am 'in their prayers'. I smile my thanks, but say nothing. I am past the angry days of questioning their God and have no desire to provoke them into an argument and attempted defence which they cannot prove, at least not to me. Nothing will make me change my mind now, and if that condemns me then so be it. I can't pretend to believe in someone who allows this to happen to anyone, let alone small children.

On Christmas Eve we do something I have never done before but always wanted to. It's a contradictory decision for me, because to do it I must go to church. And I live in fear that someone will say something that enrages me so much I won't be able to control the vitriolic words I will want to say. But, if I *did* have a bucket list, this would most likely be on it. And so we don our finest and we go to Midnight Mass. Amanda doesn't come. She thinks that if she crosses the threshold of a church she'll most likely burst into spontaneous flames given the amount of profanity and blasphemous lyrics in her song writing, so instead she goes out with the band to get pissed and wreak her usual brand of havoc on the town instead.

As we go up the aisle, I make Mum and Kate walk in front of me, Dad follows behind, and I cling on to James's arm. I avoid eye contact with anyone until we are in our seats. *This* church is more like the churches of my imagination. We have driven to the city to see it, which gave me the advantage of time to nap on the way. A priest in white and gold robes leads the service, and while I do tune out during the biblical speeches, using the time to study the people around me and the beautiful architecture of the building, there is something special about singing Christmas carols in a building that echoes. The voices of the choir can only be described as angelic, which is fitting, and their sweet tones bounce off the rafters and roll down the walls. I get chills and the hairs on my arms stick up. James holds my hand tightly throughout. All in all, it is a beautiful experience, and I am glad I did it.

Christmas Day at my parents' house, as is tradition. As is *also* tradition, friends of my parents — roughly half the town — pop around during the day to pass on their seasonal greetings and to partake in a tipple or two, to get in the 'holiday spirit'. They are mostly retired couples like Mum and Dad, with empty nests and children who live too far away to return home every Christmas. They are filled with stories about 'how well Susan is doing in her top-earning, high-flying executive job', and how 'the children really like their new nanny'. She's German, they think. Or maybe Swiss.

It makes me sad to think about it. But I can't honestly say that if I was Susan, cancer free, in a great job and living the city dream, whether I'd make the effort to come home for Christmas either. You can read all the self-help books you like, but perspective only *really* hits when you're running out of the time you need to put it in practice. Death tends to do that though; rob you of time.

It is a wonderful day. A lazy, easy, carefree day. I have my village of people around me, except Amanda who was apparently so drunk Christmas Eve she fell asleep on the roundabout in town and spends Christmas Day at her parents' house comatose on the couch and texting me things like,

Oh God, I think I kissed that guy Nate we went to school with. The one who used to eat worms. Remember him? With the weirdly straight side-part? FML.

The day is both unremarkable and memorable, for all the right reasons.

The week between Christmas and New Year is spent, as always, finishing off the ridiculously oversized ham my mother bought before it goes off, and sitting on the lawn with our feet in paddling pools complaining about the heat. Well, the others do. I don't because I love summer. Everything seems easier when the weather is warmer. People are generally less miserable.

I do two more articles for the magazine. Nadia has taken to phoning for updates now instead of visiting, and James is happy to supply her with the photos she needs. He mischievously sends in the family Christmas awful jumper photo, and none of us know until the issue hits the stand. I see the funny side but Kate is mortified. We might know it's an ironic photo, she says, but the rest of the country doesn't.

As soon as we get back to Kate's each time I head for the beach. The curved shore is mostly private and empty, and I can sit with my thoughts and be hypnotised by the waves lapping the shore. Sometimes I cry. Sometimes I laugh. I build a sandcastle, on an afternoon when the sky is the bluest blue you've ever seen and the sun is unbearably hot. Everyone else refuses to leave the cool shelter of the house so I build it alone, decorating the walls with sun-bleached shells and little sticks of driftwood. I am ridiculously proud of it, so when the tide turns and gradually washes it away I feel sad. Nothing is permanent. Not feelings, not people, not sandcastles. I strip down to my underwear and float on my back in the sea, keeping a wary eye on the shore to make sure I don't drift out too far. The memory of that dream is still with me.

Somewhere between Christmas and New Year I completely lose my appetite, along with four kilos. I can *feel* my body steadily going into decline, but I say nothing. I don't want to worry anyone else until it's unavoidable.

New Year's Eve, James and I drive to the top of the cliff that overlooks the town and watch fireworks explode in glittery bursts against a black sky. It is hard to say goodbye to the last full year on this earth that I will have lived in, even though it was the year that brought me the worst news. Despite that, and the treatments that failed to buy me more time, I don't hate the year as much as I would have thought. Because it was the year that also brought me James. And that's a pretty big highlight as far as I'm concerned.

It is terrifying to think that I am now in the year of my death. The four-digit number that will be recorded beside my name in a computer somewhere and on a headstone; it has arrived. Like a black storm cloud that has been threatening on the horizon, it is here.

Notes from Ava

(Women's Weekly January 14th)

Don't forget to take the time to enjoy the simple pleasures.

I know it's so easy to get caught up in the big things, working hard to save for a new house, new car, that expensive holiday, that we often forget to just take the time to enjoy the small stuff.

And I know that sometimes, in reality, things that sound magical all too often actually aren't. Like dancing in the rain, for instance, or buying a puppy. Rain tends to be a cold, wet affair, and puppies can be bloody hard work, given their natural tendency to pee on the carpet or chew your shoes.

Baking your own bread *sounds* a noble pursuit. Till you forget the yeast and waste an hour waiting for bread to rise that doesn't, but you bake it anyway and then wonder why you bothered when it's harder than a slab of rock and not half as pretty. Not even the birds will touch it, or the dog, and that's saying something because he eats the cat's fur balls. As for growing your own vegetables, painstakingly tending to them for weeks only to have some bastard rabbit eat them from under your nose right before harvest time, well that's just infuriating. It's so much easier to buy your lettuce in a bag and your carrots pre-peeled.

You might think a nice family afternoon walk on a Sunday afternoon conjures up images of rosy-cheeked children dashing gleefully ahead to frolic in hedges and marvel at nature, while Mum and Dad stroll hand in hand blissfully behind, over-whelmed by how blessed they are and how wonderful life is, but then you actually go on a walk. And the fight begins before you even leave the house when you have to prise your cherubs away from the TV. Before you've even gone five hundred metres someone sits down in the middle of the road, crying, because their legs are too tired to continue, the other child is in desperate need of a bath and possible decontamination because they poked a dead possum with a stick 'to see what would happen', your husband is wondering whether if 'we turned back now' we might make it back for the second half of the game, and you end up climbing a hill in an effort to get cell phone service so you can google where the nearest pub is.

It's exhausting, and not at all what you had in mind.

But here's the thing: these moments, these 'experiences', they may feel like they will break your spirit at the time, but they won't. You WILL look back on them one day and manage not to cry or cringe, and instead you'll see it for the character-building, memory-making time that it was.

When you are on your deathbed, you won't recall with any great detail the eight-plus hours you spent every day in an office, or the hour and a half you spent in the car on your daily commute. I understand the bills have to be paid, I'm not saying quit your job and run away to join the circus, or sell up and spend a year sailing around the world. What works for some is a nightmare for others. What I'm saying is, when you're dying, you won't look back and remember how horrible that picnic was because of the ants, and how hard the ground was, and because you stuck your hand in bird shit and took a bite of your sandwich before you noticed. Instead you'll remember how blue the sky was that day, how warm the sun felt, and how long and hard you laughed with your friends (or family). How good it felt to be outside, reconnecting with nature, doing nothing much in particular.

So take that walk, bake that cake with plums foraged from the neighbour's tree. Sleep under the stars, feed the birds, read the paper from cover to cover; the housework can wait.

Slow down.

Keep the balance.

Keep it simple.

37

January brings with it new resolve. I have been caught up in a downward spiral lately, focusing on the unfairness of my illness, and the impending hard days to come. I know why, of course. James. He is everything I ever wanted. Loyal, passionate, funny. When we are not sleeping or making love we are talking, about anything and everything. He tells me about the places he has been and the things he has seen and I close my eyes and pretend I was there with him, at his side all along. It's a poor substitute to actually having done it, but it will have to do.

After the hospital visit I decide I have been concentrating too much on dying, and I need to remember to focus more on actually living instead. It's hard though, when most of the time I am so tired all I can do is curl up on the couch and watch life go on around me.

Kate and my mother have gone into wedding planning overdrive. There are To Do lists stuck to surfaces all around the house, and Kate has taken to walking around with a pen tucked behind her ear so that she always has one on hand to scribble down notes in the little teal-coloured notebook that she keeps tucked under her arm. Especially useful for the many phone calls she fields.

'Who was that?' I ask one day after her phone goes for the fifth time in an hour. James has gone home to air out his house and mow the lawns, and Amanda is in the city for a few days with her band. Kate has taken a few days off this week, to 'finalise things'. The wedding is only two weeks away.

'Mm? Oh no one you need to worry about.'

'You guys haven't gone like, a bit crazy stupid, with this whole wedding thing, have you?'

'As if we would.'

'Good. So we're still on budget?'

She makes a sound that I think is supposed to signify agreement, but her eyes twitch shiftily at the same time.

'Kate.'

'What?'

'What have you done?'

'Exactly what you asked me to do. Organise you a wedding day to remember. Or celebration-of-your-life day, whatever we're calling it now.'

'Why do I get the feeling you're not telling me something?'

'I don't know. I'm not hiding anything.'

'Really? Then you won't mind if I look at this.'

I leap for her notebook but she is too quick and dives over the back of the couch where I can't reach her.

'Aha. So you *are* hiding something,' I say.

'Oh for God's sake, Ava. Stop asking questions and just wait and see. You'll spoil the surprise.'

'So there *is* a surprise.'

'You can be so annoying sometimes, anyone ever tell you that?'

'You. All the time when we were growing up.'

At the mention of our shared youth her eyes

go glassy and her bottom lip wobbles. 'If I did, I didn't mean it.'

'Don't cry,' I sigh. 'Not today. Not yet.'

'I can't help it.' She looks down at her feet. 'I'm trying to keep myself busy so I don't think about it, but it's always there. Every time I look at you, the thought of never seeing your face again . . . ' She sobs, and then claps a hand across her mouth. When she has recovered enough she removes it and whispers, 'I'm sorry. You don't need to hear this.'

I sit down on the couch and pat the cushion beside me. 'Sit.'

She takes a step and then pauses. 'Is this a trap so you can try and get my notebook?'

I roll my eyes. 'No. The thought hadn't even crossed my mind. But now that you mention it . . . '

She clutches the notebook tighter.

'Oh for . . . come on. Sit. I promise I won't try and get it.'

Still looking at me dubiously, she sits, tucking the notebook underneath her thigh that is furthest away from me. I study her face, marvelling at how familiar it is. I could close my eyes and conjure up a thousand magical memories of this girl, based on one expression alone. She has been there for me through everything. I can only hope that I have given her the same support.

'You know you're my oldest friend,' I say.

She bursts into tears.

'Wow, that escalated quickly,' I say, blinking. 'Oh, Kate, you big soppy thing. Come here.' I

287

pull her in for a cuddle.

'I'm sorry.' She sniffs.

'Stop saying that.'

'But I am. You're being so brave. And here I am being a total sook and making *you* comfort me when it should be the other way around.'

'You can't help how you feel.'

'I feel like shit.'

I pat her back. 'That's good, let it all out.'

'It's just not fair, you know?' she mumbles into my shoulder. 'Why you?'

'No idea.'

'How am I supposed to spend the rest of my life without you?'

'Again, I have no idea. But you will. You'll get through this and you'll be OK, I promise.'

'But you don't like making promises you can't keep.'

'Exactly. This one is easy. You *will* be OK, Kate. In fact, you'll be more than OK. You'll have a wonderful life, an amazing life. You'll be happy, and have a family, and do all the things you've ever wanted to do. You know how I know?'

She sniffs and shakes her head, still buried in my shoulder.

'I hope you're not wiping snot on me.'

That makes her laugh. A kind of gulp laugh, and she sits back up and looks at me, her face puffy and tear-stained.

'I know you'll be fine, Kate, because of this.' I cross my hands on my chest and give her a sad smile. 'Because of *me*. If you ever get stuck in a rut, or in a situation that makes you unhappy, promise me that you'll think about me. And you'll remind yourself that some of us didn't get to make choices, but you will, and you must. If something isn't working in your life, change it. I know it sounds too simple, and words are easy to say. But you have to promise me, Kate. Live your best life. For me.'

She swallows hard and nods.

'Say it.'

'I promise.'

'You'll live your best life.'

'I will.'

'Good.' I lean back, satisfied. 'Because if you don't, I'll come back and haunt your arse.'

She snorts with laughter. 'Yeah, that sounds like something you'd do.'

'You better believe it.'

She reaches over and picks up my hand, smiling sideways at me. 'Thanks.'

'For what?'

'Talking me back off the ledge.'

'What are friends for.'

'I love you.'

'Mumble mumble mumble.' I cough into my hand.

She cups her ear. 'Sorry? I didn't catch that.'

'Oh come on. You know I don't go in for big declarations of affection.'

'I think you can make an exception just this once.'

'Is that the time?' I pretend to look at a watch I'm not wearing.

She pounces, pinning me down and tickling me hard in the ribs. 'Say it.'

'Stop.' I giggle breathlessly. Kate used this method to coerce me into doing her will when we were small girls, and although it's been quite some time since she employed it, unfortunately for me, its effectiveness hasn't waned.

'I'm not stopping until you say it,' she insists.

'This is cruel,' I gasp.

She draws back, alarmed. 'I'm not hurting you, am I?'

'No,' I say, and then realise too late the opportunity I have missed.

'Good.' She tickles again, poking me in my sides as I contort and wheeze until finally I cave.

'Fine, fine. I love you too,' I yell.

She ceases tickling and climbs off me, her face smug. 'There. That wasn't so hard, was it.'

'Speak for yourself,' I grumble, trying to catch back my breath. 'You have an evil streak, you know.'

'I've missed this.' She smiles wistfully.

'Tickling me?'

'No, egg. This, us. Playing around. Just the two of us. Although it's great when Amanda is here too of course,' she adds hurriedly.

'I know what you mean. I've missed it too. I'm sorry if it seems like I've been so preoccupied with James lately.'

She looks down. 'It's OK, I understand.'

'I hope so. It doesn't mean I love you guys any less. You're still the best friends a girl could ever ask for.'

'I was a little jealous of him at first,' she admits. 'Which sounds completely selfish.'

'It's not selfish. You can't help how you feel.'

'I just . . . I missed it being just us, you know?'
She sighs deeply. 'But it all comes down to the
fact that all I want is for you to be happy. That's
the most important thing. And anyone can see
that he makes you that way.'

'He does. And so do you.'

'Besides, I've had you almost my whole life,'
she goes on. 'And although it's hard to share
when I know our time left together is limited,
share I must.' She sniffs nobly.

'You never were any good at sharing,' I tease.

'Hey,' she protests. 'OK, maybe not, but you
still love me.'

I give her a defiant look.

She holds up her hands and waggles her
fingers threateningly. 'Don't you . . . ?'

'I do, I do,' I say quickly before she starts
tickling me again.

Her expression turns serious. 'Oh God, Ava.
How am I supposed to say goodbye to you?'

I take a breath and breathe it out slowly,
failing to dispel the pain her words cause. 'You
don't. No goodbyes. I'll be seeing you again.
Someday, somewhere.'

'Do you really believe that?'

'I have to. Otherwise it hurts too much.'

Notes from Ava

(Women's Weekly January 28thth)

Don't leave saying something until it is too
late. You were taught words for a reason.
Use them. Unless you're angry. Then you

291

shouldn't say anything. Words said in anger can never be taken back, so don't tear someone else down just because you're having a shitty day. Stop. Breathe. Think first. Walk away if you have to.

Tell your loved ones you love them. Every single time you see them or leave them, tell them. Especially your children. Sprinkle the word on them like glitter. It will never lose its effectiveness, trust me, and it will make them feel as special and wanted as they are.

If you love someone, tell them. Because if you don't, one day it will be too late. Not might be, WILL be. We are all only a tiny cog in this great big universe for a while. Once your time is up, it's up. It's not a rehearsal. You don't get to try again. There are no second chances, no reruns. Just one chance, to make it a life you want to live. It doesn't matter if you aspire to greatness, or if you're content to live a life that others might consider average. As long as you're happy, that's a life well lived.

Cliches are cliches for a reason.

Do the things you want to do.

Don't do anything you don't want to.

Eat the things you want to eat.

Be with the person who makes you the best version of yourself.

Live truthfully, as best as you can.

DO stop and smell the roses, and the coffee, and the scent of freshly cut grass. They really are the moments that make us smile.

Look in the mirror every morning and tell yourself 'I got this'. Because you do.

Live your best life. It's the only one you'll get.

38

Something is not quite right with James. Nothing obvious, but *something* nevertheless. I can feel it. He is distant, distracted, but when I ask him if he is OK he brushes me off, saying he is fine, it is nothing. But even though he is as attentive and loving as ever, I can't shake the murky feeling that he is slipping away from me. The closer we get to the wedding the tenser he becomes.

The number of letters and packages arriving has doubled; it appears reader excitement for the wedding has reached fever pitch. When I was in hospital the magazine ran an article that basically implied I was plugged into machines and barely clinging on to life. Sensationalism at its best. I understand it sells copies, which is ultimately the magazine's intention, but it doesn't sit well with me. People up and down the country actually held candlelight vigils; Amanda shows me the photos that were uploaded on to the Facebook page. I am touched by their love, and terrified by it at the same time. These people care so much for me, someone they've never met. I worry that I don't merit it.

A week before the wedding, Nadia herself comes to the house to find out how I am feeling and how the wedding prep is going. I am sullen and mutter monosyllabic, non-committal answers in protest against her perceived lack of morals. If she notices she gives no sign of it. Mercifully, Kate and Mum are willing to discuss wedding details till the cows come home, so I leave Nadia in their capable hands and escape to the beach.

I head for the waterline and then turn south to walk along-side it. The tide is on the turn, making its way slowly back up the sand. Like the disease inside of me, its gain is indiscernible to the naked eye, but unrelenting.

It all feels like it has gotten out of hand. I am not the only person in this country dying of cancer. Far from it. According to statistics, over six hundred other people will die this year of breast cancer alone. I am just a number. A name on a list, a bar on a graph, a slice in a pie. I don't know why people are interested in me especially, but they are. And as much as I want to tell Nadia it's enough now, if reading about me makes just one woman do a self-exam on her breasts, or push her doctor for more tests, a second opinion, a proper diagnosis, then it will be worth it.

I haven't walked far before exhaustion hits, so then I sit and wrap my arms around my knees, staring out to sea. It is getting harder and harder for me to breathe with the effort of any exertion. My lungs feel as if they are stuffed full of cotton wool and only a small amount of oxygen is filtering through, leaving me weak, pale and breathless.

I am scared.

I have been to the brink and back a few times since my initial diagnosis. Or I thought I had. To be told that you are dying, while you sit there still healthy enough to carry out the basic duties of life and even experience adventure on top, is incomprehensible. It's impossible to believe that death is so close, just around the corner, rapidly approaching on the wrong side of the road with headlights on full. You, dead in its sights.

And now that I am close enough to sense the end, I am still no closer to any answers. If I thought death might bring clarity I was wrong. It only brings more confusion.

'Ava.'

I turn at my name being called. It is my father. He walks along the beach until he is at my side and then he sits down heavily beside me with an 'oof' sound as his weight hits the ground.

'You should try and lose some belly weight, Dad,' I say idly. 'It's not good for your heart.'

'Don't you start worrying about my heart. Nothing wrong with it.'

'You're working it too hard. Lose some weight. Go for a run once in a while.'

He snorts. 'Run? Have you ever known me to run?'

'Only after an ice-cream truck,' I tease, to show that I come from a place of love. 'Promise me. Now. Here. That you'll take better care of your health.'

'What's brought this on?'

'Nothing. Everything. I'm not going to be around to look after you and Mum in your old age. You've only got each other. She's going to need you.'

'Oh, sweetheart.' He puts an arm around my shoulders and pulls me in until our heads are together. 'Don't worry about us.'

296

'I can't help it.'

'I know.' He sighs. 'Listen, your mother sent me to get you. Nadia has gone. She wants you to come back and have a final dress fitting.'

'It can wait.'

'You'll get me in trouble if I go back alone.'

'I've lost another two kilos,' I blurt out. I feel him stiffen. 'Without trying. I think the end is getting close, Dad.'

'Oh, love.'

I cry, and he holds me while I do, my shoulders heaving with sobs that shake my body with such force that I honestly feel I might break all the bones in my body.

'I'm scared,' I tell him.

'Me too. Terrified. But you're not facing this alone. I'm here, we're all here.'

'I know.' I stare out to sea where a sailing ship is moving slowly across the horizon, its white sails billowing against a brilliant blue sky. I'd give anything, in that moment, to be on that ship, sailing off into destinations unknown. 'But at some point it's going to be just me, isn't it,' I say softly, through lips wearied by words of death. 'Me. Taking that final step into the unknown. Leaving you all behind.'

He tightens his grip on my shoulders but doesn't answer.

'How will I know when to let go, Dad?'

It's an unfair question and no answer comes. Just the tide. Unrelenting.

The dress, when we do go back to the house, is as I predicted. Too big. My mother frowns, pins stuck between her teeth, as she surveys the baggy material. I watch her in the mirror and see the exact moment realisation dawns. She closes her eyes tightly for a moment, calling all her strength into play, before opening them again and smiling at me brightly.

'Don't panic, but a minor problem,' she chirps. 'I mucked up the measurements last time. Completely my fault. Bear with me while I just pin it properly and then we'll be all good to go.'

'You're lying.'

'Ava Green, don't you dare call me a liar. I am your mother.'

'Sorry. I do appreciate it though.'

'I don't know what you're talking about. But you're welcome.'

'We don't have to do this if it's too hard, Mum.'

She stops pinning to look at my reflection in the mirror quizzically. 'Do what? Alter the dress? It's no problem, really. Well, for Sharon Hornsby anyway. You know I'm no great sewer but she's happy to make the alterations we need. She'll stay up all night if she needs to.' Because of the pins, her words come out all funny-sounding, but I understand her.

'The wedding, Mum. We don't have to do any of this if it's too hard on you and Dad.'

She sighs and sits on the end of the bed, spitting the pins out into her hand. 'I'm not going to lie,' she admits. 'When you first mentioned the idea I thought it was ridiculous. But then I thought about it some more, and I realised, why *shouldn't* you have the day you

298

always wanted. Besides you're right, a funeral is a horrible, morbid affair. I've never liked them.'

'I don't think anyone does.'

'Of course not. Don't interrupt.'

'Sorry.'

'I think the idea of having a day to celebrate *your* life with *your* family and friends while you're still with us is a good one. A great idea in fact. And your father feels the same way.'

'I'm not so sure any more.'

She tilts her head and sighs. 'OK. Where is this coming from? Talk to me. Tell me what's bothering you.'

'It's James.'

'Where he is? I haven't seen him today.'

'That's the point. He said something about catching up with an old friend as he practically ran out of the door this morning and I haven't heard from him since. He's barely been around much at all the last week. I don't know what happened. Everything was going so amazingly and then all of a sudden it was like he just hit the brakes, and I feel like he wants out but just doesn't know how to tell me.'

'Oh, darling, I'm sure that's not the case. He adores you. Everyone can see that.'

'Then why does he keep making excuses to leave the house?'

'They're not excuses. He does have a life outside of you, remember. A house, a business.' She says it as tactfully as she can without pointing out I am being unreasonably selfish.

'No.' I shake my head. 'Something's wrong. I'm going to try and talk to him tonight.'

'OK. But be gentle. This can't be easy on him either. You two got together so quickly, he probably had no idea what he was getting himself into.'

'That's just it though, he does have an idea.' I shrug sadly. 'He's been through it all before.'

'What are you talking about?'

I tell her about his mother's death and the effect it had on him.

'Oh.' She places a hand on her chest and looks stricken. 'Oh no, that poor man.'

'It was pretty rough on him. So much so that he tried to stop himself developing feelings for me, because he knew what I was facing and couldn't bear the thought. But he couldn't help himself. He thought he could handle this, but now maybe he's realising he can't.'

'Oh, love. That's just terrible. But I can't say I blame him. This isn't an easy ask of anyone, watching you suffer.' She chokes on the last word and swallows hard. 'You both need to have an honest conversation. See where his head is at.'

'Yeah. I know you and Dad were planning on sticking around for dinner tonight, but do you think you could make yourselves scarce? And take Kate and Amanda with you?'

'Of course.'

'Thanks, Mum.'

She stands back up and puts her hands on my hips, spinning me gently until I am facing the mirror again, with her face over my shoulder.

'You are so beautiful. Your father and I are incredibly proud of you. You know that, right?'

I nod.

'Honey, if James does decide this is too hard and he can't be here for you, try to understand. See it from his point of view.'

'I will.'

'You've always got us. We're not going anywhere.'

Her words echo my father's, but I don't torture her with the same reply. 'I know.'

'Right, let's get this dress sorted.'

39

When James gets home around seven I am waiting for him. Everyone has gone out, leaving us the house to ourselves. I have made the most of it by setting the outside table and decorating it with candles. Because it is still daylight outside the effect is lost, but I know later it will be romantic and atmospheric.

'Hey.' He smiles when he walks into the lounge. I am in the kitchen, having just poured him a cold beer when I heard his car pull up. 'Where is everyone?'

'Out.' I pass him the beer and he takes it, gulping thirstily.

'All of them?' he asks after a long drink, wiping the froth from his upper lip.

'Every last one. We have the place all to ourselves.'

'Mm, well in that case, we better make the most of it.' He pulls me in close for a kiss, and for a moment I think I am wrong, that he is still the same James he was when we kissed by the waterfall, but then he hesitates and pulls away, and I see something flicker across his face.

'What's wrong?' I ask him, trying hard to keep my voice level.

'Nothing.' He kisses my forehead. 'I'm just hungry. Shall we cook or order in?'

'I've already ordered. Thai will be delivered at eight.'

'You're pretty perfect, you know that?'

Which is, of course, incorrect. I am as defective as it gets. But I just smile sweetly and say nothing.

'OK if I just grab a quick shower?'

'Of course.'

When he emerges, damp and smelling of spicy aftershave, I feel an overwhelming surge of smug pride at the sight of him, wondering not for the first time how I got so lucky.

'Feel better?' I ask.

'Much.'

'How was your friend?'

Immediately he looks shifty. It's a fleeting look, but I know I haven't imagined it. 'He's good. It was really good to see him.'

'Is he an old photographer friend?'

'Something like that.'

It is clear that he doesn't want to discuss his day, which proves my earlier suspicions that something is wrong. But in that moment, I realise that I am scared to know the truth. If James *is* having second thoughts about us, I'm not sure I want to know, because I don't know how I will cope without him. We are both saved by the doorbell. James looks at me quizzically.

'Dinner,' I say quietly.

'Of course.' He picks up his wallet from the bench and goes to make the transaction. I sink back against the bench and breathe deeply a few times. I can't lose him. I can't.

By the time he brings the bags of food into the kitchen I have composed myself, standing with two glasses of wine poured and a smile plastered on.

'I thought we'd eat outside,' I say.

'Good idea. Plates?'

'Already out there.'

I follow him outside. The sky has started to darken, the sun on its path to awaken peacefully slumbering folk on the other side of the earth. We sit and eat, or he does. I manage a few mouthfuls but I have no appetite. The food is tasty, and once upon a time I would have eaten so much I'd have suffered from indigestion and *still* thought it was worth it. But I am on edge. I have that uneasy anticipatory feeling one gets before a storm hits; when you've heard all the weather reports forecasting doom and don't know whether to bunker down or go on one last, extravagant spending spree. James notices the food still on my plate and pauses in between mouthfuls.

'Not hungry?'

I shake my head.

'Are you feeling OK?' His voice is heavy with concern, but for the first time I notice an undercurrent of fear, almost lost in the deep timbre of his voice. It affirms my belief that he is worried about what is to come.

'Yes. Fine.'

He gives me an odd look but takes another mouthful.

'And you?' I ask.

He swallows. 'Me?'

'Yes. You. Are you feeling OK?'

He frowns. 'You mean, health wise?'

'I mean any wise, really. Anything on your mind?'

'No.'

It's there again. That fleeting look of deception. He is not telling me something.

'Tell me more about this friend of yours.'

He puts down his utensils and pushes his plate away. 'What do you want to know?'

I shrug. 'Let's start with the basics. A name. How do you know him? Is he from around here?'

'His name is Henry. I have known him for a long time, ten years or more. No, he is not from around here.'

'Is there a reason why you're being deliberately vague?'

'I'm not having an affair, if that's what you're worried about.'

'Of course not. I didn't think that for a second.'

'Then what? I don't understand what it is that you're accusing me of?'

'I'm not accusing you of anything. But you're holding back, and I know that something is wrong.' My voice becomes shaky. 'I feel like I'm losing you.'

'That's ridiculous.'

'*Don't* call me ridiculous.'

'I'm not. I didn't. Not you. I just meant . . . '

He sighs. 'Are you feeling up for a walk on the beach?'

I'm not, not really, but I don't tell him that. 'Yes.'

He stands and holds out a hand. I hesitate.

'Trust me,' he says quietly, imploringly.

I take his hand and look up into his eyes, willing him to be strong enough for me. 'Always.'

The moon, low over the water, lights our way. At first I think it is full, but closer inspection reveals a sliver missing on the bottom right side. The tiniest fraction of moon still hidden in shadow. Another cycle and her full glory will be revealed. I've always loved a full moon. For one night a month, it shines down with a mystical beauty that unleashes the crazy and the poetical within us all; a free pass to release your wild side. I kissed a stranger beneath a full moon once, something I've never been brave enough to do before or since. A whim at a teenage party on a night long ago, I'd forgotten all about it, but now the memory makes me smile. I wonder if he remembers too.

'Are you cold?'

James's voice rouses me from the past.

'No.'

'Come here anyway.'

He pulls me into his side, an arm around my shoulders. Not for the first time I marvel at how well I fit into his side, as if we were measured for this exact purpose. He kisses the top of my head and we fall into a slow walk, our feet bare in the sand, our path lit by the moon. The surface of the ocean is like a mirror, luminescent with the light from above. It is so beautiful and I am feeling so maudlin I start to cry. James stops and turns me to face him, pulling my chin up gently.

'Hey, what is it, what's wrong?'

'Nothing. Everything. The usual.'

'Stupid question really.'

I shrug. 'Still better to ask it than to not ask at all.'

'You just don't seem yourself tonight.'

'I could say the same about you,' I retort. 'You've been so closed off lately, so secretive. If you're having second thoughts about us, James, you only need to say. I don't want you to stay with me out of pity, or because you feel like you have to.'

'I don't feel like that at all.' He frowns, genuinely puzzled. 'Is that what you think? That I've fallen out of love with you?'

'I don't know what to think.' I wipe my tears on the back of one hand.

He sighs. 'Sit.'

'No. If you have something bad to say I'd rather hear it standing.'

'Please.' He sits down himself and tugs at my hand. I let myself fall carefully, until I am sat between his legs, my back nestled in against his chest. He rubs his face softly against the side of my head, his lips kissing my hair softly, and his words when he speaks are clear and unmistakable.

'I love you, Ava. That hasn't changed, nor will it ever.'

'But something is on your mind, isn't it?'

'Yes. But not what you're thinking.'

'Then tell me.'

'OK, but it has to stay between us. It's all hush-hush at the moment. My friend, Henry. He's an award-winning journalist, but more than just your average one. He's like a kind of modern-day explorer, like Cook, or Columbus.

He seeks out the unknown, or as yet undiscovered. About six months ago he found a previously unknown civilisation deep in the South American jungle. They are as primitive as it gets, and he was very nearly killed and probably eaten for dinner. But somehow, and I don't know how he does it but he has this effect on most people he meets, he won them over enough that they let him stay with them for a time, observing their ways.'

'Wow, that's . . . pretty amazing.'

'It really is. They live their entire lives hundreds of feet above the ground, in huts built into the canopy of the trees, all interconnected and pretty well camouflaged. They have their own system of catching rainwater and everything, and they only go down to the ground to hunt for food.'

His voice grows more animated as he talks, and I realise what's coming.

'He wants you to go back with him,' I say quietly, cutting him off mid-speech.

He is silent for a moment and then he speaks quietly. 'He does.'

'You want to go.'

'No.'

'Yes.'

'No.' His voice grows harsh. 'Not now. Not while you're still . . . '

I sit forward, angry. 'That's unfair. I can't be the thing that stops you from living your life.'

'Ava. Look at me.'

Reluctantly, I turn my head to look over my shoulder.

'You are my life.' His voice is raspy. 'I'm not going. I've already told him that. He is looking for someone else.'

I shake my head, hot tears in my eyes. 'This isn't fair. None of it. You didn't sign up for any of this.'

'Yes I did. I knew what I was getting in for from the start.'

'Knowing something is coming and actually having to deal with it though are two different things.'

'Ava — '

I push away from him and climb to my feet, feeling a desperate need to get out of my skin. I start to claw at myself, feeling such a hatred I have never felt before. Hatred against myself, not the essence of me, but the physical part, the part that is failing and useless and beyond my control. It is bad enough it is hurting me, but I can't bear the thought of what it is doing to him too. Sobbing, I rip at my clothes, my hair, my skin.

'Ava, stop.' His voice is terrified as he tries to stop me, but I am like a wild animal and I spin away from him, gasping, panting, heading for the water. I need to be clean, to shed this shell that is pathetic and faulty. That can't do the things I need it to do; that won't give me the future I long for and deserve.

The water is cool and takes my breath away, and I push through it until I am waist deep, then I dive, kicking away from the shore. Under the surface all sound of the world disappears. I enter a silence and darkness so complete it stills my fury. With my eyes closed, I hold my breath and let myself relax, floating, my hair splayed around me. This is how it must feel, I think. All I'd have to do is breathe out.

Then I feel arms around me, and I am jerked to the surface. The silence is gone.

'Ava, what the hell are you trying to do?' He is angry, scared.

'Nothing,' I mumble, without opening my eyes. He scoops me into his arms and I relax against his chest, weightless in the gentle embrace of the water. I am more tired than I ever believed possible.

'I'm taking you home.'

'I'm already there,' I whisper.

40

I wake up as if I am still underwater. Disorientated, unsure which way is up and which is down. The light is harsh and I blink at it, wondering why it's so bright and why it's changed shape, elongated rather than circular.

'She's awake.'

My mother's face swims into focus. Too close. I can see the remnants of day-old make-up in her creases, her eyeliner smudged beneath a bleary eye.

'Oh you gave us a fright, love.'

'Did I? Where are we?'

She puts a hand on my shoulder before she speaks, whether to comfort or restrain I'm unsure. 'Hospital.'

I frown, trying to remember my last conscious thought but feeling as if I have entered into a conversation halfway. 'How long? Why?'

'Just since last night. You were home with James, remember? He said you were acting a little bit off. Then you stopped responding to him altogether so he called an ambulance. They've run some tests which we're still waiting for the results of, but the doctor is pretty sure you had a seizure.'

'A seizure?'

'You know, like a fit,' Dad says, trying to be helpful.

'I don't understand.' I struggle up on to my

elbows. 'Where's James?'

My parent's exchange looks, and then my mother makes what she thinks is a soothing noise. It might have worked when I was four, but right now it does nothing to settle my confusion. The door opens and Dr Harrison's head pops through.

'Is this a bad time?' he asks.

'No,' my mother replies. 'Come in.'

'Yes,' I say. 'Go away.'

'Ava.' Mum gives me a scolding look. It is a reminder that no matter how sick I am, I was raised to be polite to people in authority. Out of habit, I look down apologetically.

Dr Harrison comes into the room and closes the door behind him. Closed doors mean bad news, in my experience.

'How are you feeling, Ava?' he asks.

'Confused.'

'That's understandable.'

'I don't know why I'm here. I can't remember ... ' I try again to remember something. The last thing I can remember is James. The beach. The almost full moon. His friend, the job offer.

'Confusion and memory loss are normal after suffering a seizure.'

'There's nothing normal about any of this,' I say helplessly. 'Why did I have a seizure?'

He takes a deep breath in and exhales it slowly, buying himself some time. Probably wishing he was on a golf course somewhere, anywhere rather than here. Why would anyone choose a career where you have to convey awful

312

news to good people?

'We will know for sure after a scan and some more tests, but judging from your symptoms and preliminary results, it's highly likely the cancer has metastasised to your brain.'

My mother starts to cry. My father puts his arms around her and braces himself to be the strong one today. I feel the bottom drop out of my world.

I look Dr Harrison in the eyes. 'What does that mean?'

He gives a small shrug. 'It means the disease is progressing. We do have some treatment options available.'

'Surgery?'

'No.'

'Am I going to go crazy? Before I die?'

'No, not crazy, no. But there will be . . . effects. Yes.'

I lie back against the pillows. 'I want to be alone for a while.'

'Of course.' He backs away from the bed. 'We can discuss everything more once we know exactly what we're dealing with. In the meantime you need to rest up.'

He's almost out the door when I call his name. He turns back around.

'Yes?'

'When can I get out of here?'

'I'm afraid I don't have an exact answer for that, Ava. We need to run some more tests like I said, and keep an eye on those seizures. Don't worry, this is the best place for you to be right now and we're going to take good care of you.'

'I have an important event I need to be at, on Saturday.'

'This Saturday?'

I nod.

'I can't make any promises, I'm sorry. We just have to take it a day at a time for now.'

He leaves the room and Mum comes back to my side.

'We can postpone,' she says. 'If need be.'

'Till when?' I say angrily, tears escaping faster than I can blink them away. 'It's not like I'm ever going to be feeling any better, am I? It's only going to get worse.'

She takes my hand and tries to squeeze it but I pull away. 'He's right though, Ava. This is the best place for you to be right now. The *only* place for you to be. Your health must come first.'

'My *health*,' I laugh bitterly. 'That's a bit of a stretch don't you think.'

'I know you're disappointed. And we know how much you want this.' My father has come to stand at my mother's side. 'But your mother's right. We can postpone.'

'I want to sleep. You guys should go home for a while.'

'I'm staying right here,' Mum says firmly.

'No.' I look at her pleadingly. 'Please, Mum. I meant what I said. I need some time alone.'

She swallows hard and nods, then kisses me on my forehead, her lips lingering for a full minute.

'I love you,' she says. 'So much.'

'I love you too. Both of you. I'll see you later.'

I lie there, crying and thinking, while the

shadows on the wall lengthen. I think about everything. But, most of all, I think about James. The next time I wake, the room is darker. The light has been dimmed, by who I don't know, but presumably a nurse. It takes my eyes a few moments to adjust to the shadows, and when they do I give a start. There is a figure sitting on the chair in the corner, their face turned to the window. At my sharp intake of breath the head turns and the person gets up to walk swiftly to the bed.

'Ava? Ava, it's me. James. I'm sorry if I startled you.'

'I didn't hear you come in.'

'No. You were pretty out to it. I didn't want to disturb you.' He smiles warmly, but there are new shadows underneath his eyes.

'I must have given you quite a fright too,' I say and he looks at me, puzzled. 'Last night.' I remind him.

'Oh. Yes. That was . . . pretty intense.'

'What are we doing?' I say softly.

'What do you mean?'

'This. Us. Together. It's not working, is it?'

He frowns. 'I don't understand.'

I take a deep breath and let the oxygen fill me with strength for what I need to do. 'We rushed into this too quickly, James. And the timing, obviously, is just all wrong.'

'You can't control when you fall in love, Ava. We both know that more than anyone.'

'I know. And I wish more than anything in this world — ' I give a small smile — 'more than I wish for world peace even, selfishly, that things were different. But they're not. And I think we both need to accept that. You need to live your life, James, and I need to focus on myself, and my . . . health. Something I haven't been doing.'

He doesn't angrily protest my words, which I rather expected and half hoped for. I was prepared for that. I wasn't prepared for him to walk away from me and stand by the window, his back to me. He says nothing for the longest time and I wait, wary, for his objections to come. They don't.

'Last night,' he says finally, 'I thought I'd lost you. When your eyes went all blank and you just stopped responding, I thought the life was draining out of you right in front of my eyes, and I was *scared*. More scared than I've ever been in my life. Even more than when my mother . . . ' He trails off, his voice shaky. 'I didn't know it was possible to feel the pain I felt, before you came back to me. I haven't been able to get it out of my head or my heart since.'

'I'm sorry.'

'No. I am.' He turns back around. His eyes are haunted with pain and my heart breaks at the sight of them. 'I don't know if I'm strong enough. I thought I was, but maybe I'm not. I just don't think I can survive this again.'

I smile through tears that flow faster than I can wipe them away. 'James, you've made these last few months the happiest of my life. The memories we've made together will keep me warm in here — ' I touch my chest — 'until I take my last breath. But I agree. I don't want you to stick around for what's coming. I might only have weeks left, and it's not going to be pretty. I don't want you to see me at my worst. I want you to remember me how I am.'

'I will never forget a second of my time with you, I promise you that.' His voice is raspy with emotion.

'And I will *not* be the reason you miss out on the biggest opportunity of your life.'

'Opportunity?'

'The job in the jungle. Take it, James. It will be life-changing for you.'

'No. I don't know.' He shakes his head.

'Take it. I'm not advising you, James, I'm telling you. Take it. I don't want you here any more. I want you to go, and do great things for both of us, because I'll never get that chance. I want you to go and to live the best life you can. For me.'

'How can I just walk away from you?'

I remember my question to my father on the beach, Kate's question to me. We are all scared of the same thing.

'You can, and you have to. Just don't look back.'

He crosses the room to the bed and with an angry howl he presses his forehead against mine, his breath hot on my face, our tears mingling together. He kisses me, and I feel a million lives lived in just that one kiss. A million futures together, a million roads travelled. Then he pulls away and leaves the room without looking back.

41

I can't eat. Or talk. I barely breathe. When I move, it hurts. Not physically, the pain medication takes care of that. But every movement is a reminder that I am still alive, and he has gone.

My family and friends are worried. They come and they gather around my hospital bed and they beg, plead and cajole me to take 'just one mouthful'. But what is the point of food if not to sustain life? And I don't want to sustain mine. Even if I did, the cancer has taken that decision away from me. I have no sense of control over anything, except this. So I don't eat.

The doctor puts on a stern voice and tells me I will be fed through a tube if I don't force myself to eat the food the lady in a blue smock plonks on my tray while he is there at dinner time on the second day.

'I know it's not the most appetising food in the world,' he says, poking at the brown stew on a plate, with unidentified meat and packet mashed potato that has gone hard around the edges. 'But it is food nevertheless.'

'That's the biggest understatement, and overstatement, that I've ever heard,' Amanda mutters. 'You can't call that food. I wouldn't feed that to a dog.'

I nibble enough to keep them happy and the tube away. They try to tempt me with takeaways.

French fries, pies, pizza. One night Kate brings Thai, and then sits there bewildered while I cry and wail and throw the rice and curry on to the floor.

'I thought she liked Thai?' she mutters to my mother, as they mop it up with paper towels.

'It ... was ... our ... last ... meal ... together,' I howl.

All the resolve and determination I had when I told James to leave promptly dissolved the next morning. I was wrong, I needed him. I was trying to spare him from the pain of watching me die, but I miss him too much, and I am too scared and selfish. I call him. I call him over and over and over but every time his phone goes straight to voicemail. I don't leave messages because I don't know what to say. I just know I need him.

When he doesn't return my calls and doesn't come back to the hospital, I realise that, unlike me, he has not changed his mind. I go numb. My parents, Kate and Amanda are quite rightfully confused as to why James has disappeared. I can't bring myself to explain, so I say he has gone out of town for work. They know I am lying. I do a bad job of hiding it.

I can do nothing apart from lie on my hospital bed and look out of the window. With James gone and the wedding cancelled, I have nothing to look forward to.

Occasionally, I am wheeled from the room for scans. I see no point in them now, but lack the energy to protest. They won't change the outcome. I barely listen when they rattle off results, treatment plans. None of it matters any more. I have fought, long and hard, but now I am tired.

Intervention comes in the form of my mother, as always. She arrives on the Thursday morning, four days after James left, two days before I was supposed to have the wedding day of my dreams, pushing a wheelchair into the room in front of her.

'Get in,' she says.

'What? No.'

'If I have to lift you in I will.'

I don't doubt her. But still, I don't move. I am weak and tired. When I try to sleep, I see his face, so I force myself to stay awake until exhaustion takes over and plunges me into a dreamless slumber that does nothing to ease my fatigue.

'I mean it,' she says, crossing her arms and looking at me sternly. 'Get up.'

'Why?'

'Because despite how you've been acting, you haven't lost the use of your legs.'

'Then why did you bring a chair.'

'Because, smarty, you've barely eaten so I'd be surprised if you have the strength to walk very far without fainting. Now come on, hurry up. You'll get bedsores if you don't move soon.'

'I don't care.'

'You will once you get them. Nasty, smelly things I've heard.'

'Stop trying to shock me into doing what you want, Mum.'

'Is it working?'

'No.'

She sighs. 'Ava, I don't know what's really going on with you and James, but any fool can see how much you're hurting. And I've allowed you to wallow, I have, but it's been four days now and you're not snapping out of it. If anything you're sinking deeper. Normally I'd leave you to have all the time you need to work through whatever it is you're working through. But time is a luxury we don't have. So get off that goddamn bed this minute, and *get in the bloody chair*.'

I know how unrelenting she can be, so reluctantly I do as I'm told and shuffle off the bed, pitifully lowering myself into the chair she thrusts out triumphantly.

'Where are we going?'

'Wait and see.'

I slouch down low and stare at my stockinged feet as she wheels me along corridors, through doors and eventually into an elevator.

'I'm getting out?' I ask hopefully when I see she pushes the ground floor button.

She grimaces. 'No. Sorry. I should have realised you might get your hopes up.'

'Doesn't matter.'

When the elevator doors open she pushes me out and across the reception area, towards the big glass automatic doors. I look up at her, confused.

'I thought you said . . . ?'

'You're not going home. Not yet.'

The fresh air hits like I've walked into a wall of perfume, only the opposite, sweet, natural air, so much softer than the harsh, recycled air inside that dries out your mouth and skin leaving you scaly like a lizard. It's warmer too. She takes the path that leads to the seat where I met the old lady, all those months ago. It is different now, surrounded by the lush green growth of summer. My father, Kate and Amanda are there. They have a rug spread out on the grass and are sitting around it.

'Surprise,' Dad says, scrambling up to kiss me on the cheek when he sees me. 'We thought you might like a picnic.'

'Thanks. It's a nice thought, but I'm not really hungry.'

'Suit yourself,' Amanda says. 'More food for us.'

There is an edge to her voice though, that belies any joviality her words suggest. I see Kate give her a sharp look.

'Come on, Ava,' she says cajolingly. 'Surely you can manage a sandwich? We bought your favourite cheese . . . '

'You guys can have it.'

'Oh for God's sake,' Mum snaps, causing us all to look at her in surprise. 'Right. It's time for some tough love.'

'Do you really think that's the right appro — ' Dad gingerly asks but is cut off.

Mum tips up the back of the wheelchair, causing me to plant my feet on the ground to prevent myself from falling.

'Hey,' I protest.

'Hey nothing. You're quite capable of standing, sitting and walking by yourself still, Ava.

And I won't stand by and just watch you give up. Not while you still have strength in you.'

'I haven't given up.'

'Really? Because that's how it seems to us. We've watched you retreat further and further into yourself this week, not eating, barely talking. It's like you're pulling away from us, the people that love you.'

'You heard what the doctor said, Mum. It's in my brain. How long until I don't even recognise you any more?'

'You can't think like that.'

'Of course I can,' I yell loudly, not caring who might hear. I haven't given voice to the fear I've been feeling since my admission but it's unleashed now, and I let rip. 'How can I not think like that? How can I not imagine the worst?'

'I don't know,' she yells back, and I realise she is worrying about the exact same things. 'I don't know.' She looks at me so helplessly I lose any aggression I feel.

'I just hate the not knowing,' I say, quieter now, panting. 'I have no idea what to expect and I'm so scared. And no offence to you all, because you know how much I love you, but the one person I really need here to reassure me is gone. And I don't know if I'll ever see him again.'

'Talk to us,' Kate urges, pulling me into her arms. 'That's what we're here for. Where is James?'

So I tell them. How I told him to go for his own good, that I thought I was doing the noble thing. How he didn't fight me on it. That he was

323

just as confused and scared as I was, and I couldn't fault him for that.

As I finish explaining I see Dad shaking his head, his mouth set in a tight line. 'That coward,' he says.

'He's not a coward, Dad.'

'He is. He's abandoned you, right when you need him the most.'

I look at Mum. She looks sad. 'I was hoping he'd be stronger than this,' she says. 'For your sake.'

'Please don't blame him,' I plead. 'It's as much my fault. I *told* him to go.'

'Yes, but he would have known you were just trying to spare his feelings,' Dad says. 'He didn't have to walk away. That was his choice.'

'Put yourself in his shoes,' I tell them. 'He watched his mother die, *his own mother*. He was still a kid, barely a teenager. Imagine how hard that must have been. And then for him to find me, and develop feelings for me, only to have to watch as I leave him in the same way?'

Dad's expression softens. 'Doesn't seem fair, does it.'

'No. It doesn't. It's not.'

'I guess I can understand why he's scared,' Dad admits. 'But I'm still angry with him. I don't like seeing you hurt.'

'Oh, Ava,' Mum sighs. 'What a mess, eh? Have you called him?'

'So many times. He's not answering. I think he's gone overseas.' I don't tell them about the job offer, because I promised him it would stay between us.

'Goodbyes are never painless,' Kate says softly. 'Even when they're necessary.'

'I just didn't think it'd be the last time I saw him,' I say through tears. 'And I can't bear the thought that it was.'

'As hard as it is to hear,' Amanda says cautiously, 'maybe you were right. Maybe it *is* better this way. Now, he'll always remember you at your best.'

'Maybe.'

I close my eyes and lift my face to the sky, letting the warmth of the sun dry the tears on my cheeks. Strangely, it does feel cathartic to talk about it. I should have known they wouldn't just leave me to wallow in self-pity.

'You have us,' Mum says. 'Always. No matter what's coming. We're here till the end.'

'I love you guys.'

'We love you too.'

I sniff loudly and smile bravely. 'Now, did someone say something about cheese?'

Later, when they have deposited me safely back into my room and departed for the night, I sleep easier for the first time since James left. I haven't stopped missing him, and I never will, but I have been reminded that there are others who love me just as much, and I owe it to them to give this last bit of life everything I have. I can either dwell on the unfairness and the uncertainty, or I can focus on what I have, and all that is still good in my life. I have to hold on to the belief that I made the right choice, that James is out there right now, doing what he loves, making the most of his moments.

42

'Wake up, wake up, it's your wedding day,' Amanda squeals, throwing herself on to my bed.

'Go away.' I kick out at her. 'That's an awful thing to joke about.'

'I'm not joking.'

I lift my head off the hospital pillow and peer at her. 'What?'

'Surprise!' Kate beams, waving her hands around madly. 'We're breaking you out of here.'

'Seriously?'

'Seriously.'

'Do the doctors know?'

'Yes. And they're all for it. They were going to let you go home tomorrow anyway, so once we explained how important today is they agreed one day wasn't going to make much of a difference. You just have to promise to take it easy and rest when you need to.'

'I'll promise your firstborn child if it means I get out of here. Where's Mum?'

'Finalising things at home.'

'For what?'

'The wedding. Like I said.' Amanda rolls her eyes as if I am being dense.

'Wait, I thought we cancelled it all. Or postponed it or whatever.'

Kate shakes her head. 'We decided not to, just in case. And, as it turns out, we made the right decision. That is if you still want to go through with it today. No pressure if you're not feeling up to it.'

'Well . . . ' I exhale slowly. I'd just assumed that the whole thing was off. Could I really do this today? Without James present? I look at Kate and Amanda's expectant faces and think about how much work has gone into this. And I know that if I *don't* do it today, there are no guarantees that I'll get another chance. I nod. 'Let's do it. I might not feel like partying, but I could do with the distraction. Besides, I know family and friends will have travelled from all over for this. I don't want to let anyone down.'

'They will understand if you'd rather not.'

I turn and put my feet on the floor firmly. 'No. I'm not letting this damn disease take another thing away from me. Let's get out of here, but I need to make a quick phone call first.'

Some of the doctors and nurses gather to see me off, a few with tears in their eyes. They give me a card, wishing me all the best for my big day. I am grateful to them all, but I hope, on a professional level, that I never have to see any of them again. The ride home from the hospital is bittersweet. The countryside seems brighter, but my heart is definitely sadder. My father has outdone himself and breakfast is the full monty. Eggs — both scrambled and fried — crispy bacon, golden crunchy hash browns, fried mushrooms, toast, sliced avocado, some salmon slices and hollandaise sauce. I pick and taste what I can. I still have no appetite, but I know I will need my strength.

Sophie and Kelly arrive at ten, giddy with

excitement. Seeing them, I feel affection for them both, they are lovely women who only want to see me happy. As do so many. Amanda shows me the Facebook page. There are thousands of posts wishing me all the best for the day. I feel a twinge of sadness that I was unable to take them all up on their offers of help or things for the wedding, but I just have to hope they will understand. Something tells me they will.

When Sophie and Kelly have finished working their magic I look — not healthy, I am too skinny for that — but still beautiful. I head into the bedroom alone to get dressed. Someone has placed two bags on the bed. I unzip the larger bag, the familiar one, and smile sadly as the first sliver of material is revealed. Although I have a beautiful dress hanging in the wardrobe that has been modified to fit me perfectly, this morning when I found out the wedding was going ahead I had a change of heart. There was really only one dress I wanted, and that was the dress I wore on the farm, the day James and I went for a swim in the river. So I called Sophie from the hospital and, luckily for me, I had damaged it enough that she couldn't return it to the designer, and it was still in her office. It has been dry-cleaned, I notice, because when I sheepishly handed it back to Sophie that day it was with a few grass stains around the bottom and a small tear from where I had left it draped over the tree branch. There's no sign of the tear now; whoever repaired it has done it so expertly that I can't even see where it was. I lift it to my face and inhale, hoping to catch the scent of him, but there's nothing of course. Laying it carefully on the bed, I turn my attention to the other bag. Inside I find a beautiful pair of shoes, cream coloured to match the dress. They are like ballet flats, but delicate and with an intricate lacy pattern. They are very pretty, and definitely more me than a pair of stilettos would have been.

My mother, predictably, cries at the sight of me. I have to make her leave or she will set me off, and I don't want to ruin Sophie's efforts. So she goes on ahead of the bridesmaids and me, down to the beach below Kate's house, where I decided to hold the ceremony part of the celebration. The plan is I will walk down an aisle, just as if it were a normal wedding, only instead of towards a minister and groom there will be a podium, from where I can say a few words. Wedding ceremonies are typically very short, and even though this day is not typical in the least, it's a hot day, so I'm hoping to keep this part of the day short. Then it's celebration time. Not that I'm in the mood for partying without James, but I have to try to put that behind me, just for today.

Kate and Amanda, my bridesmaids, emerge from Kate's room and I gasp audibly. 'Oh you guys, you look amazing,' I say tearfully, waving my hands frantically in front of my eyes in a futile effort to dispel sudden tears.

'Scrub up OK, don't we?' Amanda preens.

They are wearing beautiful draping dresses in a soft gold colour. With their hair loosely plaited over one shoulder, tanned skins and skilfully applied make-up, they look like Grecian goddesses.

The three of us put our arms around each other and our heads together.

'I always knew this day would come,' Kate says softly. 'That we'd be bridesmaids for each other's big days. And even though the circumstances aren't what you'd call normal, or ideal, this is still your big day, Ava. And we're here for you, whatever you need.'

'Yeah.' Amanda sniffs loudly. 'What she said.'

'And I love you both too. Thank you for being the most amazing friends. I wouldn't have had half as good a life as I have, without you two.'

We smile at each other, a little soppily, before Kate breaks apart the circle.

'Right,' she says, businesslike once more. She goes to a chiller box and opens it, revealing our large white bouquets.

'Hydrangeas,' I squeal.

'Did you think we'd forget?' Amanda says. 'Believe me, you went on about it enough that every detail has been seared into our brains for life.'

Kate checks the clock over the oven. 'OK, girls, you ready?'

We all look at each other and smile.

'Ready.'

'Ready.'

She passes us our flowers. ' 'Then let's do this.'

There's a knock on the door and Kate looks at me puzzled.

'Are you expecting anyone?'

'It's probably just a guest who got confused

and came here instead of parking at the reserve,' Amanda says impatiently. 'Leave it, they'll figure it out.'

'That's not very nice,' Kate scolds her. She opens the door.

'Hi, I'm your photographer. The magazine sent me.'

And even though it is not *his* voice, I can't help how my heart quickens. Then he steps into the room. Tall and thin, with black hair pulled back into a slick man bun. He's carrying a bag and wearing a smile that seems genuine, even if his cultivated look is not.

'Ava?' he asks. 'I'm Steve Gunning, I'll be your photographer for today.'

'Is he wearing . . . *eyeliner?*' Amanda mutters to me.

'I think so.'

'Hot.' She flicks her plait and smiles coyly at him. He blatantly looks her up and down and, judging by the way his top lip curls up in one corner, he clearly likes what he sees.

He is the absolute polar opposite of my sweet James, and he makes my eyes hurt.

Kate gives me a concerned look. 'Are you OK with this? I can tell him to leave if you're not.'

I breathe in and out, steadying myself. 'No it's OK. We agreed to let the magazine cover this and I'm not going to back out now.'

'Great.' Steve strides in.

'We were actually just on our way out, to the ceremony,' Amanda tells him. She has adopted her flirtatious manner. Kate rolls her eyes at me.

'I won't hold you up long.' He puts his bag on

the table and unzips it, then pulls out a camera with a lens so long Kate whispers to me that surely it has to be compensating for something. 'Let me just get a few quick shots of you three first, the bridal party.'

We link arms and stand on the deck as directed, and he photographs us with the trees and a sliver of ocean in the background, the clear blue sky the perfect backdrop. Every click of the shutter brings back memories, both painful and sweet, and I have to really concentrate to stop myself from crying. This isn't how I imagined this day going at all, but then that's to be expected, surely, because this day was never going to be anything but different.

Finally, he finishes. I am so nervous as we make our way across the lawn and down the path towards the trees. Mum and Dad are waiting there for me. I made the decision to have them both walk me down the aisle.

When my father sees me he takes a sharp breath in and slaps a hand to his chest. 'Oh . . . Ava. Look . . . at . . . you. My little girl . . . is all grown up.' He sniffs loudly and pinches the end of his nose.

'Don't you start crying,' Mum warns him sharply. 'You'll set me off.'

'I can't help it. She looks so beautiful.'

'She does, doesn't she,' Mum agrees.

They both look me up and down with muted expressions. It is hard to know what is going through their minds but I can hazard a guess. This is not the future they planned, when they first held me in their arms. I may not have had children of my own, but I can fathom the fierce love a parent must feel, and the anguish of knowing you only have so much control over the life of this child you have created. Some things you will be able to control, some things you won't. Unfortunately, you don't get to pick and choose.

'Are we doing this?' Dad asks. 'I'll be the proudest dad in the world to walk you down the aisle.'

He looks so vulnerable. I think about all the things he will miss out on. Grandchildren, being the big one. He would have made an amazing grandfather, with his trite magic tricks that would nevertheless have enchanted them. I am going to give him this honour, to walk me down the aisle. It's the least I can do. And later, the father-daughter dance. My parents are being forced to endure the unendurable. It is not fair on them, just as it is not fair on me.

'OK.' Kate turns to me. 'Wait here. We'll go first, and then when you hear the music you follow. Are you sure you're up for this?'

I nod.

She kisses me on the cheek, tears glistening in her eyes. 'You look amazing. I love you.'

'I love you too.'

She and Amanda disappear into the trees, down towards the beach. Steven follows to find himself the best vantage point from which to photograph my entrance. Alone, I can let my facade slip, but I don't allow myself to cry. Without James in my life, it all seems meaningless. But I have to respect his decision and his reasons behind it. He's not a bad person, I know that much. And he loved me, I know that just as sure as I know the grass is green and springy under my feet, the sky blue overhead. He loved me. So it wasn't an easy decision for him. I know that, and the knowledge should bring me comfort. It doesn't, but it should.

I take a deep breath. This day may not be the day I have been dreaming of since I was a young girl. But it *is* the day I have been dreaming of since I was told I was dying. A lot of work and planning has gone into it. I will enjoy this day, as much as I possibly can. Tomorrow I can fall apart, but today I will be strong.

I hear the first few notes of music drift up to where I am standing. I left the song choice up to Amanda, trusting her taste implicitly, and now I recognise it instantly and smile. Ed Sheeran's 'Photograph'. One of my favourite songs of all time, and oh so very apt, but also, so very painful right now. I close my eyes and breathe in and out slowly. My eyes fly open when the singing starts. It's her, Amanda. She's singing the song herself and it's hauntingly beautiful. She will go on to great things, I am more sure of it than ever. Carefully, I make my way down the path, towards the outpouring of love I know awaits me.

I step out of the trees, and into a sea of people. There are my close family and friends, seated, and then beyond that, standing all around, are hundreds of faces, all smiling at me. I stumble under the weight of their stares.

'Who are these people?' I ask Mum.

'Readers of the magazine mostly.'

'But why are they here?'

'So many people adore you, Ava, and want to see you happy. It's a public space and we didn't have the heart to turn anyone away, but if it's too much I can ask them to move back and give us some space.'

I scan the crowd, recognising familiar faces. Ruth from Marmalade Farm. Kelly and Sophie. The mayor. My seventh-form geography teacher. My ex-boyfriend and his wife and children. People I have crossed paths with, both in the past and more recently. They are all here to see me. Old ladies with handkerchiefs at the ready beam at me myopically. There must be a hundred people or more. I should feel intimidated. Normally I would. But the love that radiates off these people is palpable and fills me with strength.

'No. It's OK.' I nod. 'They should be a part of this too.'

'Are you sure? There are an awful lot of them.'

'I'm sure. I want them to hear what I have to say.'

'You have a wonderful heart, Ava Green.' My mother smiles.

'You might be slightly biased.'

'Maybe. But I don't think so.'

I pause to close my eyes and breathe in the salty air, capturing the moment, squeezing the life out of it. There is only one thing that would make it more perfect. Well, one person. But he is not here.

43

The music swells. This is it. My moment. I lift my chin and step forward, feeling like the princess I always dreamt of being, determined to enjoy every step. I take my time, smiling at everyone I pass. I feel special, and loved. When we reach the end of the aisle, Kate is standing by the wooden podium. My mother and father kiss my cheeks, tears in their eyes, and take their seats. Without them at my side, the nerves come back and I almost lose confidence, but then I hand Kate my bouquet and turn, focusing on the faces staring back at me, and a sense of calm washes over me. My mother was right. These people are not strangers. Their faces represent a lifetime, *my* lifetime. My journey to get to this point. They are all on their own journeys, of course, but our paths have intersected somewhere along the way, and we have added our own paragraphs and pages to each other's history books. Sometimes the impact has been brief, a footnote. But it all has meaning. It all adds value. It has all shaped the woman I am, standing here today. This day is as much a celebration of *them* as it is me, because without them, my journey wouldn't have been half as enjoyable, or epic. Kate passes me a microphone that is connected to an outdoor speaker system and then retreats.

'Thank you,' I say, clearing my throat, hearing

my voice bounce back at me through the sound system. 'For being here today. I appreciate it. As most of you will know, I'm not much of a public speaker. So I'll keep this reasonably brief. I've spent a lot of time thinking about what I was going to say today. I kept coming up with pithy little speeches, and words that I thought were very wise and considered.'

I frown, adopting a serious, scholarly face and hear a few titters. It encourages me, I feel my voice strengthen.

'Words that I could pass on to you, and you would go forth and live your best life, remembering my advice, and me, always. Because that's been my biggest fear, you see. That you'll all forget me. I wanted you to dwell on my memory, and fester on the sadness; because I thought that would show that you still cared. But last night I realised I've been thinking about it all wrong. I know you won't forget me, although you'll probably think of me less and less as the years go on, and I've decided I'm OK with that. Honestly. You shouldn't dwell. You *should* move on. If there is anything I know better than most, it's that life really can change in an instant. Death *will* come to us all — sorry, that's morbid I know and I notice a few of you shuddered when I said that word — but here's the thing. It shouldn't be such a taboo subject. We talk about anything and everything these days. Our sex lives, cosmetic surgery procedures, even the most ridiculous ones you can think of. I saw a programme the other week about labia enhancements for God's sake. Sorry, Dad. You probably didn't think that's a word you'd hear your daughter say at her wedding.'

People chuckle.

'Death is a natural consequence of life. You can't have one without the other. It is one of the only things, apart from birth, that we all have in common. No matter how we live, or where, or how much money we have, we all leave this world the same way. So don't waste time being miserable, or weeping for me. Do I wish things were different? Hell yes. No question. I don't want to die. I'm not ready for it, and I'm terrified. But I will, and soon probably. Grieve for me for a short while, and then be thankful for each day that you are still here. Some things we can't control, but there is so much we can. *Choose* to be happy. *Choose* to be grateful, for both life and the small moments it consists of. *Choose* kindness, and love over hate. Always choose love. Even if you are as scared as you can possibly be, choose love. When you are face to face with your own mortality you don't want to be thinking, if only I'd been braver. *Be* brave now. Take chances. What have you got to lose?'

I pause, and someone starts to tentatively clap. It makes me smile, but it's not what I want. I hold up one hand.

'Wait,' I say. 'I'm not finished. I know that you've heard all this before. I'm not going to stand here and pretend that I'm the first dying person to come up with these nuggets of wisdom. I'm not. And I won't be the last. But here's the thing, I didn't understand just how important these words, this advice, is. Not until I was dying myself. And if that's the one thing I can get through to you today then I'll be happy. *Don't* wait until you're dying to start living. Think about what I've said to you, really think about it. I know life can be busy and hard and there are a million little mundane things that have to be done each day in order to just survive. But surviving isn't enough. You have to live, *really* live. Because before you know it, your time will be up too, and you want to look back and be satisfied that you gave it your very best shot, and you lived your very best life.'

I have no idea if I'm getting through to them. I can see a few people crying. And couples embracing each other, heads bowed together. I hope I am. That's all I can do.

'OK.' I smile. 'That's enough of that. I love you all. I will treasure the memories we share until I take my last breath, but I want this day to be about living. So, please, as well-meaning as I know you all are, I'd appreciate it if no one tried to use today to tell me goodbye. I'm not dead yet, and I'm not ready for that. So let's all get a drink and enjoy the best that this fine town has to offer. I want you all to enjoy yourselves, please, that's an order. Or I'll take it personally.'

I poke out my tongue and people laugh.

Despite my light tone, my speech has drained me emotionally. I step away from the podium and start to step down when I hear a voice.

'Wait!'

My heart quickens and I search the crowd for the owner, needing confirmation, even though I know of course who that voice belongs too. I'd know it anywhere. I just don't want to hope in case I am wrong.

I am not wrong.

James is standing there, at the bottom of the path. He is wearing a black suit, and is panting as if he has been running. I stare at him, every fibre in my being afire with love at the sight of this man who has captured my heart so completely. I stop breathing, my ribs tight. The crowd is silent as people swivel their heads to look at both James and me. As far as I'm concerned though, we are the only people there, everyone else has receded into the background.

'You came,' I say.

'I had to.'

He starts striding forward. I hitch my dress up with both hands and step down from the podium quickly. We meet in the middle of the aisle, pausing for the longest heartbeat to stare in each other's eyes first. He looks tired and bedraggled, but perfect. I see myself reflected back at me. And I see his love, his urgent craving for me. Then I am home, in his arms, and everything in the universe falls into perfect alignment.

'These last few days without you have been the worst of my life,' he says raggedly, his voice choking on his pain. 'I got on a plane, but the second we were in the air I regretted it. I made it as far as LA and then spent two days flying the longest way home to get back to you.'

'I missed you so much. I thought I'd never see you again . . . ' My voice chokes in my throat.

He silences me with a kiss, desperate and urgent. When we pull apart we are both breathless and unsatisfied. I realise that I will never have enough of this man. But now that he is back in my arms, I plan on doing a damn good job of trying.

'Remember that day, at the farm?' he asks. 'When we were in the paddock and you asked me all those questions.'

'Yes.'

'You asked me if I'd ever been in love. And I told you I had, once. Remember?'

I nod, unsure where he is going with this.

'I was wrong. That was nothing compared to what I feel for you, Ava. It's all-consuming, how much I want you. How much I need you.' He lifts me up and holds me tightly, our faces pressed together. 'You are my everything, my world. Hell, I would lasso the moon for you. I want to give you everything you deserve, anything you want. Everything you need.'

'You already have. You. I don't need anything else.'

'I love you, Ava Green. I will love you endlessly and always.'

'Oh James, I love you too.'

He lowers me back down to my feet gently and then he drops down to one knee on the flower-strewn sand, fishing in his coat pocket. I realise instantly what is happening of course, and clap my hands over my mouth.

'Ava Green,' he says solemnly, pulling out a little black box and holding it aloft, 'will you do me the most profound honour of being my wife, and making me the luckiest man in the world?'

I fight my instincts to scream the answer. 'Are

you sure about this?' I ask in a low voice. 'You know how rough it's going to get. I can't promise you it will be easy.'

'I've never been surer about anything in my life. I don't want easy. I want you. And I will be there for you every step of the way, through both the good and the bad. You're not getting rid of me again.'

'I never wanted to get rid of you in the first place.'

'So is that a yes?'

'I'm not sure.'

His smile slips off his face and he looks at me, worried. 'Why not?'

'Well I mean, I haven't seen the ring yet.'

He closes his eyes for a moment as his smile grows again. Then laughter bubbles out of him. 'Jesus, Ava, you had me really worried there.'

'I'm sorry.' I half smile, half cry, though they are happy tears. 'I'm kidding of course. I don't care what the ring looks like, it's a definite yes. Yes, yes yes!'

He woops loudly as the crowd erupts into woops and cheers and I remember for the first time that we have an audience. I laugh through joyful tears as he climbs to his feet and picks me up to spin me around. When I protest, laughingly, that I am getting dizzy, he puts me down and slides on the ring, a beautiful emerald the colour of the lake at the bottom of the waterfall. Then my father claps him on the shoulder and James turns to talk to him. Kate taps me on the shoulder and I turn around.

'I've just been informed that the Mayor

happens to be an ordained minister,' she says quietly. 'Shall I fetch her?'

'Yes.' I smile at her. 'And quickly. I don't want to waste another second not being this man's wife.'

Hearing the word, James turns, groaning, and pulls me into his arms again. 'Those are the most beautiful words I have ever heard you say.'

I kiss his chin. 'I bet you say that to all the girls.'

'Only the cute ones.' He winks.

44

At 4.49 p.m. on my 'wedding' day, I officially become James's wife. It is the happiest moment of my life, and the most emotional by far. Afterwards, we don't let each other go, not for a second. Well, apart from bathroom breaks. After the ceremony on the beach, we head to the surf club rooms, which have been decorated beautifully enough to mollify even my mother. There, we dine on the freshest bounty the sea has to offer, as we celebrate our new chapter with the people who helped write the book of my life.

Surrounded by love, we dance on the balcony under the stars, until we are too sleepy to shuffle another step. Then we are chauffeured to a motel where we tumble into a mountainous bed and gently consummate our marriage.

It feels like a dream, and yet it is the most genuine thing I have ever done.

We honeymoon on Stewart Island, where we make love in a glass igloo under the blazing glory of Aurora Australis, the Southern Lights. I cry at their beauty, and marvel at the magnificence that is this planet upon which we live.

We fool ourselves, James and I, wrapped in our little bubble of love, that I am well, and that James has sole claim on my body, not the cancer that ravages the inside. But we can only pretend for so long, and two months after the wedding, two glorious, wonderful months in which we only strengthen our love, I develop pneumonia and quickly begin to go downhill. Almost overnight it seems, my body betrays my will and I begin what I know is the start of The End.

True to his word, James is at my side through it all. The last-ditch medical procedures that fail to buy time, and the conversations that no one ever wants to have, but must. I am admitted to hospital while the doctors attempt to bring my pain under control. It is in the hospital that I become aware that eventually I will be on so much medication I will lose awareness, and assumedly my death will thereafter briefly follow.

The idea of Hospice is mentioned, and shot down by me. I don't want to die in a strange room. When it becomes clear that I am in the end stages and there is nothing more to be done, I ask to go home. A hospital bed is set up in Kate's lounge, near the window. James sleeps either in the chair beside me, holding my hand, or on the couch. My parents move into our old room. When it is fine I ask for the French doors to be opened. I want to die with the smell of the sea in my memory.

Time passes. I don't know if it's days or hours or weeks any more. A palliative care team visit daily. The morphine helps, for a while, but the pain is constant and gnawing, unlike anything I could have ever imagined. I am not ready, and I am scared. I don't pretend to be brave to spare anyone's feelings. I cry when I need to, which is often.

Blink.

In my dreams, James and I live for ever, in a tree house beside a waterfall. We have five beautiful babies, with their father's eyes and their mother's tenacity.

Cancer is no longer, a cure has been found. No one suffers. At least, not from this.

I hear them. The voices. Muffled, tearful, weary. I hate what I have put them through. Continue to do. Is it my fault? That I am still here? Am I hanging on when I should be letting go? Have I failed at the very thing that comes to us all?

Blink.

I dream of him. With the water on his skin and the sunset in his eyes. The timing was all wrong. And yet, the timing was perfect. I wonder where he is, and what he is doing. Then I remember. He is here, at my side, where he promised he'd always be. I can't bear for him to touch me any more. My skin is so thin it hurts. My bones so brittle they could break. I miss him with a longing that never ends.

Blink.

I tiptoe amongst the stars, along the Milky Way. Hitch a ride on a comet, dance with the man in the moon.

I am star dust; blow on me too hard and I will disintegrate.

Blink.

Epilogue

(Written by James — printed in the Women's Weekly)

When I was asked to write a few words, not long after Ava's death, I initially said no. The pain was too raw, my grief unrelenting. It still is, and shows no sign of waning. But then I remembered how much comfort Ava drew during her final months from you, the readers of this magazine. She cherished each and every letter, and was grateful to be included in your thoughts and prayers. So I do this for you, and for her.

After our wedding, Ava and I, we thought we still had time up our sleeve. That turned out to be wishful thinking. The cancer was too aggressive, and had spread too far. She became seriously ill very quickly and was admitted to hospital. When it was clear that there was no longer anything that could be done for her, we brought her home, at her request.

One night she asked for a sip of water, and in the brief moment that I turned around to pick up the glass and straw, she slipped into an unconsciousness from which she would never awaken. Her family, closest friends and I spent the next eight hours at her bedside, reminding her of how much she is, and always will be, deeply loved. We told her it was OK for her to let go, to seek an end to her pain and suffering, and that it wasn't goodbye, because we would see her again some day.

Ava died just after 5 a.m. on a Saturday in March. As the sun rose over the sea she took her last breath. The end, when it came, was peaceful. For that I will always be grateful.

We buried her in a pine casket in the cemetery that occupies a sharp corner on the road leading out of town. She rests on the tip of a hill, overlooking the ocean, where she is buffeted by wind and salt spray, which I can't help thinking she would have liked. Ava drew comfort from feeling alive, and nature is a good provider of that. I visit it often, although to my dismay I don't sense her presence there. She is gone, dancing amongst the stars somewhere, pain free and forever young. Her grave is merely a place to rest flowers and my weary head, and I have fallen asleep there more times than I care to admit.

*   *   *

Time moves on. I'll be honest, and admit I'm struggling, desperately. I was blessed with the love of the most amazing woman, and I am grateful. But I am also selfish. It wasn't long enough. Not by a long shot. I remember a few weeks before she died, I told Ava I had no idea how I would go on living without her.

You'll find a way to manage, she said. *People still live after losing a limb.*

She was more than just a limb though. She was my whole heart.

I will try my hardest to live my best life,

because I promised her I would, and because she taught me not to make promises you can't keep. But she can hang on to my heart, until the day we are reunited again.

Acknowledgments

This book would not be in your hands if it weren't for the tireless belief of my wonderful agent, Vicki Marsdon, who keeps insisting that I have talent, and who is relentless with her encouragement. Thanks to Emma and Anna at Piatkus, who believed in this story based purely upon the strength of a few paragraphs. You saw the potential, and I'm hugely grateful for that. Thanks also to the wonderful teams at Hachette New Zealand and Hachette Australia for your amazing support and efforts, especially Sacha, who is very clever and very kind.

Amanda Shapleski, Andrea Sheffield, Jo Edwards, Michelle Barbridge, Richard Lloyd-James, Cara Randall-Hunt, Tara Lyons, Kelly Thompson, Micaela Bretton, Yvette Hurst, Gail Shaw, Robyn Jan Geiger, Gilda Galluzzo Seager, Emily Ciravolo, Emma Green, Rebecca Raisin, Fiona Wilson, Shelly Feetham, Mark Paxton, Tracy Bain, Casey-Lee Vautier, Rachael Albert, Bonnie Whittaker, Janelle Harris, Michelle Vernal, Donna Moran and Donna Young — you guys are all special to me and your support doesn't go unnoticed.

Jennifer Allen, Caroline McCormack, Brenna Nicholson, and Corina Douglas, thank you for reaching out and making me feel less alone in my new home. Let's do that girls' night out again soon!

My family, especially Tony Ryan, Patrice Ryan, Rob Ryan, Kerrie Ryan, Ange Ward, Jacqui Morrissey, Catelyn McCarty, and Jack Morrissey. I love you all so very much. My welcoming new family, Christine and Ian Robinson, Rachel and Mark Barker, Wayne and Nikki Robinson.

My very, very dear friends who *feel* like family, Kevin, Lorraine and Rachel Tipene. We'll come and see you in France one day, I promise!

And lastly, my hard-working, tremendously supportive husband Karl, and our precious cherubs Holly, Willow and Leo. You make every day chaotic and loud, but also fun and wonderful. I love that every time I drag you into a book store and point at the shelf you still say 'Mummy's book!' with as much enthusiasm as the first time. Long may that continue.

We do hope that you have enjoyed reading this large print book.

Did you know that all of our titles are available for purchase?

We publish a wide range of high quality large print books including:
Romances, Mysteries, Classics
General Fiction
Non Fiction and Westerns

Special interest titles available in large print are:
The Little Oxford Dictionary
Music Book
Song Book
Hymn Book
Service Book

Also available from us courtesy of Oxford University Press:
Young Readers' Dictionary
(large print edition)
Young Readers' Thesaurus
(large print edition)

For further information or a free brochure, please contact us at:
Ulverscroft Large Print Books Ltd.,
The Green, Bradgate Road, Anstey,
Leicester, LE7 7FU, England.
Tel: (00 44) 0116 236 4325
Fax: (00 44) 0116 234 0205

POP!

and

Mum Has a Ban

PHASE 2
AND 3

/j/v/w/

Level 2 – Red

BookLife
Readers

Helpful Hints for Reading at Home

The graphemes (written letters) and phonemes (units of sound) used throughout this series are aligned with Letters and Sounds. This offers a consistent approach to learning whether reading at home or in the classroom.

HERE IS A LIST OF PHONEMES FOR THIS PHASE OF LEARNING. AN EXAMPLE OF THE PRONUNCIATION CAN BE FOUND IN BRACKETS.

Phase 2			
s (sat)	a (cat)	t (tap)	p (tap)
i (pin)	n (net)	m (man)	d (dog)
g (go)	o (sock)	c (cat)	k (kin)
ck (sack)	e (elf)	u (up)	r (rabbit)
h (hut)	b (ball)	f (fish)	ff (off)
l (lip)	ll (ball)	ss (hiss)	

Phase 3 Set 6			
j (jam)	v (van)	w (win)	x (mix)

Phase 3 Set 7			
y (yellow)	z (zoo)	zz (buzz)	qu (quick)

HERE ARE SOME WORDS WHICH YOUR CHILD MAY FIND TRICKY.

Phase 2 Tricky Words			
the	to	I	no
go	into		

Phase 3 Tricky Words			
he	you	she	they
we	all	me	are
be	my	was	her

GPC focus: /j/v/w/

TOP TIPS FOR HELPING YOUR CHILD TO READ:

• Allow children time to break down unfamiliar words into units of sound and then encourage children to string these sounds together to create the word.

• Encourage your child to point out any focus phonics when they are used.

• Read through the book more than once to grow confidence.

• Ask simple questions about the text to assess understanding.

• Encourage children to use illustrations as prompts.

PHASE 2 AND 3
/j/v/w/

This book focuses on the phonemes /j/, /v/ and /w/ and is a red level 2 book band.